THE Mañana Treehouse

THE Mañana Treehouse

Bruce McLean

thistledown press

Thistledown Press Ltd.
410 2nd Avenue North
Saskatoon, Saskatchewan, S7K 2C3
www.thistledownpress.com

Library and Archives Canada Cataloguing in Publication

Title: The mañana treehouse / Bruce McLean.
Names: McLean, Bruce, 1929- author.
Identifiers: Canadiana (print) 20200279874 | Canadiana (ebook) 20200279882 | ISBN 9781771872058 (softcover) | ISBN 9781771872065 (HTML) | ISBN 9781771872072 (PDF)
Classification: LCC PS8625.L422 M36 2020 | DDC C813/.6—dc23

Cover illustration by Paul Wohlstetter
Cover and book design by Jackie Forrie
Printed and bound in Canada

Thistledown Press gratefully acknowledges the financial assistance of the Canada Council for the Arts, SK Arts, and the Government of Canada for its publishing program.

For my wife, the late Pauline St-Pierre Dion who showed as much concern for me as for herself after she came down with Alzheimer's and enabled us to ride it out together, living as happily ever after as was possible under the circumstances. She liked pink carnations.

"I can't believe that!" said Alice.

"Can't you?" the queen said in a pitying tone. "Try again: draw a long breath, and shut your eyes."

Alice laughed. "There's no use trying," she said. "One can't believe impossible things."

"I daresay you haven't had much practice," said the queen. "When I was your age, I always did it for half-an-hour a day. Why sometimes, I believed as many as six impossible things before breakfast."

— Lewis Carroll's *Alice Through the Looking Glass*

CONTENTS

ONE

TWO

ONE

1. Yarn spinning

KISH HAS A TEASING AFFINITY with words. Fine words, fancy footwork giving voice to the richness of her imagination. As a children's storyteller, she comes by it quite naturally. She brings it into play while trying to help me come to terms with her Alzheimer's. It leaves me on the receiving end of her caregiving when it should be the other way round. Listen to her, coddling me, suggesting that it would be easier for me if I thought of it as what's-his-name's disease.

"You know that little joke, 'I'll never forget what's his name,'" she says. "I know that it's not a knee slapper. But in the Alzheimer's context of forgetting, what's-his-name's disease is kind of funny. Don't you think so, Max? It's funny peculiar."

Funny peculiar? I sink into thinking that it's funny futile. *Ahhh Kish.* Breathing her name to myself, I'm indulging my soft spot for her surname as I have all along. Her name is Connie Kish. Constanze Maria Kish on her birth certificate. I may call her Kish as long as I don't resort to any sappy kiss-Kish alliteration. She had her fill of such teasing — Hey Kish! What a dish! — from randy high school boys when she was a teenager.

With Alzheimer's haunting her for some thirty years, Kish wasn't surprised when it stepped out of the shadows and into the open. Ah yes, an acquaintance of long standing. In the cards for her all along. A spook keeping her under surveillance since she was a girl of fifteen and saw the surrender in her father's eyes while she laced up his shoes in the morning and buttered the toast for him. Her Uncle Will also became incurably forgetful and withdrawn. She knew all about the fifty-fifty odds that later on she could be singled out for the family strain of Alzheimer's. And now, when it touches her on the shoulder with a sly come hither, she lets on that it's a liberating moment. She's ready for it. She can't nip it in the bud but she can shrink it down to size by calling it Alzheimer's Lite.

Ahhh Kish. It's as close to praying as I can get. The only thing I'm any good at is worrying. It's touch and go. At times, in certain denial. It can't be Alzheimer's. Then, switching from uncertainty to hoping against hope and from there, goddammit to hell, comes my muffled anger about what's happening to her. I'm on a merry-go-round, circling back into denial, insisting that Kish is an alert, wryly intelligent woman and a gifted storyteller. Her memory is in good working order. At the age of forty-eight, she's too young for it. I can't allow it to exist.

"What's-his-name's disease," she says, savouring that little tidbit and jotting it down in the coil-bound notebook she uses in her work as a storyteller. All joking aside, she gets back to describing her dementia as Alzheimer's Lite. She intends to mention it to the neurologist who has been reviewing her case. She has an appointment with him this morning. She'll ask him to apply it to her as a formal diagnosis. Alzheimer's Lite, an alternative to Alzheimer's Regular Strength.

We're having breakfast — granola with milk and banana slices — where else but in the breakfast nook? It's a welcoming little alcove, as bygone as a kitchen icebox, with the charm of an archway, padded benches and a pink laminate table. Her notebook lies open on the table. Over recent days, it has been evolving entry by entry as an agenda for her session with the neurologist. It won't be a consultation. It will be a negotiation with him. She's draws me into her scheme of things with a rich and sugary voice. Put her in a symphony orchestra and she'd be one of the cellos. Mellow-toned, seductive and winkling a smile out of me by rhyming off a joke about the ditsy blonde who gets Alzheimer's only to find that her IQ goes up. Kish asks me if it's funny enough for her to tell to the doctor, first thing, to break the ice with him.

"Sure Kish. It's funny and I want you to know that it only hurts when I laugh."

"That's the spirit!" she says.

"What I mean to say is that it hurts even more when I laugh."

"Oh Max, my love. I know. I know. I know what you mean. But whatever you do, don't give up . . . Don't quit on you and me . . . We're going to get through this. You'll see."

Here I am, ashamed of myself for settling in under her wing and yet finding it a pleasant place to be. We've seen better days during our twenty-three years together. But we've never been closer, sitting over coffee. Killing time until we leave, she engages me by playing around with a Brothers Grimm fairy tale.

"I'm Gretel and you're Hansel," she says. "We're tormented by a wicked witch in a darkening forest. But fear not, dear Max. We'll have our own trail of bread crumbs leading us out of the forest. We may not live happily ever after. But we'll live as happily ever after as can be expected under the circumstances."

Kish turns to homing in on Alzheimer's. "Conjure that word up in your mind," she says. "Alzheimer's. Look closely at it. What do you see?"

"Three syllables? Is that it?"

"Yes, but there's more. Do you see the glowing in that shiny little vowel in the heim part of it?"

"Let me take a closer look."

"Yes, let go of yourself and you'll see that it's Freddie the firefly with a sparkly magic wand lighting up that syllable."

Her next target is the word diagnosed. "I'm going to be diagnosed by that dementia doctor," she says. "Well, let me tell you, that word has me squirming. It's those ugly consonants. Di-agg-nozed. And rhyming with exposed the way it does. Ex-pozed, making it sound as if I've been tainted with something.

"Oh Max," she says. "I don't want you giving up on me. The diagnosis is not a done deal. We shall see what we shall see."

Getting ready for the doctor, deciding what she'll wear. She has it narrowed down to her platinum pantsuit with a duster-length coat or the Harris Tweed suit in a light brown. She frets about being late and asks again, What time is it? She makes a note of the neurologist's name. Dr. Winkler. She'll address him by name and let him see that she can remember it. She's anticipating his list of questions. Her friend Liz Fogarty recently went through them with her stricken mother.

"Liz told me about all the questions," Kish says. "They are humiliating. Oh what fun! Having a neurologist ask me if I know what day it is. I'll make a note here as a reminder that it's Monday, January the fifteenth. And when he asks if I know where I live, should I have it written out, thoroughly locating myself? The way I did as a schoolgirl? Carefully, line by line, with my name and address on Medana Street. In our city of Victoria. In the province of British Columbia. In Canada with the maple leaf on our flag. And on our Mother Earth in the Milky Way and beyond to the Universe."

She wonders what the neurologist will say about her defying Alzheimer's.

"I'm not expecting it to go easy on me," she says. "But surely I have a right to some fairness in the process. It starts with having me forget myself and putting the wine glasses into the microwave as if they belong there. Shouldn't I then be allowed to forget it altogether? But no. I'm left struggling to remember those blank moments in front of the microwave. The doctor will be asking me about it. Well, I won't be apologizing for it. What happened, happened. And that's all there is to it."

Ahhh Kish. I guess it's the dementia that has her thinking that a disease should play fair. But there's nothing hazy or forgetful about the way she insists that she can make special arrangements with it. She's in command with that high-powered imagination. I'm trying to keep up with the storyteller Connie Kish and that reassuring cello voice tempting me to think that she cannot be denied. I'm along for the ride wherever it takes us.

2. A promise of remission

DR. WINKLER HAS US SEATED in matching ginger-orange chairs with puffed, velvety arms touching. Kish and I are in synch with these warm and friendly chairs, our arms nudging together in a united front. Looking just great in the platinum pantsuit, she starts in breaking the ice with her joke about the ditsy blonde. The doctor has a comeback, asking her if she realizes that one of the good things about Alzheimer's is that you get to meet so many new people.

In my clichéd thinking, a neurologist would be middle-aged, old for his years, and turned out in a dark business suit. But this Dr. Anthony Winkler is much younger, wearing a wrinkled white smock over blue jeans, purple gym shoes, and a yellow T-shirt showing Harold and Maude tearing along on a motorcycle.

Before getting down to business, the doctor has a surprise for us. Going back two decades, he remembers Kish as a children's storyteller. He's one of the hundreds of people around town with Connie Kish fixed back in their childhood. She has made such a success of the storytelling that there's a fan club. Nothing official with a president and regular meetings. Just a goodly number of people, now two generations of them, with Kish fondly remembered from one of her storytelling engagements.

"I should have twigged to your name," the doctor says. "But it was the sound of your voice. While you were telling that joke that the penny dropped. I remember you telling stories at the daycare centre I went to."

"Which one?" Kish asks.

"Happy House."

"They were one of my first clients."

"Do you still wear the high pointy hat with stars on it?"

"Same old, same old," she replies.

He can't hold back, recalling what a joy it was for him as a boy, singing along with her rendering of the Muffin Man who lives in Drury Lane. There's also his favourite story, *Miss Twiggley's Tree*, and getting his mother to buy the book, reading it to him at bedtime until he had it memorized.

"Do you remember how it starts?" he says, reciting it.

Funny Miss Twiggley lived in a tree
With a dog named Puss And a color TV.

Kish joins in with what I take to be the second verse.

She did what she liked,
And she liked what she did.
But when company came
Miss Twiggley hid.

The doctor chimes in with another verse.

She named her dog Puss
But he didn't mind that.
"My very best friend,"
He said, "is a cat."

Kish doesn't miss a beat.

Now Puss was clever —
A smart dog indeed.
He did the shopping
For things they would need.

"I'm impressed," the doctor says. "You're nailing it."

"Well so are you."

"Yes, but it's the only story I know word for word. For you it has to be one of dozens and dozens of stories on your list."

"Yes, but it's fresh in my mind because I've been going over it again, rehearsing it for an engagement next week."

Their sojourn into rhyme puts a different light on things with the doctor deferring to the patient even after he returns to the business at hand.

"I have a list of questions here to see how your memory is functioning," he says. "But it won't be necessary for me to ask you if you know what day it is, now will it?"

"I'm disappointed," she says. "I have the answer written down."

The doctor wants to know about anything recent, any new developments.

"New developments?" Kish says. "Well yes. Last evening. Putting the wine glasses into the microwave. Max saw me doing it."

The doctor has me recalling that we were at the kitchen sink after dinner. She was drying the wine glasses. I heard the clunk of the microwave door opening and turned to see her put one of the glasses in. She held the other glass up to the light, perceiving a smudge, buffing some more, then putting it into the microwave and carefully closing the door.

Kish tells the doctor that I tried to comfort her, pointing out that the stemware cupboard is directly above the microwave and saying that it was an easy mistake. No worse than the night before when I left a carton of cherry vanilla ice cream melting away on the kitchen counter.

"Of course," she says. "You and I know, don't we doctor, that there is a big difference between what I did and Max forgetting to put the ice cream back into the freezer."

"Can you tell me, Mrs. Kish, what you were feeling at the time?"

"Helpless," she says. "I can see myself standing in front of the microwave . . . feeling helpless . . . You know that little row of dots when there are no words in a sentence? Well, I'm in there with the dots . . . and then somewhere else . . . drifting away, coming back . . . Not knowing where I've been."

I'm wondering if the doctor questions, as I do, how she could be aware that she was unaware. If Alzheimer's telltale amyloid plaques and tangles are spreading in her brain, could she really remember not remembering? Or is she imagining a process that would make sense to the doctor and to me? Either way, she's impressively vivid in the way she talks about it.

The session with the doctor turns out to be a process of elimination. Mostly sorting through the results from an MRI scan and from testing for small strokes and for vitamin or other deficiencies. He also has the family history to consider. Having taken that into account along with the test results, the doctor has only one explanation for what's happening to her. He's down to the last culprit left standing. Alzheimer's. But he's dodging around the word as if he can't bring himself to apply it to her.

"That's it, isn't it?" Kish says, taking him off the hook. "It's Alzheimer's."

"We can never be one hundred percent certain with a diagnosis," he says. "But the indications are that that's what it is."

So there it is. Alzheimer's. Served up ungarnished on a silky platter. The doctor has come as close to making it official as he can get. Kish responds to it by becoming the silky dame, delving into the lower reaches of her contralto voice with nary a hint of anger about the di-agg-nosis. But I've got that covered — goddammit to hell. I'm crushed and angry enough for both of us while she's stringing the doctor along, asking him to call it Alzheimer's Lite. He has her file on his computer screen.

"That's an intriguing diagnosis," he says, sounding relieved. "I'm typing it in here. 'Alzheimer's Lite'. I take it that you're spelling it L-I-T-E. Well, it summarizes your situation pretty well. I can see from your test results that even with your memory problems, you're up on a plateau. You're functioning at a high level overall. Your vital signs are good. I wish my blood pressure was as good as yours. At your age — only forty-eight — we're dealing with early onset Alzheimer's. Yes, quite early. A mild cognitive impairment. You can think of it as early days."

Clearly, the doctor is soft-pedalling it. He knows better than to suggest that early days is a positive thing. I've been on line, consulting Dr. Google and his colleagues about Alzheimer's when it happens to somebody Kish's age. They call it Early Onset Alzheimer's Disease, EOAD, as opposed to another snug little acronym, LOAD, for Late Onset Alzheimer's Disease, which shows up in the age range after sixty-five. What they have discovered is that generally, EOAD patients show a more rapid cognitive decline than those with LOAD. In my online questing, I also encountered Alzheimer's first identified victim in Germany in the late 1800s. There are faded sepia photographs of the gaunt and haggard Frau Auguste Deter who became a patient of Dr. Alois Alzheimer, a neurologist with a bushy chevron moustache and wearing pince-nez spectacles.

Kish and this doctor with the loud T-shirt are leaving me behind. Of all things, she has him considering the option of a brain transplant as a surgical remedy for Alzheimer's. At first, letting on that he's warming to the idea, the doctor says that with a brain transplant there would be an advantage. Because the brain is an immunologically privileged organ, he explains, rejection would not be a problem. But he then holds forth with a Catch-22.

"With a transplant," he says, "the organ donor would have to be brain dead before it would be ethical to transplant the brain from the donor to the donee."

"Quite right!" Kish says. "Who needs a dead brain? You know, don't you, that brains can be vastly overrated. Do you remember the Wizard of Oz in the movie saying that brains are a common commodity and that every timid little creature that crawls on the earth or slinks through the slimy seas has a brain?"

Their bantering about a brain transplant has me off by myself and wondering about the feasibility of transplanting neurons from one brain to another. Wanting so badly to do something for her, anything, I'm thinking it through. Alzheimer's comes about when the flow of neurons carrying thoughts and memories zipping hither and thither around the brain is jammed up by the amyloid plaques. The human brain, having in the order of one-hundred-billion neurons, could spare several billion of them. I'd willingly lie down beside Kish with a hookup in place and have my supposedly hale and hearty neurons soldiering forth from my noggin into hers. If it would help to invigorate her brain, I would do it for Kish.

Truly, I would, in the same way that half of my liver or one of my kidneys are hers for the taking.

Sitting sedately in the orange chair, briefly coming out of the closet as an Alzheimer's victim, she's notching down the charm and sounding impersonal when she asks the doctor about the prospects for a cure for Alzheimer's.

"Well," he says, pausing. "I'm very sorry to have to tell you that we don't have a cure, and there isn't likely to be one for some time."

"Well if it can't be cured then I guess that it must be endured," Kish says.

"I wouldn't put it quite that way. One of the things that we can do is to get you on Aricept and see how it works for you. Generally, it provides some improvement in awareness and ability to function."

In a time's-up gesture just before noon, the doctor turns off his computer, rolls his high-backed chair away from the desk, and turns to face Kish and tell her about another one of his patients.

"He's almost as resourceful as you are about his dementia," the doctor says. "Instead of defining it as Alzheimer's Lite, his approach is to try to dismiss it altogether. He has this slogan, 'Alzheimer's Schmaltzheimers. Forget about it.' It seems to work for him. It's helping him to get on with the rest of his life, at least as far as he's able to do that."

"I like it," Kish says. "It's the nice echoing of that "heim" sound. There's rhyme and rhythm to it. And it's funny, don't you think, for him to be telling people to forget about Alzheimer's? I'm going to make a note of it."

She takes out her notebook. Alzheimer's Schmaltzheimers? It's too big a mouthful to serve as a chant in a nursery rhyme. But it could work for her as an incantation.

"One more thing," the doctor says. "The referral informs me that you're walking your dog a couple of times a day. Well, keep it up. Regular exercise is as important to you as it ever was. It helps to maintain a good blood flow to the brain. And you, Mr. Kish. You should be out there walking with her."

It's not the first time I've been called Mr. Kish and occasionally I let it go. But this time, I decide to straighten things out.

"Yes, doctor, I'm the husband, but my name is Max Osborne. She let me keep my name after we were married. Wasn't that nice of her?"

"Sorry about that, Mr. Osborne. But let me say again, Ms. Kish. You're functioning at a high level overall. When Alzheimer's comes into the picture, most people throw up their hands and say, game over. But it's not. There are degrees and you seem to be aware of that. You're seeing yourself as a special case with your own strain of Alzheimer's. The Alzheimer's Lite. You should trademark it as a coping mechanism. My hope for you is that you stay up on that plateau you have created for yourself."

It's the second time he has mentioned the plateau, prompting Kish to inquire about it. Schmoozing away, she has him going beyond the science of medicine and into the healing art of it.

"Now about this plateau, "she says.

"It's all yours," the doctor says.

"Tell me, please. Just how healthy would it be up there?"

"As healthy as you want it to be."

"It seems so far away," she says. "It's drearily flat and barren and exposed to the westerly winds. There are no trees up there."

She's asking the doctor and me if we're familiar with the story about the Swiss Family Robinson who lived in a treehouse on a tropical island.

"Yes, I saw the movie," the doctor says.

I chime in, "And so did I."

"I have it on my bookshelf," she says. "The Robinsons were shipwrecked and alone on their island. They built a treehouse with a rope ladder hanging down from it."

Hands folded in her lap, she's a picture of serenity and confidence. "Can you feel the little surges of inspiration," she says. "They have this tree growing from a winged samara seed pod . . . a leaf, a twig, and a branch at a time . . .

"It's the cool shade that I need," she says, pausing again.

"And listen to the rustling of the leaves . . .

"I'll need a place to sit . . . "

She has me leaning forward and tuning in to what a lucky few can do when giving leeway to the vitality of their imagination. I'm holding my breath while Kish has another treehouse magically taking shape, phrase by phrase.

"I'll have a rocking chair with a blue and white cushion up there.

"Now it's a treehouse . . . the Mañana Treehouse. There's something about that word, isn't there? Mañana. Can you hear it? Soft sounding. An indefinite tomorrow, going on forever as a place of remission, staving off all sickness and disease . . .

"And do you know what? I won't be needing a rope ladder. I'll get up there with a hop, a skip, and a jump."

Well aware of my doubting Thomas tendencies, she turns to me. "Can you see me up there?"

"Yes, Kish. I can see you. Looking good. Looking very good."

Dr. Winkler is also buying into it.

"Yes, Ms. Kish," he says. "Come to think of it, it's an offshoot of Miss Twiggley's treehouse. And with your very own treehouse, who needs a plateau?"

He takes a moment to explain what he meant when he said that Kish was a special case. Normally, with a referral like this, he wouldn't be seeing her again. He would hand her back to her GP and that would be the end of it for him. Instead, he intends to take her into the fold and have her on his list of patients.

"You're a very interesting case, Ms. Kish," he says. "So I don't want to lose track of you. On your way out, have the receptionist make an appointment to see me in a month. Have her set up regular appointments. Once a month. We'll be running a few tests to see how you're getting along in that treehouse of yours."

I am meanwhile beginning to see the light. What did she say about the Mañana Treehouse? A place of remission, staving off all sickness and disease? She'll use it to buy time for herself between now and when it starts getting dark again. Vague about the future, she's hanging on to her identity as a wry, intelligent woman. I'm wondering what she'll say when I ask her to shove over and make room for me in her rocking chair.

3. Trees

IT COMES AS NO SURPRISE to me that Kish would find solace in a treehouse. It fits right in with the close affiliation she has with trees. Going back to when she was a teenager smoking marijuana in the upper reaches of a particular tree on the Douglas Street side of Beacon Hill Park. I think of it as Our Tree with the capital letters to acclaim it for bringing us together.

Much later on, she was the tree hugger, doting over the Spartan apple tree we have in our garden. In keeping with ancient lore, she planted it during a waxing phase of the moon to foster flourishing roots. She was the tree lady, talking to the sapling while watering it three times a week. She made it part of the family with formal introductions, presenting me to the tree as Maximillian Osborne and the tree to me as *Malus domestica*.

Recently, in the park after a windstorm on the first day of spring, we came upon a hemlock blown over with its root system torn up, exposed, and dying of thirst. The tree was leaning precariously, rubbing with a groaning sound against another tree and lurching down a few feet at a time as the branches on the supporting tree snapped off under the weight of the falling hemlock.

"Ah look," Kish said. "And listen to the poor thing, hanging on and struggling to stay alive. And that other tree, holding it up and trying to save it."

Also on her care list is the solitary fig tree growing in the lobby at the Capitol 6 movie house in Victoria. *Ficus carica*, twenty-five feet high, close to forty years of age and looking healthy enough, with lush and shiny palmate leaves. Skin-deep beauty, says Kish. Looking under the bark, she sees the tormented heart of a tree reaching in vain for sky and sun above the glass dome that imprisons it. She has it darkly brooding in solitary confinement and waiting for the right movie to come along. Perchance a film set in Azerbaijan where fig trees were cultivated centuries ago. As she would have it, such a movie would be the cue for this captive *Ficus carica* to erupt into a botanical Godzilla, uprooting itself, exploding through theatre walls, arm branches thrashing around with fury as it stomps down the aisle, and vanishes into the movie screen to make good its escape and settle contentedly in Azerbaijan with kindred trees on a fertile slope overlooking the Caspian Sea.

Over the years on our walks around the park, in a little game we played, I would try to coax us along the pathway leading past Our Tree.

"Hey, look! There it is, over there!"

I wanted to have a little brass plate inscribed, *Where Max met Kish* with the date it happened and tack it high up on the trunk of that tree. To commemorate the occasion, I also wanted us to climb the tree so that we could smoke a joint up there together. But Kish always declined.

"You've got some nerve," she said. "Getting me mixed up with one of the drug-addicted floozies you were hanging out with as a teenager."

But she had a soft spot for that tree. I could hear it in the warmth of her voice.

"Oh you and your darn tree," she would say as she pulled at my arm and led us off in the other direction.

It has been that voice all along. The first time, a young version of it calling down to me from that tree on a summer evening. I was walking my Aunt Sarah's dog in the park. The perky little mutt, a Cesky terrier, pulling away to the end of the leash, cocked a hind leg and peed on the tree trunk, at which point that voice came down to me with a proclamation.

"Hey kid, this my tree!"

She would have been fifteen, but sounded older and sure of herself, taking outright possession of the tree and calling me kid.

"Okay! It's your tree," I said.

"Well then, why did you let your dog pee on my tree?"

"I didn't let him do it. He didn't ask me for permission. He just did it."

"But you're holding the leash. You're responsible for him."

She had me on the defensive, lovelorn at seventeen and in general trepidation of the female species. Peering up, all I could make out in the gloaming was her silhouette. But the voice was clear enough, asking me why, before Oscar took to irrigating her tree, I had been walking around it. My explanation was that I was listening to a birdcall that intrigued me. I couldn't see the bird but I could hear it coming from her tree. Just two notes. Really sad. She asked me to sing the notes and instead, I whistled them. Eeee-oooo.

"Good ear there, kid," she said.

Up there, in what I now fully conceded was her tree, she had also been listening to the bird. She hadn't seen it either but she knew that it was a black-capped chickadee. She informed me that the more familiar call of this bird was a quicker dee-dee-dee-dee sound. The birdcall we heard that evening was the slower, descending eeee-oooh. Like this, she said, singing the two notes precisely and informing me that in music it was a minor third. She said it sounded like a pathetically hen-pecked male calling out for a mate with a reputation for sleeping around. I was emboldened. We were talking. We had that cuckolded chickadee in common. I liked her, sight unseen. I was taken by the sound of her voice.

"What school do you go to?" I asked.

"Are you flirting with me?"

"I wouldn't call it flirting."

"I would. And I don't flirt around with guys I don't know."

"Would it be flirting if I told that you my name is Max and that I go to Oak Bay High?"

"Definitely flirting," she said.

"What if I asked you for your name?"

"Same deal."

Oscar was tugging from the end of his leash, wanting me to get back to the dog walking. Just then, I picked up on whiffs of marijuana smoke.

"So that's what you're doing up there," I said. "You're smoking pot. Toking up. I know what it smells like."

"You're wrong, kid. It's tobacco. It's a Turkish cigarette."

I lowered my voice as close as I could get to baritone level and let on that I smoked marijuana all the time, calling it weed, when in fact, I had smoked it only once with my brother Conrad.

"I suppose you want to come up and smoke one of my Turkish cigarettes," she said. "Well you can't. Oscar can come up if he wants. But you're going to have to find your own tree.

28

This one's taken . . . Now seriously, I'd like to know how I'm supposed get down from this tree."

"The same way you went up?"

She reviewed the fundamentals of tree climbing. "It's easier climbing up because you can see your way. But it's harder going back down because you can't see below your feet and where you're placing them and you're trying to avoid the places where some dog has been whizzing."

"Are you barefoot?"

"No. But really kid, I shouldn't have to put up with it."

She asked if my aunt lived nearby. "Just a few blocks away," I said.

"A stepladder would be helpful."

It was agreed that Aunt Sarah would have a stepladder and that I'd go and get it. On my way back, the girl said, I'd be passing the drive-in on Douglas and I could pick up a couple of ice cream cones there. She liked vanilla.

It was the least I could do. Away I went, with Oscar trotting along, back to Aunt Sarah's house and returned awkwardly, carrying the ladder and the ice cream cones in a tray, only to find that the girl had climbed down on her own and was nowhere to be seen. The ice cream was melting quickly. Oscar turned up his nose at vanilla, leaving me to console myself, slurping back and forth to keep up with the melting.

In the course of my dog walking for the rest of that summer, I would just happen along under that tree, casually glancing up into it. Regrets were piling up. Why hadn't I climbed up there in a he-manly way — me Tarzan, you Jane — in hopes of getting acquainted and toking up with her? As it was, I had no idea what she looked like. All I had to go on was the sound of her voice.

Ten years later, I was bowled over by those sugary contralto tones, so deeply imprinted that I recognized them immediately, flowing from the larynx of Connie Kish, a novice teacher at the elementary school where I was in my first year as a vice-principal. Renewing acquaintances one morning in the staff room, I recalled our encounter in the park. I avoided any mention of the pot smoking.

"Don't you remember me?" I asked and followed up by whistling that eeee-ooo chickadee sound.

"Oh yes!" she said with a smile that lifted my spirits. "I remember."

"It's that voice of yours," I said. "I'd know it anywhere. Why didn't you wait?"

"You're mistaken, Mr. Osborne. I waited but you didn't return. Okey-doke!"

Saying okey-doke the way she does to this day, Kish gives equal weight and rhyme to the syllables with a direct and quiet authority. It's her way of saying subject closed and let's move on.

I thought that by declining to remember our encounter, she would have me forget that she was smoking marijuana when she was fifteen and too young for it. But over time, bit by bit as we became friends, she confided in me. Not only was that tree a hideaway for toking up, it was her escape from the Alzheimer's that was tearing her family apart. An only child, she was losing her father and an uncle to it. Her mother, distraught over what was happening, was also an absentee parent. Kish was doing more than her share in looking after her father and wondering about the fifty-fifty chance that she would inherit his dementia.

After school, she took him for walks in the park. They went to that drive-in for vanilla ice cream cones. In rare moments of intimacy, he'd laugh and they'd smile back and forth as he lapped away at the ice cream like a little boy and wanted more of it. She looked after him willingly and lovingly. Her main regret was having to miss choir practice at school. Evenings and weekends taken up with his care, she lost touch with school friends; she felt increasingly alone and turned to smoking marijuana in that tree.

During her first year as a teacher, her classroom tended to be a noisy place. As a novice, she was easy pickings for the unruly ADHD kids. The only quiet time in Classroom 5 was story time. With Kish telling the stories, all of the children, even the rowdy ones, sat quietly and listened. As a Connie Kish aficionado myself, I would find some reason or other to duck out of my office, meander down the empty hallway and pause outside Classroom 5 to listen to her. I was stalking that voice. I couldn't get enough of it.

At the end of the school term, Miss Kish and Mr. Osborne, teacher and vice-principal, came to an understanding. It was agreed that she didn't have the temperament for school teaching. "What did the cross-eyed teacher say to the vice-principal?" she quipped. "I can't control my pupils." Leave it to Kish to josh about her shortcomings as a teacher.

As for Kish and Max, well our universe was unfolding as it should. She went along with my regaling her as a storyteller and in time she eased into it as a career, and I moved on to become the vice-principal at another school. She was no longer under my authority. It would therefore not be inappropriate for us to go out for dinner and a movie. By then, beguiled as I was by that surname, I was calling her Kish.

It sounds made up but it's not. Although it's commonly a Jewish name, in her case there's a gypsy connection. It goes back to her great-grandmother who was born into a Romany

31

clan and lived the caravan life in the early 1900s in the south of France until she and her husband and their daughter Constanze became lace-curtain citizens of France and settled in Marseilles. Constanze later married Jacques Marchand, a watchmaker and goldsmith. Under women's rights rooted in the French revolution, Grandmamma Constanze Kish kept her birth name and brought it with her when she and Jacques came to Canada and settled in Victoria.

I was falling for Kish and I couldn't fall fast enough. The attraction started with that voice and extended to the woman overall. Much later on, when she asked me if I thought breast enhancement surgery would make her more alluring, I said of course it's your bod and do as you want, but please, put away the measuring tape. In the eyes of this beholder, the existing topography is perfectly fine. It would be pointless to try to improve it with a boob job. I also cast my vote against any peekaboo, over-the-forehead hair styling that would cover up that cowlick of auburn hair growing slyly against the grain. Same goes for any orthodontic tampering with the slightly crooked tooth on the left side of her smile.

A few months later, after we discovered the meaning of andante in the sack, she said how nice it was to find that a discerning ear for chickadee calls wasn't my best feature. A secondary consideration was that I could laugh at myself. She also liked what she described as my craggy good looks. The craggy part was my nose, twice broken, the first time while getting sozzled on beer at the students' pub at university. Talking when I should have been listening. A surly classmate, showing me the error of my ways, threw a punch that realigned my schnozz and left it bearing off to the right.

The second nasal readjustment happened on Yates Street during our first movie date — *Tootsie*, it was — after I interceded on her behalf when she was confronted by an inebriated passerby who thought she was a former girlfriend named Delores. Afterward, Kish said it was gallant of me, rallying to her defence. My natural fight-or-flight response in such situations tends toward flight. I don't know what possessed me to stand in there. Not stalwart exactly but, as Kish described it, more in the tradition of Sir Percival, according to chivalric lore, a gentle and reluctant knight. I didn't actually engage in manly fisticuffs on her behalf. We made do with the singular fisticuff.

Only one fist was thrown and I was on the receiving end of it. Arthur punched me squarely on the right side of my nose. This served as rough-and-ready cosmetic surgery, realigning said nose and leaving it somewhat thicker than before. Kish, mopping with a tissue and touching my face with her warm hands, remarked that my craggy good looks would be even craggier than before.

We were married six months later and spent a month resort-hopping in the south of France on a trip that was financed with a gift from Grandmamma Constanze. But I don't think of it as our honeymoon. That distinction belongs to a weekend jaunt to the village of Ganges. Kish's gift to me on the occasion of our first anniversary in exchange for the pair of Picasso prints that I gave to her. She made all the arrangements. The ferry to Salt Spring Island, the hotel booking, and dinner reservations.

"It's all yours," she said. "All in your name. If you don't have anybody else to go there with you, then I'm available."

"Let me check around," I said. "I'll get back to you."

That weekend, on the Sunday, the desk clerk at the hotel suggested that we go oyster digging. He provided a shovel, an oyster gun he called it, for digging up the oysters and a billycan for stewing them in sea water over the little fire we would have on the beach. He pointed us in the direction of the oyster beds on the shore of a little cove a few minutes' walk from the hotel.

For our seashore lunch that day, we had a baguette, a quarter pound of butter and a bottle of champagne — the wine that goes with oysters — in a thermos bag to keep it cold. While we were digging into the sand for the oysters, Kish informed me that the womanizing Casanova, an authority on aphrodisiacs, made a habit of fortifying himself with a plateful of oysters for breakfast.

During that excellent repast, I contrived a few changes in Omar's *Rubáiyát*. A jug of wine/A loaf of bread/A few puffs of pot/A bowl of steamed oysters/And thou. I know it doesn't scan worth a damn. But let me say that it was a true honeymoon interlude, passing the 'thou's back and forth in the wave-swept seclusion of that beach.

Returning to Victoria, sitting out on the deck of the ferry sailing south on Haro Strait, in the anniversary spirit of the occasion, I let her know that our first year together had been enlightening for me.

"I want you to know that I've become a one-dame man."

"Well then," she said. "We've had a two-way conversion. By my troth, I'm a one-man dame."

"Well that's just dandy. And I want to tell you something else but only if you promise not to tell anybody else."

"That depends."

"It's a relief for me to say this and get it out into the open. I've come to realize that you're more insightful and intelligent than I am."

"Do you really think so?"

"Yes, you are."

"I don't think of you in those terms."

"You're smart as a whip without cracking it over me."

"That's just your self-deprecating humour at work there, Max."

"Not quite, my love. There are times when I have no choice but to defer to you and take myself down a peg."

"Are you doing that now?"

"Ah, Kish. It happens when you get the upper hand in some discussion we're having and I say, 'There you go again, Kish, running rings around me.'"

"Yes, I remember. And then I say, 'There you go again, Max. So sure of yourself that you can take yourself down a peg.'"

"That's only because you make it safe for me to do that."

"That's me. Good old, safe old Connie Kish."

"That's right. I can safely take myself down a peg because I know that you'll notch me back up a peg. Building me up."

There, on the ferry deck, she was holding her hat in the wind and radiating intelligence. I wondered if she could see the inner sheen I derived from knowing that a woman like her could love me and endow me with a high opinion of myself.

"What we have here, my good man, is a quid pro quo," she said.

"There you go again, running rings around me with all that scholarly Latin."

"The quid part of it is me building you up. The pro quo is you praising me as a storyteller and telling me I could make a career out of it."

"Aw shucks, ma'am. 'Tweren't nothin.'"

"Thanks to you, it's starting to shape up as a career."

"About time, too. Otherwise, you'd be a kept woman."

"Is that so? Well, being a kept woman is vastly superior to being a debauched vice-principal sneaking along the hallway and stalking one of the teachers."

"So, you were onto me."

"Yes. Really, Max. Helen Marlowe, the teacher across the hall, saw you hanging around."

"How can you associate with such a shady character?"

"Such a wonderful man. I knew you were at the door listening and I liked it. And something else. As a teenager, I hated my voice. I hated being different. I didn't want to be the contralto soloist in the school choir. I wanted to be a soprano like the other girls. Then you came along and changed that. Oh, Max. Without you, I wouldn't be a storyteller."

That reaffirming weekend left me with renewed confidence in the warmth and affability we had as a couple. It flourished in the morning, first thing, just the two of us tethered together by brain waves crackling their way across our bed. Kish, childlike and open to possibilities, would be teasing them out into a meeting of the minds. She had me believing that simply by activating her brain waves, she could wake me up right after waking up herself, usually around seven thirty.

To this day, I have no inkling as to what was going on in that first breath of her waking up. It never worked the other way. When I woke up before she did and tried to will her into waking up, my brain waves fizzled and failed to make the connection. Kish on the other hand had only to open her eyes and invoke some spooky remote control to have me responding. I had various explanations. I wanted her to consider that we could be synchronized in the wake-up physiology of our rising heart rates and respiration. Or could it be that I was responding to the immediacy of her radiating warmth and her stepped up vibes when she woke up? I was dubious about brain waves actually sparking their way through her skull to go exploring across the bed.

"Listen to the brain boffin holding forth," Kish said. "Well, you know what, smarty pants? Sometimes brains think too much."

She didn't want me gearing it up with science. She wanted the magic of soulmates waking up together. What made her utterly convincing was the heart and soul she put into having us start our day in harmony and unison. If a flow of brain waves didn't work for me, she would have me think of it as love reaching across the bed. How I woke up was of no consequence. It was entirely her doing.

Here I am now, years later, recalling it far more fondly than she would. As she would see it, her Alzheimer's has been softening me up and has me going overboard, striving to remember her the way she was and trying to keep her that way.

I miss the fringe benefits. The way it was, being there with her under the fleecy nap of a Hudson's Bay blanket and the warm caress of the sheets. Even as a staid-as-they-come high school principal, how could I resist becoming a privileged character with entree to her world? It was ahhh so good to be floating quietly into our morning and looking over at the window curtains billowing in with an ocean breeze from the Strait of Juan de Fuca a few streets away.

I relished feeling superior to the morning people who are upbeat and chatty first thing. Kish and I would be sulky and at peace together. Brain waves, softly beating hearts, with the pillow talk held to brief mutterings. And, until quite recently, there was time for renewal, for belonging, simply not being alone, spooning together or for sharing a dream one of us might have had.

Until quite recently? There it is again. Goddammit! That lowdown little qualifier. The new demarcation in our life together. AA, After Alzheimer's and BA, Before Alzheimer's, when Kish could wake me up with a brainwave blink of her eyes. She's not as open to enchantment as she used to be, not with the dementia tapping into her vitality, short-circuiting the brain waves and leaving me to jump the gun, waking up separate from her and alone.

Or last night, going to sleep, fretting about what the future holds for her, wondering if her brain would be more vulnerable to an Alzheimer's ambush under the cover of darkness while she sleeps. This morning, I lie in bed worrying about what first thought will surface in her mind and swim into her consciousness when she wakes up. What could be worse for her than to start her day face to face with Alzheimer's?

I don't know what's up with her, away over there on her side of the bed with her head under the pillow. My guess is that she's pretending to be asleep. If she was really asleep, I could wake her up by touching her shoulder. But off in the shadows, faking it, she's a world away and beyond my reach. I'll stay on hold and wait for the sound of her voice.

4. Oh me of little faith

THERE'S ANOTHER TANGIBLE WHIFF of magic hereabouts. More specifically, being in two places at the same time. In the realm of religion, it's known as bilocation. To cite an early example, there was St. Isidore of Seville, a farm labourer, circa 520 CE. As a young man, before ascending into saintliness, he claimed to be kneeling in prayer at church while at that very moment, he was out conscientiously ploughing in the fields. One of the spins that could be put on it is that this ambitiously pious farm hand was fibbing in the hope that it would persuade the powers to turn him into a saint.

However, there can be absolutely no doubt, none at all, that Kish can be sitting with me over coffee in the breakfast nook and simultaneously lolling back in her rocking chair in the Mañana Treehouse. She's on a roll, upbeat and quirky, being herself, a fascinating woman. She isn't silly superficial. She's silly wry, whimsical and thoughtful all in the same breath as a free spirit. She can be everywhere and she can be nowhere, ascending and descending in a flash between the bliss of remission up there while down here the dementia war is raging. When I ask her what it's like up there, she says that it's as close to being an angel she'll ever get.

"What else do you want to know about it?" she asks.

"You must have a pretty nice view."

"Yes, you can see forever and beyond to a healing spa in Shangri-La. Oh Max, I'd really like you to see it for yourself."

"You've read my mind. I was about to ask you to make room for me in your rocking chair."

"You mean a rocking chair built for two?

"Why not? We have a bicycle built for two. Just think how cozy it would be for us, sitting side by side, taking in the view from your arboreal abode."

"Arboreal abode?"

"Well that's what it is, isn't it?"

"Really Max! Arboreal abode!" she says scornfully

"I'm just trying to be supportive."

"Arboreal abode! Oh Max, you're making fun of me."

"Ahhh Kish, I would never make fun of you or trivialize something as important as this is. It's just that I went on line, about treehouses, and it popped up out of nowhere. Abi's Arboreal Abode and Hammock Haven. It's for rent, in Kentucky I think, for seventy-one dollars a night."

"Well, I don't want you Googling my treehouse to death. Bilocation? Arboreal abode? Listen to those words. How contrived they are."

"Well, I didn't mean to trivialize your treehouse. Far from it. I can see how well it's working for you."

"But it's not working for you. Is that it, Max?"

"Well, you know me. The smarty pants."

She's up in her treehouse, disappointed and talking down to me.

"Okey-doke?" she says with certainty, meaning that the mañana promise of remission from the dementia is her affair. I've become prince consort to Her Kishness. Deferring to her even as the closet goddammit guy, too angry to be a true believer. I know that I'm missing out on something and settling for a compromise, second best to being up there with her. I have the satisfaction of knowing that she wants me with her in the treehouse, sharing in her magic. In that sense, we're in this together, which is where I want to be. Sheltered with her in spirit. Trying to believe in this tree of life — more to the point, the tree of our life — and knowing that she's better off without me and my doubts about it queering it for her. Oh me of little faith.

She has a *New Yorker* magazine cartoon pinned up on the noteboard next to the wall phone in the kitchen. It's a Robert Mankoff drawing with a bearded, portly figure wearing a monk's robe and sandals and carrying a sign that says, "The end is nighish."

Tinkering fancifully, Kish has nighish slotted into a procession.

"Nigh, nighish, nigher, nighest," she says. "Creeping up on me like the Alzheimer's. Nighish. How does that sound to you, Max? Nighish. That's where I am now."

5. Dickering with dementia

WE'RE GETTING BACK AS CLOSE as we can to ordinary days. It's happening in a familiar place, the breakfast nook, as dated as the house itself with its flagstone pathway leading in from the sidewalk and shiny stained glass in leaded panels around the front door. Along the wrap-around veranda, we have a row of lilac bushes. They're *Syringa afganica*, and in this the month of May, they're in blossom and perfuming the street.

However, this morning, the way things are, it's dull and blustery out there on the other side of the breakfast nook window. Gusts of rain are pelting at the glass while we're having breakfast. It's my turn at the kitchen stove. I'm cooking a savoury oatmeal with pepper and salt instead of sugar and cinnamon and a poached egg on top.

Over coffee, Kish informs me that she'll no longer be answering our phone. She won't be available to any callers except her cousin and dearest friend, Hilary, who is a lawyer with a family in Vancouver. In childhood, they lived on the same street here in James Bay. If anybody else calls, I'm to say that Kish isn't available. She's taking a sabbatical, time away from friends looking embarrassed and at a loss for words now that they know about the Alzheimer's.

"I've been getting that 'oh-you-poor-thing' look," she says.

"Well yes, but isn't it because they care about you?"

"Yes, I know. And I guess I would have been doing the same thing to Liz Fogarty's mother after she was diagnosed last year."

In my new role as social secretary, I'm left to deal with a dinner invitation from the Etheringtons, Carl and Helen, for next week. We've been friends for years, going to concerts and dining together. We spent ten days with them on an ocean cruise to Alaska. Now, it's their turn to have us over for dinner and Helen has phoned about it. We've always enjoyed going there. She's a violin teacher and a good cook and they're an interesting couple. They started out as Kish's friends, as is the case with Hank and Susan Green, Sukie and Malkait Gill and Anita Stokes who lives next door and all of our friends. Kish cultivated these friendships and I latched onto them. The few friends I had as a teacher and school principal have drifted away. The same goes for the friendships I had as a schoolboy and university student. It's one of my shortcomings. I'm too passive. Out of sight, out of mind. I don't seem to get around to doing what it takes to keep friendships alive. This leaves me with two friends, Kish and my brother Conrad, and possibly Flora, our Scottish deerhound. I'm hesitant about including her because I'm not sure what she would think about such an arrangement.

"What do I say to Helen?" I ask.

"You could go," Kish says.

"No I couldn't do that."

"I'm not really saying go by yourself. I want you to deal with it. Just tell Helen that we can't make it. She's not the type to get all huffy. Who knows, she might be relieved. I'd be the Alzheimer's elephant in the room, making everybody uncomfortable."

It's left to me to dish out what remains of our season tickets to Victoria Symphony concerts. There's been six of us with

43

the Etheringtons and the Gills in the front row, lower balcony at the Royal Theatre. Great seats with a bird's eye view down into the orchestra. Having decided that she won't be going to concerts, at least for this year, Kish wants me to give our tickets to the Gills with the understanding that they consult with the Etheringtons about who gets our seats for the remaining concerts.

"Are you sure that's what you want? We've had those seats for ten years."

"You could still go to the concerts. I won't mind. Really, Max. I want you to do that. And you should go to the Etheringtons for dinner."

"Without you? Ah, come on. It wouldn't feel right. We're friends with them as a couple. I'd be the elephant in room."

"I know that I'm making things difficult for you, Max. And I'm sorry about that. I'm hoping that you'll bear with me "

"But you're cutting yourself off from all of your friends. Are you sure about that? They're such an important part of your life. Mine too."

"I still care very much about my friends. That hasn't changed. It's just that I need a little time to come to terms with our new situation. I'm just not there yet. I'm feeling very insecure."

"What can I do to help you with that?"

"You're already doing all that you can. It's just that I want to consolidate and get down to the basics. To you and me. When we get that sorted out, we can start expanding and get back with our friends."

This evening, we're watching television, *Jeopardy* at the moment. I'm musing to myself, so far, so good. As far as I know, her day has passed without any memory lapses.

It's almost as if this thought is a jinx and it tips her into an Alzheimer's moment. Intending to raise the volume on the TV, she's pointing her cell phone and jamming away at it in frustration, saying that the batteries need changing. I'm genuinely sympathetic, decrying the surfeit of technology laid out on the coffee table in an assortment of control devices with their hooded, beady little eyes. One gadget for the television set. One for the DVD player. A third for the video recorder and yet another for the CD player. And to boot, her phone, which she has handy because she's expecting a call from Hilary.

"Oh Max," she says. "You do go on. Why not just come out with it and say that the phone is for phone calls and this remote is what I need when I want to turn up the sound on the TV?"

"Well, it's because you already know that. You simply picked up your phone without realizing it. I could have done the same thing."

"Yes. But you would have noticed right away that the volume control on the phone doesn't look the least bit the way it does on the remote. You wouldn't have kept on mindlessly pushing buttons while you were looking right at the thing."

"But were you really looking at it? Knowing what it was? Or were you frustrated, not really seeing it and thinking this darn thing isn't working the way it's supposed to?"

Kish has a state-of-the-art bullshit detector. It's finely tuned and has kept me on my toes over the years. I know that it has been activated when she cocks her left eyebrow and shifts into her Gallic shrug. What gives this detector extra clout is that it speaks pidgin French. It's another inheritance, along with the voice and the Gallic shrug, from Grandmamma Constanze. After settling in Victoria, she made the transition from French to English with the aid of such expressions as *c'est le gros boo-ul shee-it*. She also Anglicized the word *grand-mère* into grandmamma, pronounced grandma-MAH, and wanted to be addressed in that way. I never met the woman but from photographs of her that I've seen and what Kish has told me about her, I know that she was a proud, somewhat aloof old dame and that when she said C'est le gros boo-ul shee-it it had the weight of a royal proclamation

Kish wants me to give her the name of one person I know who tries using their phone as a TV remote. As everybody knows, the rule of holes is that when you find yourself in a rapidly deepening chasm, you stop digging. And yet here I am, madly shovelling away, making the point that these contraptions on the table look much alike. They're black, hand-held and have rows of buttons. Kish saves me from myself, coming up with another way of minimizing the lapse with her phone.

"What would be involved?" she asks. "I'd say it was no more than sixty seconds before I realized my mistake."

Well, yes, as far as we know, the confusion over her phone was her only lapse of the day. So that would be sixty seconds over the course of the day that she was off kilter. The rest of the time, say for sixteen waking hours, she was functioning normally. It's been that way for most of her lapses into dementia. They're sad little glitches, bouts of Alzheimer's Lite, a matter of seconds off the beam.

"We'll call it the sixty-second rule," she says, tapping into the magic of the Mañana Treehouse. "If a spell of forgetfulness lasts sixty seconds or less, well then we don't have to worry about it now do we? And where's my notebook? I want to make a note of this."

"Yes. You can be a little forgetful for a few moments, no problemo. You're like that commercial for Ivory soap claiming to be ninety-nine-and-forty-four-one-hundredth percent pure."

This sixty-second rule reassures her when she looks down at the beaded moccasin slippers that have found their way onto the wrong feet. The rule also covers another wayward moment out in the garden when she pours dog kibble onto the platform feeder for the birds, much to the soulful dismay of Flora. Playing out my string of denials, I'm saying not to worry, Kish. Those old slippers are loose-fitting and interchangeable. And that gaffe at the bird feeder was a whoops-a-daisy moment.

"There's something else." she says. What did Dr. Winkler say? 'Alzheimer's Schmaltzheimers! Forget about it!' Yes, I made a note of that didn't I?"

I'm nodding along with her and trying it on for size — Alzheimer's Schmaltzheimers. I notice that she said *we* don't have to worry ourselves about brief lapses. I take it to mean that she's thinking that this is a team effort and I want to keep it that way. What matters is that we're together, in our shelter, denying the undeniable and holding the fort. Momentarily subdued, Kish says that there are small mercies at her disposal.

"Small mercies," she says. "I've always liked the sound of the expression. Small mercies. Grandmamma called them *les petites miséricordes*. She thought they were nice things to have. I've read somewhere that there's no pain associated with Alzheimer's. So I won't be needing a pain pump. I guess that's a small mercy."

Quick and inventive, she moves along to wondering why she shouldn't be able to negotiate what she'll be allowed to remember and what she'll forget. Once again, dickering with dementia. She has my name at the top of her list and wants to keep it forever. There would also be the names of cousin Hilary and her husband, Jim, and their boys, Sean and Eric.

And Flora of course and a few close friends. What would she trade away for that list of names?

"All my recipes," she says. "The ones I know by heart. My favourites, the Chicken Dijon and the egg frittata with leeks and fontina cheese. I'd also give up remembering how to knit and how to clean the oven."

"That's very noble of you. Next thing I know, you'll be giving up on your share of the vacuuming and scrubbing out the shower stall."

Well, yes, she'd be willing to make the supreme sacrifice and bargain away any and all housework on condition that she doesn't become so forgetful that she loses her touch as children's storyteller. The Alzheimer's has her wondering how long she'll be able to continue what has been her working life for twenty-three years.

She's not, as is often assumed, a library volunteer reading from storybooks and holding them up to show the pictures to the children. The stories Kish tells she knows by heart. She spends hours rehearsing them in her studio. She's professional in the sense that she's adequately paid. Her going rate is one hundred dollars an hour. She leans toward the classics, *Aesop's Fables*, the Brothers Grimm, Hans Christian Anderson, and Beatrix Potter. She also has a repertoire of children's songs and accompanies herself on the guitar.

Her rendering of the Barney Google song is something to listen to and to behold with Kish costumed with the pashmina shawl and the star-studded Harlequin hat, chording away on the guitar left-handed the way she does. If you believe that the devil is a southpaw, you'd know there's something a touch demonic in her singing about Barney Google and his goo-goo-googely eyes with Kish herself going cross-eyed and leaning out toward those kids sitting on the floor, giggling their hearts out. She also dances the hokey-pokey, step by step, and has the children following along.

At her peak, she was performing regularly at two daycare centres, the kids' section at a bookstore, a branch of the public library and at children's birthday parties. She started cutting back last year and has it reduced to one of the daycare centres and an occasional birthday party. Striving to stay tuned up as a storyteller, she's spending more time than ever rehearsing stories and songs in her studio.

This afternoon, she's appalled when she finds herself groping for a moment for the name of the street we live on. Then she recovers on her own, remembering that it's Medana Street.

"Well, not to worry," she says, making allowances.

"Right on there, Kish. All together now, 'Alzheimer's Schmaltzheimers. Forget about it!'"

"I've been thinking about that," she says. "I'm going to write to the people at Hallmark and suggest that they put it on a get-well card for people with Alzheimer's. They could illustrate it with a picture of some poor benighted soul on the cover and inside in big red letters, 'Alzheimer's Schmaltzheimers. Forget about it!' What do you think?"

"I think that it's as absolutely off the wall as you can get."

"Would you send me a card like that?"

"Ah, Kish, that's a bummer."

The next morning, Alzheimer's swims front and centre in her thoughts when she wakes up. She turns to me with what amounts to a confession about killing a spider last evening. As if the kitchen sink was the scene of the crime and a red-striped tea

49

cloth was the murder weapon, it's afloat in her conscience that she swatted one of the spiders nesting in this old house of ours.

"I can still see myself standing at the sink with the tea cloth in my hand and the spider lying there."

What's bothering her is the lapse in her veneration for life. Over the years, she has made a habit of fussing over spiders and liberating them. Her live-and-let-live policy extends to water-seeking spiders in the sink or the occasional housefly buzzing around the place. For this eventuality, she has a high-tech fly swatter. Instead of splatting the fly dead against the wall, this device, with its fine polyester fibres, has a stunning effect. Amazing, isn't it? She paid fifty dollars for it with the benevolent expectation that she would take the dazed fly outside to a safe place on the back porch where it would regain consciousness and start buzzing around all over again.

Whenever a daddy longlegs showed up in the sink, she would get out her spider rescue kit — a water glass and a little square of clear plastic — and place the glass over the spider, then carefully slide the plastic under the glass. Following Albert Schweitzer's concept of reverence for all life, she'd take the trapped spider out onto the back porch and release it. Presumably the spider would then be at liberty to hunt down any dazed housefly that happened to be out there, spin it into a webbing and stash it away in the arachnid pantry.

On one occasion, showing me the bug in the glass, Kish said, chortling, "You never know. This could be the itsy-bitsy spider who climbed up the water spout."

She can't explain what went amiss when she went blank at the kitchen sink, forgetting who she was and killing the spider and then having to relocate herself and realize what she had done.

"It happened so quickly," she says. "And you know when that kind of thing occurs, it's like that vague awareness you have when you're typing at a keyboard and one of your fingers hits two keys at once. You sense it. You know that you've made a mistake but you don't know what it is until you look."

"Yes, Kish. And with the spider, it would have been all over in a jiffy. It's covered by your sixty-second rule. You don't have to worry about it."

"That may be so," she says. "But it didn't do the spider any good, now did it?"

6. Out and about in the neighbourhood

THE DOWNSIDE OF THESE ORDINARY days is that we're not going out any more. No matter what I suggest — dinner and a movie, lunch or brunch on a Sunday morning — she's standoffish about it. I miss the enthusiasm she had for routine shopping together or driving out to Sooke for dinner at that restaurant on Whiffin Spit Road. She'd also have me keyed up over the prospect of heading up to Mount Washington for a weekend of skiing or taking a summer drive up to Long Beach as we have several times. The night before, she'd roast a Cornish game hen, glazed with crab-apple jelly and load it into a picnic hamper for a roadside lunch with bread rolls, a green salad and a bottle of chardonnay. She'd have us up at dawn for a full breakfast, then driving north, getting a head start on the world with the sun just coming up on our secret open road.

This morning, I wonder what's up when there's a flash of that lost enthusiasm. Soon after breakfast, she wants to go car shopping. She is trying to persuade me to trade in my set of wheels for a car with a sunroof. "Not some stingy peekaboo place," she says. "Let there be loads of light and cool air coming through." At the dealership she says I should get something classy and that we'd have the back seat removed from the car allowing rangy, long-legged Flora to sit on a blanket on the floor with her head out of the window on the passenger side. Flora and I, two of a kind, would go anywhere with Kish.

And soon we're proceeding off the car lot in a gas-guzzling, dark-blue sedan with a push-button roof that's roomy enough for Kish to be standing up in it. She's Lady Baltimore wearing wrap-around sunglasses, a purple jacket with the collar turned up, and a long, coiled scarf trailing back while she deigns to take in the urban panorama with Flora sniffing at it from her window. I'm not about to be the killjoy, telling her ladyship about the risk of having a cop present me with a ticket for allowing her to ride without her seat belt.

There's just no nitpicking allowed. I'm trying to get on her wavelength and plug into the neighbourhood she knew as a girl. It's a balm for what ails her. She wants to keep it alive in her imagination. This patch of Victoria is part of her story, her birthplace, mine too. We're parochial, thinking of it as the little acorn as opposed to the big apple. But this is all about Kish. I'm merely along for the ride.

"I've been forgetting and losing touch," she says, talking down to me through the roof opening while we wait for a traffic light to turn green. She wants to get back to the sense of place and belonging she had as a child at South Park Elementary School. Here it is, half-forgotten, half-remembered, on Douglas Street, overlooking Beacon Hill Park. What was once upon a time her school is a handsome structure, solid red brick, built ninety-five years ago and now with the playground devoid of children in July. We're parked in front of it. In a sweetly voiced falsetto, in the carefree rhyming of a ditty that goes with it, Kish becomes a schoolgirl skipping rope.

Dolly Dimple walks like this,
Dolly Dimple talks like this,
Dolly Dimple smiles like this,
Dolly Dimple throws a kiss.

From South Park Elementary, I am bidden to head deeper into old town James Bay to the very heart of it at 207 Government Street with Kish standing tall in the sunroof and Flora gazing out of the window as we drive through the wrought-iron gateway onto a circular driveway in front of a yellow house with twin gables and a string of pendant knobs hanging from the rafters like Christmas ornaments. Emily Carr (1871–1945) lived here as a child, and Kish came here as a child herself on a school field trip. Now, paying her respects to Emily Carr, she says, "How sad and frustrating it was for her. Ahead of her time as a painter with a new way of seeing her beloved West Coast. And nobody buying her pictures."

A few minutes' drive takes us for a jaunt into the Beacon Hill Park she knew as a girl, notably going to cricket matches on Sunday afternoons with Grandmamma Constanze. Going all out, becoming Anglais, she took an interest in the most English of all games and joined the local cricket club.

"You should have seen us," Kish says, sprucing up old memories. "Sitting in the pavilion during a tea break in the cricket match. I'd have an orange squash and Grandmamma would be sipping tea. And during the cricket match itself, after something or other was well played, we'd be joining in the polite titters of applause. It was all so controlled and civilized. It was that way when I played grass hockey at school and university. Quite the opposite of what you see from the spectators, fans as fanatics, at hockey and football games on TV."

We're driving through Cook Street village and its profusion of chestnut trees. Heads are turning in surprise from the sidewalks at the sight of Kish who pretends not to notice them from her lordly station in the roof opening with Flora, also taking in the view. As we approach the end of Cook Street, we emerge from its canopy of trees with fresh light expanding above us. It's airier. Well before we can see it, we know from the dawning of light that the ocean is out there waiting for us. And now in plain sight as we swing onto Dallas Road. Flora has her forepaws up on top of the car, and she's rearing up through the roof opening right next to Kish, a touring spectacle heading along toward Clover Point.

As close to sea faring as we can get on four wheels, we're parked half way along this narrow, rocky squirt of land jutting out into the Strait of Juan de Fuca. Kish has plans for this leg of the tour, once again, dredging up her childhood, going back to the way it was before her father was overwhelmed by Alzheimer's and could introduce her and her cousin Hilary to the sport of flying kites. Clover Point is where kite flyers gather. It's also a launch pad for kite surfers and parasailing. In the trunk of the car, Kish has a kite, a single line, store-bought delta-wing striped with the colours of the rainbow and a three-strand tail. According to the specs, it will take to the sky in a wind as low as eight kph.

And fly it does, even though it's such a rare and windless afternoon that there are no other kite flyers on Clover Point. The motion of the car provides the wind power. Kish stands on deck in the roof opening, holding the kite string. She's facing backward and looking up at the trailing kite, a falcon on a leash, dipping and rising. The seagulls and pigeons are watching. I'm the irrelevant chauffeur and caregiver, holding at ten kph, crawling along the road. After a few minutes, Kish hauls the kite back down and sits beside me before we turn back onto Dallas Road. Flora, with the back seat all to herself, is flying solo in the roof opening.

"Thanks for putting up with me," Kish says.

"Putting up? Enjoying myself is more like it. Armchair kite flying is the only way to go."

"But you missed out on it," she says. "We should have changed places. Let's go back and I'll drive and let you do little kite flying."

"Let's do it on another day. It's getting close to dinnertime."

"Yes. I've got a tuna casserole ready to go into the oven. And besides we've had more than enough nostalgia for one afternoon."

"Right, that's what it was. A nice nostalgic afternoon."

"Is that the same as an Alzheimer's afternoon?"

"Well, Kish, you were so on the ball that Alzheimer's never occurred to me."

"Are you sure about that? There's a lot of it going around."

7. Drawn-out days

HERE I AM AGAIN, WIDE AWAKE and trying to anticipate her frame of mind when she wakes up. If she knew about this, she'd tell me to quit stewing about things that are beyond my control and to see what I can do about having a nice day myself. Now, she's awake and cantankerous. "Tell me it isn't so," she says. "Tell me that you didn't kiss me on the forehead."

It's not as I thought at first, some new anxiety about Alzheimer's. She's scowling with questions about what happened last night. My defence is that I was kissing my favourite forehead. She insists it was a peck. A peccadillo on my part. I'm left reminding her that last night, just as we were getting into bed, she wanted to make sure she hadn't left the garage doors open. I went out and checked them for her.

And when I got back, I thought she was asleep and I didn't want to wake her. I did what we normally do when one of us is getting back into bed or getting up during the night. Either way, it's to be done carefully, sliding out of bed and easing your weight off the mattress so as not to disturb the other. Returning, you must see that the other is properly tucked in and then slide carefully back into bed. As Kish would have it, even if — as the tuckee on the receiving end of the tucking — you don't wake up, deep down you're aware that you're being fussed over and that you're cherished. That's what I did last night. I tucked her in.

I now realize that she was awake. Whatever it was that I planted on her forehead, Kish, on the receiving end, found it too brief and tight-lipped. It would have been acceptable if I had dallied and followed up with a softer mouth and moved on, kissing further afield. She informs me that even with the Alzheimer's, I am still her husband and she is my wife with a libido that's quite undiminished. Furthermore, there's no pecking allowed. She's addressing me as Maximillian. The way it works, when she's vexed with me, Max becomes Maximillian, signalling that I must listen more closely to her. When I want to get her attention, I call her Ms. Kish.

We have a rule, out the window now I guess, that we don't argue in bed. There's a place for that, sitting in Adirondack chairs on the front verandah. Outside, we keep our voices down and get it over with. At this moment, I'd be ill-advised to suggest that we adjourn to the verandah. Better to ride it out and look contrite. I still think that, given the circumstances, the peck was appropriate. It would be a mistake to kiss her now and try to put a little more oomph into it. That would only make things worse now that she's refusing to let go of it.

"Maximillian," she says. "You're a man. You're not some chicken pecking away at me. Next thing I know, you'll be calling me ma'am and putting a hot water bottle at my feet."

She rolls onto her side to face the other way. What can I say that wouldn't sound patronizing? She looks so frail. I guess it's the Alzheimer's. I can't go much beyond another peck on the forehead. It seems to me that I'd be taking advantage of her. It's also my libido that's in question. My sensory nerve ends aren't as alert and tingly as they used to be. I'm fifty-one, not all the way over the hill, but on the crest of it, with the glimmer of a bald spot and a paunch pressing out against my belt.

It's going to be one of those sombre, drawn-out days and we're getting through it with vague regrets over what didn't happen in bed last night and leaving it at that. Anticipating that we won't be making love tonight is something new for me, for Kish as well if that's her situation. It's been a long time since we've expected anything close to a daily romp. Until recently, there was the lingering possibility that it could happen on any day of the week. That little zing we had has faded away. I hope it hasn't fizzled out entirely.

Our lovemaking has matured over the years. We've been learning how to make it sing with what she said was a touch of rubato, slowing it down a little then picking up the tempo at our discretion. We became an ensemble, sorting out the difference between the erogenous zones and the erroneous zones and game for new things. Until recently, we were coalescing occasionally and yet often enough in the morning for her to keep a roll of breath mints handy in a bedside drawer.

Coalescing is the word we use for making love. We don't actually speak the word itself. But we think about it that way in our trying to be exact where words are concerned. After we discovered what we had together, we wanted to be precise about it. Making love seemed to be off the mark — as if it could be manufactured. Fucking came up of course and was rejected after we looked it up. Early 16th century: of Germanic origin, possibly from an Indo-European root meaning strike. As an epithet, the F word conveys annoyance and contempt. All that anger and pounding aggression didn't apply to what we had together, courtly coalescing, sometimes not so courtly. Kish came up with coalesce, the particular definition: to cause to unite in one body or mass.

On occasion, she would have tea lights glowing around the bedroom and rose petals on the bed. We pampered ourselves with warm baths together, fragrant oils and back massages. Having no children, we were devoted entirely to each other. Coming and going as we pleased and free to stay out as late as we liked. Yesterday, when we talked again about not having children, Kish lapsed forgetfully for a moment and couldn't remember why.

"We have this big house," she said. "What is it? Four bedrooms? Why don't we have any children?"

In our dealings with Alzheimer's, I have learned not to give lengthy explanations. They only intensify her confusion and have her squirming with embarrassment.

"Well, Kish my love," I said. "I guess it was the Alzheimer's."

"Oh yes. Oh Max! Here I am again, forgetting that again. It's just that I was wondering about those empty rooms.

"Childlessness," she said out of nowhere with her fondness for words glowing through the haze of her forgetfulness. "Childlessness . . . With all those esses . . . Sounds so desolate. Like wilderness."

With a tired-out smile, she was groping in confusion, momentarily unable to remember deciding years ago that she wouldn't run the risk of passing Alzheimer's from her father down the line through her to any children we might have. We didn't need friends with children telling us what we were missing. We already knew.

When I was courting Kish, I knew what I was getting into. By that time, her father had been placed in one of the care facilities on Shelbourne Street. Shortly before we were married, she took me to visit him. Poor guy. At first, in bewilderment, he didn't know who she was. Then he remembered her vaguely and started in on me. He accused me of raping his daughter. Cursing a blue streak. Throwing a half-eaten tub of chocolate pudding in my direction. By taking me to visit him, she let me see what might be in store for her, for me. After the visit, she came to the point.

"Yes, I know. The poor guy," she said. "Of course you realize that if you marry me, you'll have the possibility of dementia as a dowry. Sometime in the future, you could have a poor-guy wife with Alzheimer's."

There it was. Fair warning. The odds were fifty-fifty and I accepted them. I like to think that I would do it all over again. Later on, regrets about not having children closed in on me when I saw my brother Conrad kitchy-kitchy-kooing over his three grandchildren. It hit home that I'd never be a grandfather. Kish made up for it by going all out in her work as a storyteller. She became another kind of mother in the guise of a fairy godmother, nurturing girls and boys with stories. She's had them riding in a coach carved from a pumpkin or tagging along with Alice picking daisies and with pink-eyed White Rabbit ducking down a hidey-hole and Alice tumbling down there after him.

"What do you think now?" she asks. "About our not having children?"

"I can't help thinking what a wonderful mother you would have been."

"How can you know that?"

"I'm absolutely sure of it. It starts with that rich and mothering voice of yours. The perfect voice for comforting a baby and singing lullabies."

"But do you ever second-guess my decision not to have children?"

"No. It was the right thing for us."

"If we had children, we wouldn't be indulging ourselves the way we are."

"Yes, Kish, we're lucky that way."

"Do you really think so?"

"Not really. I'm saying that we're making the best of it. We have Flora. You decided not to expose any children to what is now happening to you."

"Yes, but there was that test I could have taken to find out if it was safe for me to have children."

She wants to be reminded that the test wouldn't have given her any certainty. She went through this on her own before we were married and a few times in the early years and needs to go over it again.

"They wanted to put me under a microscope," she says.

"A magnified Connie Kish! Now wouldn't that be something to behold?"

"They wanted to see if I had the apolipoprotein E-4 gene. That's ApoE-4 for short . . .

"Listen to me showing off. Apolipoprotein!" she says, referring to the presence of a gene that indicates a higher risk for Alzheimer's. The catch is that some people who have the gene don't catch Alzheimer's. And sometimes, people who don't have the gene do come down with it. That's why Kish decided not to take the test. Simply not knowing and hoping for the best would be better than taking the test and not knowing for certain one way or the other and waiting for the worst.

We talked about adopting children and delayed it for a year and somehow never got around to it. We were putting the downsides aside and living our lives, with no colicky baby wailing at us first thing in the morning. No nuisance toddlers who would want to join in the fun of a kneesies encounter under the breakfast nook table. It's some time ago now that, after a leisurely Sunday brunch and a couple of mimosas, our touching knees would occasionally come into play as erogenous zones arousing enough to send us back upstairs to the bedroom. It's not that we were pawing away at each other all the time. But it happened often enough for us to know that it could happen at any time. But certainly not now, not with Kish turning in bed to face away from me. I pretend not to notice the silvery end of the roll of breath mints couched in her hand.

"Please, Max. Please," she says, turning back to face me. "You're looking at me without really looking at me."

We ride out the rest of the long summer day. Still talking to each other. No silent treatment from Kish. She's not the sulky type. And neither am I with my preference for being miserable and at times silently angry, rather than being even more miserable without her.

8. A lazy Sunday

LUTHER, A ONE-LEGGED CROW, is out there in the gnarly
old oak tree in front of the house. He's like a character in a
minimalist novel, alighting on the page without much in
the way of a past life and with a hazy future. No longer agile
enough to battle for his share of road kill, he has latched onto
Kish for survival. I admire his chutzpah, carrying on as if he
has two sound legs under him. Wily and adaptable enough to
get by without crutches, he's cawing away and rousing us out
of bed.

I'm grateful for this squawking reveille. It gives Kish
something real to wake up to even if it is one of the most
godawful sounds in nature. If you didn't know about this
raucous corvid trait, you'd think that Luther was choking to
death on a fried-chicken bone. He is perched on a branch
extending close to the open bedroom window. He knows
where Kish lives. Calling to her on this Sunday morning, he's
close enough to watch her getting out of bed. Street smarts also
run in the corvid family

While we make our way downstairs to the kitchen, Luther
launches himself out of the oak tree and into flight around the
house to the back yard where Kish has been feeding him every
morning. He comes to rest on the phone cable running from
the back of the house to the alley. He bounces on the wire, then

bellies down onto it for better balance while peering into the kitchen window.

Flora looks anxiously at her feeding bowl. Given that she lives here and has her own room — a converted pantry with a mattress and blanket for a bed — she expects feeding priority over a transient, one-legged crow. As the royal dog of Scotland, she has lineage going back to days of yore. According to Kish, she's a Hebridean princess. According to me, Flora is your basic good dog, a graceful soul and like dogs generally, better than people deserve.

Since she saw Kish feeding her chow to Luther, Flora has been skittish and watchful. She's aware that things aren't right with Kish. She may be able to sniff out dementia the way some dogs detect the presence of cancer cells. Kish fills Flora's bowl with kibble then puts on her sandals and goes out wearing a light grey cardigan over her nightgown.

It's my turn to attend to breakfast. I'm shifting from the window, keeping an eye on Kish out in the garden, and back to making an omelette with mushrooms and chives, chopped sundried tomatoes and gratings of Parmesan cheese. As a cook, I score myself as a six out of ten. I have a few moves in the kitchen. I can crack and spill an egg with one hand. I'm familiar with several recipes, one of them a pasta primavera. I also take pride in serving up a mint-crusted rack of lamb with roasted carrots, parsnips, and red onions for Sunday dinner. What I lack in gastronomic skills, I make up for with relish and enthusiasm when presenting a meal as if it is a culinary masterpiece.

From the back door window, looking out through the gauzy curtain, I watch Flora and Kish on the garden path out past the apple tree and the patch she has for growing herbs. I'd have a better view from the big window in the breakfast nook, but I'm minding my manners, standing where I can see without being seen while she pours a mix of coarse birdseed onto the feeder for Luther. Flora is keeping an eye on things, raising a hind leg to scratch her belly. It's not a dog's typical hard scratching. It's a dainty balancing act, a dog on four stilts with one of them raised and carefully daubing at the itchy spot.

It's dicey, figuring out how long Kish will be out there and timing the omelette accordingly. The garden is full of distractions. There's her wheelbarrow. I was with her at the hardware store when she bought it, after taking the heft of it, wheeling it up and down the paint aisle and calling it Barry. Now, she's tipping the orange vinyl bucket forward to empty out the rainwater. She'd be empathizing over Barry's indignation after spending a night in the rain, forgotten and abandoned by her yesterday. She's making amends by hosing out his bucket and putting him near the garden shed to dry out in the sunshine. The shed has a horseshoe above the door. Kish nailed it there. According to the superstition, it's a witch repellent with its crescent shape resembling the new moon much feared by witches and warlocks. Another blessing perceived by Kish is that swallows nest under the shed's overhanging rafters. It's reassuring to know that we have such a lucky garden shed.

There's another delay now that she's talking over the back fence with Anita Stokes who is accompanied by her duo of Manx cats, one of whom is cross-eyed. I have the table set in the breakfast nook. The plates are warming in the oven. From the back door, I call out. Kish says she'll be right in. This is my cue to pour the omelette into the frying pan and turn on the coffee maker and plunk the bread down into the toaster.

Breakfast is ready but she isn't. Ahhh Kish. Dammit! Off on an impromptu walk with Flora on her leash, going out through the back gate. They'll be heading out toward Douglas Street.

My concern is that Flora, close to fifty kilograms, is strong enough to take charge. I'm fretting about churchgoers' traffic on that street this time of the morning. I turn off the stove and shift the omelette pan off the burner, then hurry out to the closet at the front door, kicking off my slippers, stepping barefoot into brown loafers and heading out the door with an umbrella. It's raining again. I'm off, down the front steps and along the sidewalk, breathing easier when I see them at the end of the block.

Good dog Flora, stepping along at Kish's side, shepherding her, a caregiver I like to think, not striding off ahead the way she usually does. Kish, wet and shivering, is surprised to see me.

"Well, fancy meeting you here," she says. "And what's this? A new trend in walking attire? No socks and in your dressing gown?"

"Look who's talking?"

"Ah, touché. So what brings you here?"

"I'm out looking for Connie Kish. We had a date for breakfast and she stood me up."

She looks away for a moment, a light going on as she joins me in taking a third-person look at herself.

"Yes, she did, didn't she? She stood you up and she's sorry about that. And she's grateful to you for not asking for an explanation because she doesn't have one . . .

"Ah Max, my love," she says and moves in under the umbrella and takes my hand. "Let's go home."

Flora proceeds ahead of us, straining at the leash, leading the way up the front steps, across the porch, all the way back to the kitchen. I intend to dump the now-deflated omelette and make another one. But Kish, having changed into a dark green Argyll tartan dressing gown, has other ideas. She takes over, sidling me away from the stove to sit in the breakfast nook while she starts in. She's spritely, in good humour and coasting along on her treehouse remission.

"I'm looking at this omelette," she says. "And do you know what I see? I see a Max Osborne creation. I see TLC. Now, if I dared to scrape this treasure into the garbage, Hestia, the goddess of kitchens everywhere, would strike me dead. What say you, Hallowed Hestia? Thirty seconds at medium heat in the microwave? Just let me make sure there aren't any wine glasses in here."

What a thing to say. Do I laugh or commiserate? It doesn't matter. Kish wouldn't notice. She's all wound up, heart and soul, in consultation with Hestia about resurrecting the omelette. They have it sliding out of the pan and onto a platter and lightly nuked in the microwave. Kish applies a fingertip to see if it's hot enough, then confers with Hestia about bringing the omelette back to life as if some form of mouth-to-mouth resuscitation is required.

"What say you now, Hestia? A touch of . . . "

There's a pause. Kish looks at me quizzically. "What do you call it? That yellow stuff. You know. We put it on toast?"

Forgetting a word isn't necessarily a symptom of Alzheimer's. We all have occasional blank spots. I know what not to do when it happens to Kish. She doesn't want me coming on as the eager beaver supplying a word that she can't find. It's wait, wait, don't tell me, allowing time for her to come up with it on her own. If she can't, it's permissible for me to help out, providing that I do it subtly.

"It's on the tip of your tongue. It's got that buttery taste."

"Good one there, Max."

She's so enthusiastic about the omelette that she's unabashed over the blank spot, knowing as she does that it's covered by her sixty-second rule.

"What say you then, Hestia? Just a light daubing of butter and another twenty seconds in the microwave? Yes that will do it."

This resurrected omelette is scrumptious fare. Obviously, Kish and Hestia worked some culinary magic on it. More coffee, Max? Don't mind if I do. Kish is pouring and making more toast and informing me that the word toast derives from the Latin *tostum*, to scorch, and that the Ancient Romans were partial to a slice or two of tostum in the morning. She's been rhyming off tidbits like that for years. Whereas I wouldn't have known *tostum* from Postum.

Are we having fun yet? I think so. I'm content with another slice of *tostum* with an English brand of coarse-cut marmalade. Kneesies anyone? Well, we're not having that much fun. She has shifted far enough along the bench to avoid any contact with me under the table. I'm not in the mood and Kish would know that. Sitting around munching on toast and marmalade is less challenging than kneesies and nooners.

Cycling has been a Sunday thing for us, riding on Lizzie, our bicycle built for two. She's vintage Schwinn with a pale blue frame, a wicker basket and a silvery bell on the handlebars. Kish usually occupies the front seat and it takes all of her finesse and gearing down to get Lizzie to bear up under the strain of pulling the trailer we have for Flora. This is a bit much for Lizzie who is, after all, built for two, not for two plus a trailer and a big dog. Flora is able to keep up, loping along behind Lizzie for a mile or so. Then she'll park herself in the middle of the cycling path and wait for us to circle back and let her hitch a ride in the trailer. I want to head out after breakfast but Kish balks at the idea.

"In that rain!" she says.

"I'd like to go. We've got rain outfits. It's a warm rain. We could use the exercise."

"But it's pouring, Max. You go if you want but I'm staying home."

The way it works out, instead of riding in the rain, we are doing the crossword puzzle. This used to be a Sunday diversion for us but not for a while now. I've been wary of crosswords on grounds that the Alzheimer's would be nipping away at her vocabulary. But Kish has the newspaper folded open to the crossword page and she's telling me to scootch over so that we can sit side by side at the breakfast nook table.

"Now there's a good crossword word," Kish says. "Scootch, seven letters meaning to move your derriere."

We're sitting close together so that both of us can read the clues. I'm the scribe with the ballpoint. And never mind that I taught high school English for a couple of years and should be good at this, Kish has the bigger vocabulary.

The top left part of the puzzle comes quickly. I like proceeding methodically, working through the across clues all the way to the end and then dealing with the down clues. Kish flits around, switching back and forth. It usually results in quicker gratification, this time filling all the squares in the upper left, including ear candy, her input as two words for Catchy pop tunes. The upper right also falls into place after we take a chance by putting in the S for three plural endings.

This is where the jumping around pays off with the words stabs, rosas and mitosis across and the down words assisi and systs (for Operating procedures, abbr.). It takes us just over half an hour to finish the puzzle. I manage a couple of tricky ones. There was tee for the clue, one may have a ball at the country club, and do to a T for execute perfectly. But Kish is the wordsmith. She gets seisms for tremors, ampere for current amount, Bali for the Hindu part of Indonesia and a Wagnerian word, sieg for victory. Finishing crossword puzzles is old hat for us. But from the way she's carrying on, you'd think it was a first.

"You look surprised," she says.

"Surprised about what?"

"That we got through the whole thing."

"Why would I be surprised? We've been doing it for years."

"You were expecting me to get confused about it. You were feeling sorry for me."

I can't win. No matter what I say, she goes one better. She's right about me feeling sorry for her. But she's making too much out of it. Feeling sorry for her shouldn't be such an issue. We're both in retreat. Time for another cup of coffee. Flora is more solace to her than I am. She's always been Kish's dog. She tolerates me. She has picked up on the slump we are in and mopes around, following Kish wherever she goes.

"I can take a hint," Kish says. "We're going for another walk."

Walk! Flora knows that word and goes directly to the front door and waits while we put on our shoes. The walk takes us down through Beacon Hill Park, across Dallas Road and into dog territory where she can strike off on her own. She knows about the ordinance requiring that she be on a leash in most of the park and that south of the road, along a stretch of oceanfront, she can run free. Eight years old, up there in the lifespan of her breed and hitting her stride, she's a flat-out reddish blur. Normally, she goes tearing off in the direction of Clover Point and is out of sight for a few minutes, but this time, she doesn't go that far. She has us in sight at all times and cuts her workout short and comes back to us, turning her head so that Kish can clip on the leash.

This has me imagining that Flora believes that she's in charge. She wants Kish on the other end of the leash so that she can't go wandering off. Even though I'm walking close to them, I'm at a loss, estranged from them, excluded from the treehouse and such a loner that I'm wondering if Flora would mind if I clipped myself onto her leash so that I'd have a sense of belonging.

9. Décolletage to die for

KISH IS WORRIED about her storytelling engagement this afternoon at the Pooh Cottage Daycare Centre. It's more than the brief spell of performance anxiety she normally has just before she takes her place in the story time chair in the Tigger Room. Expecting so much of herself, as she has all along, she's always on edge until she settles into the first story on her list. But here after breakfast, she's struggling with a different kind of apprehension. Awake half the night worrying about it, she's afraid she'll forget everything and embarrass herself. And she doesn't want to put her memory to the test beforehand by having me as a rehearsal audience.

When she started out, it was a regular thing for me to be her sounding board. She'd have me traipsing back into the mindset of a boy of five to listen to her telling such stories as "Jack and the Beanstalk" with her dredging down into a heavy contralto to become the menacing giant, stomping around and telling the story. "Fee-fi-fo-fum. I smell the blood of an Englishman. Be he live, or be he dead. I'll grind his bones to make my bread."

Most of the time, I'd think that she nailed whatever it was. But she wouldn't take yes for an answer. How could she make it more compelling? Okay, consider slowing the delivery down a bit to load up the Fee-fi-fo-fum with more tension. I'd go from sounding board to mirror for her. As the children's kindly fairy godmother, she'd have to work a pile of magic to become a scary giant in their eyes. She wanted to know if she looked like an ogre, rearing up and rocking slightly from side to side, scowling with her brow deeply furrowed. Obliged as I was to comment, I'd say, "Well, if you bared your teeth just a little, this little boy would run and hide in the next room."

Kish was always refining her delivery even with stories she had told many times over, the likes of "Goldilocks and the Three Bears" or "Hansel and Gretel" or "The Princess and the Pea", which is a favourite of hers, having lived it as a child herself, imagining that she was the princess with a fanny so royally tender that it was sorely bruised by a pea hidden under a pile of twenty mattresses and twenty feather beds.

She was a spellbinder. One of the managers at the public library urged her to write a book about storytelling. She was interviewed three years ago on a television show called Folks of Vancouver Island, answering questions from Debbie Donaldson, who also did the weather reports on the news broadcasts. I have a video of Debbie setting up my few seconds of fame by asking Kish what made her want to be a storyteller in the first place.

"It was my husband, Max Osborne," Kish replies. "He thought I had a flair for it."

After that, it is of course all anti-climactic, but the Q&A goes on with Kish relating that storytelling is a three-sided affair. There's the story, the storyteller, and the children.

"Once you've got a good story," she says, "You make it your own, telling it from the heart, not from the book. You inhabit the story. It becomes second nature to you and the story and the children will carry you along in the telling. Most of them already know the story. I like to tease them once in a while, asking if they know about Goldilocks and the five bears. You should hear them piping up, 'Oh no, no! It's Goldilocks and the three bears.' Oh dear, I'll say to them. I've forgotten. Now, just who are the three bears? And they'll tell me who they are."

She goes on to say that storytelling relies heavily on children's imagination. It's as natural as breathing for them to be riding along with Cinderella in a splendid coach that's been carved from a pumpkin. The closest thing Kish has to a prop is a low table with a scattering of books of stories and nursery rhymes as a reminder to the children that what they're hearing from her can also be found on the printed page. She wants them to want to learn to read.

This morning, I have a suggestion. Why not have the book handy in her lap this afternoon? If there's a memory lapse, she could glance down to refresh her memory and carry on from there.

"Maybe I should just resign and get it over with," she says. "I'll wait and see how I feel about it after lunch."

There's a phone call from Hilary. She wants to know if I can talk.

"Sure. Kish is at work in her studio." We both know this is a do-not-disturb block of time.

"How is she?" Hilary asks. "How's she feeling about herself? And how's the drug, what's it called?"

"Aricept. She has her difficult moments but she's functioning normally most of the time. And she won't tolerate fools gladly. She calls us as she sees us."

"That does sound normal."

"You know that squelcher of hers. *C'est le gros bool shee-it?*"

"Oh that," Hilary says. "What about those difficult moments? Is it still Alzheimer's Lite?"

"No. I don't know. Yes, actually, I do know. It's still Lite. The neurologist said that it summarizes her situation and that she should trademark it."

There's really not much I can do to comfort Hilary. I don't know if Kish has mentioned the Mañana Treehouse. All I can say is that she's doing as well as can be expected. I know that's a lame thing to say. Trying to convey that it's not all doom and gloom, I go out of the living room and hold the phone at the door to the studio so that Hilary can listen to Connie Kish, storyteller in rehearsal, singing the Barney Google song.

"Well, that tells us something," Hilary says. "She's having to rehearse a song that she's been singing for years and years. Is she still doing her crossed-eyed routine?"

"Yes, she most certainly does. And those kids can't get enough of the googling."

"Connie was always good at going cross-eyed," Hilary says. She confesses that she was jealous, seeing the boys at school making a fuss over all the different ways Connie could go cross-eyed.

I've heard all this before, of course. By age seven, Kish had developed a fine control over her lateral rectus muscles. Going beyond simply crossing her eyes, she could turn her left eye upward and the right one in toward the nose and then reverse the process. Her windup finale, a double whammy, had her cranking both eyes in so far that the centre patches seemed to disappear under her nose leaving the blank whites of her eyes.

I remember when I was a boy, learning to wink with my right eye. I progressed from that into trying to go cross-eyed, striving at a mirror, bearing down, contorting my mouth, pleading with my eyeballs to turn in toward my nose. A boy at school told me that a jellybean might help. As a final inducement, as if my eyeballs had a candy craving, I Scotch-taped a pink jellybean on the end of my nose. Still I failed to master the basic swivelling of the eye centres. They wouldn't budge. They stared defiantly straight out of the mirror at me.

When Kish and I were young and giddy and newly in love, she could crack me up by twisting her mouth into a lop-sided leer and going cross-eyed. Merry brown eyes going round and round, hither and yon, up, down, and sideways. But I have to say those zombie-like blank eyeballs left me squeamish and wondering if she exposed the children at Pooh Cottage to the whites of her eyes.

The time, one-fifteen. Kish, having apparently decided that she's up for another afternoon of storytelling, is holding her red and black Harlequin hat and wearing the pashmina shawl, a tasselled, teal-blue cashmere creation. I think it's new. She has a cluster of helium balloons, yellow and purple, floating over her head.

"How do I look?" she asks.

She has asked me that many a time. Usually, I say that she looks just great, something along that line. Today I make a production of it, musing and stroking my jaw as if pondering the imponderable.

"Well Kish, that's a tough one."

"I can't look all that bad."

"The thing is, I'm looking at a work of art. Like the Mona Lisa. You can't take her in all at once. I'm going to have to give it some thought. Are you asking me about the storyteller Connie Kish?"

"Yes that's what I want to know. How does she look in five words or less?"

"Exciting. Mysterious and spooky. A spell-binding Scheherazade."

"Hold it right there. Too many words."

"I'm just getting started. Connie Kish the light of my life? Those eyes, those gorgeous gypsy imports from the south of France? Then there's the voice. I'm thinking synaesthesia, but what colour is that voice? Teen-age sweetie pie hiding up a tree? How's that?"

"Okey-doke. Time to go," Kish says, glancing at her watch.

"No wait. Wait. So you're asking me how you look? Well, I'm admiring the way that shawl exposes your right shoulder and that finely delineated display of muscles and clavicle bone. Not everyone has that fine bone structure. It leaves me achingly aware that the reason for the décolletage is as supporting structure for what swells out so beautifully below."

"Oh you do go on. I'm going to be late."

"What? I'm not allowed to savour you."

"Sure you are. But you're all talk. I'm still looking forward to a little action *dans le sack.*"

"Well, just one more thing there, Kish. Go easy with the décolletage at the daycare centre or you'll drive those little boys out of their minds."

"Mustn't disappoint the little darlings," she says.

"They should be so lucky."

She won't let me drive her. The Alzheimer's leaks into everything and has had me trying to finagle my way into every kind of helping out. I'm unable to persuade her that a performer of her ranking should have a chauffeur-cum-roadie to look after the driving and carry her guitar and set up the balloons on the story-time chair. She looks at me with quiet exasperation. She wants to go it alone to prove that she can.

"Onward ho," she says, going out the door.

From the back door window, I watch her walk out through the bright summer garden to the garage.

10. Trusty John, a.k.a. John the True

LATER THAT AFTERNOON, DRIVING HOME from Pooh Cottage, Kish was in a line of vehicles on Douglas Street waiting for the traffic light to change at Fort Street. As she told me later on, she noticed a pedestrian walking unsteadily along the roadway. She got out of her car and guided the old fellow back onto the sidewalk. The traffic light turned green and the driver behind her car was honking away at her. She hurried back.

Thoughtfully, she had left the car with the motor idling so that she'd be able to drive off without delay. Not so thoughtfully, when she closed the door, she had locked up the car. There they were. Kish helpless, her keys dangling from the ignition, engine running, her guitar, the shawl and pointy hat in the back seat with the balloons floating up against the rear window of the little red hatchback that was obstructing rush hour traffic at one of the city's busiest intersections.

Along came Sergeant Angus MacAskill of the Victoria police department. He assigned another policeman to drive her car to an impound lot. Her encounter with the sergeant quickly softened from a stern interrogation into a chatty social occasion after he recognized her as the story lady at Pooh Cottage. Last week, waiting there to pick up his grandson Ryan, this brawny cop had been captivated by her rendering of

"Jack and the Beanstalk". There at the intersection, he wanted Kish to know how often Ryan raved about her storytelling.

The sergeant seemed to fill the front door frame when he came in after driving Kish home. She introduced him to me as Sergeant MacAskill. "Make it Angus," he said and took off his policeman's hat. He called her Connie. We were friendly over coffee and engaged in serious conversation about going googly-eyed. Angus told us his grandson Ryan was so enthusiastic about Miss Kish singing the Barney Google song that he keeps trying to go cross-eyed himself.

"I should take it out of my routine," Kish said. "A few of the parents think that going cross-eyed could be harmful to the eyes. There's that old saw about eyes locking up and staying permanently crossed. But one of the fathers suggested that I give lessons showing the children how to do it."

Angus said he would sign up for the lessons himself. I joined in, saying that I would as well.

"And so would my grandson," Angus said.

About to leave, he put his hat back on, making it known that Sergeant MacAskill was back on duty and obliged to broach the subject of Kish's driving. "We have to talk about what happened this afternoon," he said.

"Yes, I know," Kish said. "I was holding up traffic and you're going to give me a ticket. Well, it shouldn't be a problem. I haven't had a ticket since they stopped me for speeding on the way to the airport. It must have been twenty years ago."

"There'll be a little more to it than that," said the sergeant. "What concerns me is what you said while your car was being driven away. You said, 'Don't mind me, sergeant, you see, I have Alzheimer's.' I have to ask you, was that a joke or is that the situation? Have you been diagnosed with Alzheimer's?"

"Yes, by a neurologist."

"Well, I'm really sorry to hear that," the sergeant said. "You have my sympathy. I've had to deal with a few people who have it. And I have to say, the way you carry on a conversation, you don't sound like a person with Alzheimer's. If you hadn't told me about it, it would never have occurred to me."

"Nice of you to say so," Kish said.

"I hope you understand that there will have to be a report to the Motor Vehicle Branch. They'll look into it. They'll want an opinion from your doctor about your fitness as a driver. You may have to take a road test to see how you're doing."

"So. They're going to make me stop driving."

"Sorry to say, that could happen."

"You can stop right there," Kish said. "I won't be putting you through all that. My mother did that after she had to stop driving. She was well past it. But she complained about it for years, going on and on, saying that she'd been a good driver for sixty years, never had an accident, and they had no right to make her stop driving."

"Well, it's a hard thing to let go of," he said. "I'll probably be like your mother when my time comes."

"Yes," Kish said. "But we don't get to keep on driving for ever and ever, do we? Now tell me, what if I decide to take a shortcut through all that rigmarole? I guess I could give up driving voluntarily."

"I had an uncle who did that a couple of years ago," he said.

"Well that's what I'll do," she said, removing her wallet from her purse, taking out her driver's licence and presenting it to him.

Just like that. Kish turned in her driver's licence. It may have been the right thing to do. She's so compliant. It would make more sense for her to be angry about what's happening to her. She's forgetting how much she's always enjoyed driving. As a driver, she's a natural. With her behind the wheel, the car becomes an extension of her hands and feet. We used to have one of those garishly long, eight-cylinder gas guzzlers with the ugly tail fins. She could handle it better than I could. Parallel parking was a breeze. She'd pull it off in one pass, backing into a space just big enough for one car, angling the wheels, and there we'd be, right on the curb.

She's been driving for thirty-one years and never so much as dinged a fender. And ever the storyteller, she gives full credit to Trusty John, a.k.a. Faithful Johannes, who came to life as a stalwart with a reputation for looking after things in a Grimm Brothers' fairy tale. I've heard her say, Thank you John, after a close call in traffic or when she found a parking space downtown right where she wanted it. For as long as I've known her, she's had Trusty John as a watchful presence in the back seat of her car.

11. Hiccups and earthquakes

I'M EMBARRASSED, SILENTLY BERATING MYSELF. Goddammit man! Get a grip. I'm taking deep breaths — in through the nose, out through the mouth — in an effort to stave off the onset of crying while we're on our way to the impound lot and it's drawn to my attention that I have stopped at a green light.

"Hate to bring this up," Kish says. "But does this mean that you're going to be driving straight through at the red lights?"

Hands folded primly on her lap, she's joshing, offering to take the wheel, then reaching across the console to hold my hand. She's sweetly reasonable and above the fray, at treehouse level while I'm hunkered down well below it, with my anger and embarrassment and a white-knuckle grip on the steering wheel. Now that the traffic light has turned red, I have the car idling and I face a little off to my left so that she won't see the *verklempt* look on my face.

I'm overwhelmed about what's happening to her. I can't risk making eye contact and have it open a little valve somewhere behind my eyes, turning on the waterworks. I've recently become familiar with the build up to such an event. The lump in the throat. Blinking a little faster. That fullness behind the eyes, like the bunging up of a head cold. And the world getting blurry. And then taking those deep breaths to hold back the tears brimming at the back of the throat and tasting like olive brine.

I'm close to blubbering out of control. It hasn't happened yet and at this moment, I don't dare to try talking. It's embarrassing to realize how vastly superior to me she is in the crying department. On the rare occasion that she's reduced to tears, she can talk clearly and cry at the same time without any blubbering and lurching sobs. It's probably the theatrics of her work as a storyteller that gives her enough control to talk through her crying. I can't do that. I'm a wreck. With that pressure building up behind my eyes, if I were to let go, there'd be a little storm of hiccups and earthquakes.

Kish knows what I'm going through. It's typically perceptive of her to see a parallel between pity and the kind of crying that equates with snivelling and feeling sorry for yourself. She has read somewhere that there are two kinds of pity. There's the pity that tends toward empathy and helps us to hold out against sentimentality and be supportive in a beneficial way. She stacks that up against the puny, mawkish kind of self-pity that insulates us against the suffering of somebody else.

"Crying can be the same thing," she says. "It can be feeling sorry for yourself."

What has me on the verge of crying in the car is how calm and thoughtful she is. "I guess we'll have to pay a fine at the impound lot." she says. "And they'll charge us for the towing. That's what they'll do, isn't it, before they let me take my car back."

She's holding the spare set of keys for the hatchback. She has forgotten about giving up her driver's licence and that I've arranged to have Conrad drive me out to the impound lot tomorrow so that I could drive her car home and that this was just a trip to get her stuff.

84

"Silly me," she says. "My guitar and shawl and the hat are in the back seat. And don't forget the balloons. I didn't forget them. Before I left, I went back to the Tigger room and gathered up the balloons. But I won't be needing them anymore."

That has me asking why, prompting her to explain that she had forgotten to tell me that she's no longer the storyteller at Pooh Cottage.

"Things were just fine this afternoon with *Miss Twiggley's Tree* and two other stories," she says. "The children seemed to enjoy themselves. I had them dancing the hokey-pokey. But on my way out, the new manager called me into her office. She explained to me that the children must come first and that we couldn't put them at risk and how sorry she was about the Alzheimer's. I could see that she was leading up to saying that she would have to let me go and that it was difficult for her. So I saved her the trouble and said that I would resign. I guess they'll have to print new brochures. They have my picture in the one they're using now . . . Oh and something else. They still owe me six-hundred dollars for three engagements this month."

I come close to losing it again when I realize how innocently considerate of others she has been. Surrendering her driver's licence to Sergeant Angus and seeing things from the new manager's point of view and quitting as the storyteller and concerning herself with Hilary's distress and with mine as well.

"Are you disappointed in me?" she says.

"Ahhh Kish, don't say that."

She's the caregiver again, going easy on me, sympathetic when she realizes that I've been close to crying, then treading lightly, wanting me to know that in our case, with Alzheimer's in the picture, there's no crying allowed.

"Come on, Max," she says "You can be such a woebegone worrywart at times. I don't mean to be unkind. I know things are difficult for you. But your angry fretting doesn't do either of us any good. And it's upsetting for me. I can't allow myself the luxury of anger. If I were to blow my stack, I can see myself falling endlessly and never coming out it. And I go into a panic at the mere thought of crying because once I start, I'll never stop. I'll just melt away. Or I'll reach the point where I won't be able to cry at all. So there'll be no crying. Okey-doke."

There's that gentle certainty. She's applying it to herself and expecting it from me. And that's what I'll have to deliver. Woebegone worrywart? Max, Max, giving myself a scolding and pledging to soften my anger and try to kick the crying habit. She's got so much more to cry about than I have. It also occurs to me that even worse than being unable to stop crying would be the desert of drying up and left unable to cry at all.

I'm trying to reassure her, saying, "Sure Kish. No more crying." I'm also holding back, knowing that all along, in our dealings with each other, soppy has been avoided at all costs with a tendency toward restraint and the calmness that goes with it. Basically, not having a drone of idle chatter going all the time and not going overboard, spouting the I-love-yous so often that they become as trivial as saying have a nice day.

At the impound lot, parked next to her car, there's a finality to the business of moving her guitar and the helium balloons, the pointy hat and pashmina shawl and the books out of her car and into mine with the awareness that she won't be needing them and that she'll no longer be driving the red hatchback. This has me asking her about Trusty John and wondering what's going to happen to him.

"Are you making fun of me!" she says.

"Of course not. It's just that the way you talk to him, I want to play it safe and believe in him myself."

I'm making allowances for Trusty John, her silent partner, taking the afternoon off when he didn't stop her from locking herself out of her car downtown. He may not be foolproof, but the way things are, Kish and I need all the help we can get. It's not that I really believe. I'm within a whisker of saying the wrong thing and offending her when I suggest that we can't abandon Trusty John by leaving him in her car. In her scheme of things, he would know that she won't be driving any longer. To my relief, it's the right thing to say.

"Oh Max, that's so thoughtful of you," she says.

"I thought you'd like to have him riding along with us in my car. Do you think you could arrange to have him switch over?"

"This is your car, isn't it? Your new car. It's up to you."

"I don't think he would listen to me. He's your guy. He's been with you longer than I have."

She insists that if I have it right in my mind, I can have Trusty John as a presence in my car. I'll also have to make another adjustment in my thinking. It's not my car any longer. It's our car, with Trusty John riding along, looking after things for both of us.

12. Moving away

KISH HAS BEEN BUTTERING ME UP. It's what she does when coaxing me into going along with something she wants. Most of the time, I'm onto her and she knows it. She'll make the egg frittata with leeks and fontina cheese for me for a weekday breakfast or slip a Burnt Almond chocolate bar into my briefcase for me to find at work as a nice little surprise. This morning, she's offering to take me out on a date, her treat, dinner and the movie of my choice.

And now, getting down to business, she invites me back into the breakfast nook after lunch. Instead of sitting at the window, she parks directly across from me, within kneesies range without actually touching. On the table in front of her, she has an agenda of some kind written on a clipboard. She's apologizing for it.

"It's just that I need it," she says, rambling. "You know ... To keep track of things ... I should have updated to a smartphone instead of sticking with my Blackberry. And now I just can't seem to make the darn thing work for me anymore ... I get confused ... I forget what I'm trying to do ... So you see it's easier for me ... You know ... To write things down in my notebook ... the old-fashioned way."

From what I can see upside down, she has a list of notes on the top sheet of the clipboard with little squares drawn in for the check marks after they've been dealt with. She taps her pen on the first item.

"I don't want you to be slave to me," she says.

"Neither do I."

"Well then, why aren't you going to work every day?'

She's pinning me down. I haven't resigned as a high school principal but I've arranged to take a leave of absence. Without having told her about it. I'm going to let it play out into early retirement. I don't see this as a big sacrifice. I was never cut out for the administrative side of education. Once upon a time I wanted to go back to teaching English. But my father would have thought less of me. He would brag to anybody who'd listen that I was the principal — the head honcho, he'd say — at a school with 800 students and a staff of sixty. My view of it was that I belonged in the classroom, teaching.

"Not to worry, Kish. I'm just taking a leave, that's all."

"No way," she says. "Nobody should have to dedicate themselves entirely to somebody else. It's slavery."

"That's pushing it. A slave has no choice in the matter. I'm free to come and go as I please."

"You should be protecting yourself."

"Protecting myself against what in particular?"

"You should be thinking ahead to when I won't be who I am and protecting yourself against that."

"What about me looking after you?"

"Oh, Max. There's really no need for that. What you should be doing is thinking about what's best for you in this."

"And what would that be?"

"For you to survive! Oh Max. That's what I want you to do. Survive!"

"That's what I'm doing."

"What I'm saying is that things have changed."

"It doesn't mean that we have to change."

"Ah, come on there, Max," she says looking down at the clipboard. "I've been a burden to you. The way I am, having to ask you to drive downtown to help me find my car, for instance. And . . . And . . . "

Here they are again, the dementia devils, clouding up her mind, then punishing her again, having her go back to an incident well before she turned in her driver's licence. She had parked her car downtown and forgotten where it was and then, compounding it, decided that she must have taken the bus downtown in the first place. I remember the wounded pride on her face while I drove her around. When we found her car parked on View Street, she was more resentful than grateful.

"But it was nothing," I say. "What? A few minutes of my time."

I should know better than to try to downplay it.

"Ah, Max, please don't go there," she says.

Next on her list is Strathaven Place, an extended-care home. We both know this facility, having gone there to visit my Aunt Sarah, who spent the last two years of her life there because she couldn't look after herself after Uncle Frank died.

"Your aunt liked it there," Kish says.

"That's not the way I remember it. Every time we visited her, first thing she would ask if we had come to take her home."

"But my situation is quite different from your Aunt Sarah's."

"Yes. You're much too young for a place like that."

"Too young?" she says. "Well Max, you're only two years older than I am. That makes you much too young and much too alive to be saddled with a wife who has Alzheimer's."

Now it unfolds that she's planning to move into Strathaven herself. She's making the case for it and dismissing my reminder that twenty years ago, we promised that neither of us would put the other one into a nursing home.

"But you aren't putting me into Strathaven," Kish says. "I'm doing it on my own. Okey-doke?"

She works around to telling me that she's already done it. I'm prying it out of her, bit by bit. She went to Strathaven Place two days ago in a taxi and they took her on a tour of the facility. And now she's tugging a brochure out of the clutches of the clipboard and showing me the floor plan sketch for the Ashwood suites. One of them, Suite 932, happened to be vacant and she signed a one-year lease for it.

"But you're not even close to needing to go into to a care facility."

"I think that I am."

"Did you consider talking to me about it beforehand?"

"Yes, Max, I did, I really did. But I thought it would be easier on both of us for me to go it alone."

"But this affects both of us."

"I know. I know."

"What would you say if I decided to move away without talking to you about it."

"You didn't tell me about taking a leave from the school."

"But you're moving away!"

"You shouldn't think of it as moving away."

"How should I think about it?"

"I'm doing it for you," she says, reading from her notes again. "And I want you to go back to your work as a high school principal. You should have a life of your own. I just can't have you hovering and looking so down in the dumps the way you are. Flora is the same, following me around all the time, with those doleful eyes. She makes me want to cry. But never mind that. Think of it this way. I won't be that far away. Strathaven is only five kilometres from here."

It leaves me wondering if as an Alzheimer's patient, she has the competence, legally speaking, to sign a lease without me as a co-signer. The answer is, yes, she has and she exercised it after talking to Hilary, a lawyer, about how far she could go in managing her own affairs. Hilary advised her that it was a question for Dr. Winkler. He in turn, at her last appointment with him, tested her with a list of questions and tallied up her answers. He then wrote a letter about his findings and it's now on file with her medical records at Strathaven Place. She has a copy of it for me.

It's addressed: To whom it may concern. As one of the whoms, I'm advised as follows: "Ms. Kish was in my office for a physical examination and a Mini-Mental Status Examination. She scored twenty-six out of thirty on the mini-mental examination. The physical examination was normal."

There are several web sites dealing with this test for cognitive impairment. MMSE they call it. Thirty questions about the country and province you're in, the time of day, day of the week, and so on. Here's where it gets interesting, saying that any score greater than twenty-seven points out of thirty indicates a normal cognition. Kish, scoring twenty-six comes within a whisker of being normal. Does it mean that with one more point, she wouldn't have Alzheimer's?

"In conclusion," the letter says, "I consider Ms. Kish to be fully capable of managing her affairs."

I'd like to talk to the doctor about that score of twenty-six out of thirty. I'm wondering if Kish and I should get a second opinion from another neurologist. What does the score really indicate? Alzheimer's Lite, meaning that she's up there in her treehouse rocking chair, in remission and buoyed up with confidence and certainty? She has that letter from Dr. Winkler. It's her okey-doke way of saying Alzheimer's Schmaltzheimers to anybody — me included — who questions her competence.

It's all coming straight out of the blue. She hasn't seen fit to talk it over with me. No heads up. Goddammit, leaving me out of it altogether. I'm overwhelmed. I can't think of anything more to say. She doesn't need me as a caregiver or as a guardian co-signing that lease. In her words, I now have a high-maintenance wife on my hands. We're looking at close to six-thousand dollars a month for the Oakwood suite and the level of nursing care she'll need in addition to such incidentals as the TV cable hookup, laundry, visits to the hair dresser's salon on the main floor. It rounds out to eighty thousand a year.

The money won't be a problem, not with a sizeable inheritance from my father three years ago after he passed away following a stroke. His will provided a bequest of just under three million dollars, my half of the proceeds from the sale of his five lumberyards and a ready-mix concrete business. A few years earlier, Kish and I would have invested half of it and lived it up on the other half, travelling to Europe and splurging on winter vacations somewhere close to the equator — preferably, according to Kish, going back to a Mayan village in Mexico where she could pick mangoes right off a tree.

But with Alzheimer's in the offing, we played it safe, paying off the mortgage, having a new roof put on the house, having it repainted and socking the rest of the money away. We drank a toast to my late father for setting us up as leisure class, yearly income, $150,000. It occurs to me, even in this darkest of dark moments, that whatever happens now, we'll be able to pay the bills.

After apologizing for the clipboard and fumbling at times, she's back up in the Mañana Treehouse and into remission. She's been typically thorough and gutsy. I admire her for it and all in the same breath, I think that she's away ahead of herself. Moving into a care facility in a few years maybe, but not now. It's barely eight months since her diagnosis. I'm making the best of it, trying to put on a happy face. But it's saddening to realize that she doesn't need me for anything more than seeing to it that there's enough money in our chequing account to cover the monthly payments. That's the full extent of my involvement in the process of Kish moving out of our home and into Strathaven Place with a one-year lease to stay there.

13. Kish doesn't live here anymore

LUTHER THE CROW is even cannier than I thought. After only two days without Kish feeding him, he switches allegiance to Anita Stokes next door. First thing this morning, I watch that two-timing corvid go gliding out of the oak tree in front of our house and over to the tree in front of Anita's house. With his raucous cawing, he harasses her into feeding him.

Flora is unable to match Luther's sly flexibility. Every morning since Kish moved out, she comes loping up the stairs and circles the bedroom. Then she'll take a long, accusing look up at me and I'm scowling down at her, saying, "What in the hell are you are you looking at!" I'm trying to vent my anger against Flora. But she's so calmly benign that it rolls right off her. Having established that Kish hasn't returned overnight, she goes back downstairs to whatever it is that she has in the way of a life of her own. Surely she hasn't been relying entirely on Kish and me. I have to hope for Flora's sake that there's more to it than being a pet. What does she do? What does she think about when she's by herself in the pantry or in the back garden?

She would be deeply offended if she knew that Kish doesn't want to see her at Strathaven Place. There are sundry dogs on leashes and assorted cats, one of them on a tether and others underarm or in cages. They are paraded in as visitors. When I mentioned that I could bring Flora in for a pet-together, Kish ruled it out, saying that she doesn't want Flora seeing her at Strathaven and that later on, she would come home to visit her.

It was a particularly low point for me when Kish asked me to change the message on our telephone answering device. It now informs callers that they have reached the residence of Max Osborne, making it clear that Connie Kish doesn't live here anymore. She has me stewing to myself, Aw shit, Kish. How could you?

It's of no concern to her when I tell her our Spartan apple keeled over last night. She adored that tree. A few years ago, when it started bearing fruit, she became the happy harvester, picking the apples and gift-wrapping them in little baskets for our friends. When we planted the tree, we didn't realize that we'd placed it too close to a concrete retaining wall. The root growth on that side was so stunted that fifteen years later, it wasn't Spartan enough to stand up to a strong wind. When I describe what a sad sight the tree is, knocked flat with its root system naked and exposed, she writes it off as firewood.

"Anita has a chainsaw," she says. "She'll help you to cut it up. If you don't want it for the fireplace, Anita would like to have it because it burns slowly and gives off a sweet aroma and nice colours and sells for two-hundred dollars a cord."

And when I tell Kish about Luther taking up with Anita, she's matter of fact about the corvid family of birds and how smart and perceptive they are, making plans for the future.

"Just think for a moment, how practical it is for Luther to be adapting to a new situation," she says. "You should be taking the same approach."

I get around that by saying that I've been adapting by planning to sell the house.

"That's a good idea," she says.

This was her idea in the first place. She wants me to sign up with Anita as the realtor for the sale of the house and the purchase of a condo. Anita, Kish's friend and our neighbour, took up selling real estate after the death of her husband. I'm clutching at straws, guessing that part of Kish's defence against Alzheimer's may be to limit how much she cares about anything, even the house we have called home for twenty-three years. That's my hang-up about selling the place. I'm left hoping that all's well between Kish and that other abode, the Mañana Treehouse.

I wake up even wearier than I was when I went to bed. There's a void, a cold spot on her side of the bed. I miss hearing the sound of her voice first thing. Otherwise, not much has changed. It's my same old wondering. How's her day starting? Her brain waves are no help to me now. They don't have enough voltage to bridge the gap from Strathaven Place to my noggin here at home. Kish was right about the distance. It's 5.4 kilometres. I've clocked it on my car's odometer.

14. A blessing in disguise

WHAT'S REMARKABLE ABOUT SUITE 932 is how small it looks. It would have been a finicky process for the architect having to cram a living room, kitchenette, bedroom alcove, and bathroom into an area of 420 square feet. However, according to Kish, it's not constricting in the least. I don't have the heart to remind her about our rambling old house and say that this new abode is about the size of our living room.

She has the suite furnished with a torchiere lamp behind a beige recliner chair. Facing the TV set, there's a pair of teal-blue armchairs, quite close to the colour of the comforter on her bed. On the wall in the bedroom alcove, she has hung the two Picasso reproductions, *Harlequin with Violin* and *The Old Guitarist*. It pleases me to see that she still thinks highly enough of my first anniversary gifts to have brought them from her studio at home. She makes it clear that she likes it here. She finds it homey and reassuring. She knows exactly where everything is.

"It has simplified things for me," she says.

Running true to form, she doesn't need my help with any shopping for the kitchenette. She has managed it on her own. She opens the small refrigerator stocked up with a carton of pineapple juice, coffee cream, half-a-dozen eggs, marmalade, cream cheese, red grapes, and a netted bag of oranges. In the cupboard, she has a loaf of bread, shredded wheat, and a package of English muffins.

She tells me she intended to have breakfast here on her own. "But this morning," she says, "I went to the dining room and enjoyed it so much that from now on, I'll be going to there for all of my meals. I won't be needing the eggs or the shredded wheat and I want you to take them home."

She also asks me to take a garment bag with some of the clothing she brought with her from home. There isn't room for it in her closet, a narrow enclosure that holds several new outfits. She's wearing one of them, beige drawstring slacks with wide and narrow stripes and a darker beige pleated blouse. She has a toned-up look. She's been going to the exercise room on the main floor. She's in good humour, buoyed up and coasting along on her treehouse remission and adapting to Strathaven. It's surprising how at home she seems to be.

"I feel safe here," she says. "The best part of it is getting together with my friends in the dining room."

"Making friends. That's good, Kish."

"Yes, we're getting acquainted and we're comfortable sitting together at our table. We can be who we are. We can remember each other's names or forget them and it doesn't matter either way."

Apparently anticipating that I'm wondering where I fit into this arrangement, she says that both of us need time to adjust to it.

"Some care facilities have a rule that new residents aren't allowed to have visitors for the first month so that they can settle in properly. Lucky for us, Max, they don't do that here. But I do think that we need to give ourselves time to settle into our new situation."

This turns out to be process of nudging me out onto the fringe of her life at Strathaven Place. Where do I fit in? She decides that visiting hours for me are from 4:15 to 4:45 p.m. A meagre half-hour. And when I show up, I'm to knock on the door and wait for permission to go in. Not that I'd be brash enough to go barging in. She wants it understood that the suite with her name on a scroll-fringed plaque next to the door is also her boudoir.

"Do you know that boudoir is from an old French word for sulking place," she says. "And as such, it should be every woman's entitlement."

I'm not to feel singled out. She has this arrangement with everybody. The nurses and care aides and new friends are required to knock and to pause for a moment before they go in. I guess this is her way of staying in control of the inevitable process of losing control. She has me dutifully carrying home the groceries and the unwanted clothing.

For the next few weeks I show up every two days with a dozen hot-pink, large-blossomed carnations, a favourite of hers.

"It's nice of you to remember," she says. "But you're overdoing it. She puts me on notice. "Pink carnations only on Sundays."

When I ask what she would like in the way of flowering plants for her window sill, she says none at all. She doesn't want the responsibility. Connie Kish, ardent gardener, is afraid that she would forget to water a couple of plants.

Trying to find a bigger niche for myself at Strathaven, I offer to work out with her in the afternoons. I could use the exercise. But she tells me that it's residents only in the exercise room. In yet another exclusion, the ninth floor dining room is off limits for me. When I ask if I could have dinner with her there, just occasionally, she fobs me off, explaining that there isn't room. There are three other residents, Mrs. Ritter and Belinda and Bob Jones at her table. Kish thinks of them as a family unit. They are settled into a routine. Breakfast at eight, lunch at noon and dinner at five, every day of the week at their assigned places. If I showed up, I'd be out of place, wedged in at a corner of the table.

"You could crowd in and sit next to me," Kish says. "But that would put you too close to Bob and he would find it very upsetting."

Bob, I'm told, has a peptic ulcer that flares up when he's confused. It has taken him several days to get used to having Kish at his table as the replacement for the late Mrs. Ludwig. Kish tells me that Bob and his wife Belinda have a nicely dovetailing arrangement for looking after each other. He's late seventies, physically robust with Alzheimer's and confused to the point where he thinks that Strathaven is a holiday resort. Belinda, the same age as Bob, is mentally sharp, paraplegic and needing help to get around in her wheelchair. Bob attends to the wheelchair pushing and Belinda looks after the thinking.

"Yesterday at lunch," Kish says, "Bob was looking across the table at Belinda and asking her, 'When are we going home?' And she reached across the table, put her hands over his and said, 'Bob, my dear, we are home. This is it.'"

15. A not-so-big kahuna

KISH MAY NOT HAVE ROOM for me at her table in the dining room but she wants me to think there's a place for me in her bed. She has invited me to show up early on Saturday afternoon, just before three o'clock. After I knock on her door and she calls out for me to come in, I find her in bed. She has the torchiere turned down to a soft setting. She's wearing a mauve bed jacket, one that I haven't seen before. She lifts her right arm to raise the sheet and blanket.

"Ahoy, mate!" she says. "Come on. The cold air is getting in."

I glance away from her, avoiding eye contact after noticing how frail she looks and thinking I'd be taking advantage of her. That's not all that's turning me off. I can't get my head around the idea of cozying up in a hospital bed. I'm not sure that she can either. Considering all the other ways she has been shutting me out of her life, I can't help thinking that she doesn't really want me in bed with her and that this is a game of some kind.

"A little loving will do us a world of good," she says, revving up the charm with her sugary tone of voice. "All this celibacy is bad for my health. Yours too. And you know, don't you, that Alzheimer's isn't contagious?"

The medication she's taking for the dementia could be sparking her libido. I've been on line inquiring about the side effects of the Aricept prescribed by Dr. Winkler. There's nothing conclusive about it. But Aricept raises the level of acetylcholine in the brain and this would have a stimulating effect and could ramp up the patient's sex drive. With Alzheimer's generally speaking, there's no single pattern of change in sexual behaviour. Some people cool off altogether. The other extreme is an aroused libido, breathing fire. It can also happen that the Alzheimer's victim has powerful urges but can't remember how to satisfy them.

Kish and I have always been able to say, Not tonight, dear, without recrimination. But I've been saying it for quite a while. I can't apologize or reduce her to hearing me say that there's no other woman in the wings. What's different this time is that she's persisting with her come hither.

"I think I'm coming down with something," she says with a grin and limply holding the back of her hand to her forehead. "You remember, Max, that dreaded Hawaiian disease. We've joked about it. What do they call it?"

"Lack-a-nookie," I submit, filling in the blank for our made-up word.

"That's it. Lack-a-nookie. And you're the big kahuna with the cure for it."

I'm turned off even more by this kind of talk. It sounds more like a prelude to fucking than the coalescing we had together. Finally, she turns sarcastic.

"Whatever happened to the décolletage man? Look at you. So healthy. You should be coming on to me."

I'm reduced to explaining that I need more time to get used to Strathaven and the risk of having a care aide come in unannounced and interrupt the proceedings. Lowering my voice I'm so straight-laced that I'm leery about talking about sex where we could be overheard. Kish has that covered, assuring me that at three thirty, all of the staff are tied up at the shift-change meeting and that it takes about twenty minutes. She says that there would be the thrill of taking a chance on getting caught. A little danger to spice things up.

"But never mind," she says. "Even if they didn't catch us in the act, they'd know. They'd see it on my face and they'd think highly of you. They'd respect a man who's doing his duty as a husband."

She leaves it there with a Gallic shrug, adjourning our love life, saying that I seem to be out of the habit. And it's a darned shame and that I should find out what's happened to my libido. If and when I get it back, she can't guarantee that she'll still be available. She's so brittle and smirking that I think this was a big tease right from the start.

"It's dinnertime," she says. "Time for you to run along and get a life."

She sends me packing at quarter to five. From the tone of it, you'd think I'd been here all day, hanging around and in the way. I guess there would be times at places like this with visitors staying longer than they should and polite residents acting as if the visitors can stay as long as they want, while thinking to themselves that they won't object when the visitors leave.

What have I done to make her so abrupt and indifferent? This is not the Kish I know. I shouldn't think this way but it bothers me to see her getting so involved with other residents and starting to feel at home at Strathaven.

On the main floor, getting off the elevator on my way out, I'm asking myself, is that Mrs. Booker? Still alive? She's more slumped in her wheelchair than I remember her. But it's her. Still wearing those cat's-eye upswept spectacles and wheeling herself across the lobby toward the elevator. She's too far away for me to be certain, but I think she's doing a double take herself, looking in my direction and remembering me. I step back onto the elevator, making my getaway. I'm not in the mood to be renewing old acquaintances. The doors are closing between us but she's close enough for me to see the saddened look in her eyes when she realizes that I'm avoiding her.

I got to know Mrs. Booker while coming here to visit Aunt Sarah. During those visits, I mastered the niceties of visiting family or friends at an extended-care home, or thought I had. I learned to glance away from the importuning old eyes of strangers to avoid letting them glom onto me. It sounds hard-hearted I know. But take my word for it. The prudent thing is to pass them by and go about your business and minimize contact with residents in hallways. If they greeted me, I'd say hello back, then keep my distance and move on.

But it didn't pan out that way with Mrs. Booker. Outside her room a few doors along the hall from Aunt Sarah on the fifth floor, she gave me a lingering glance. The cagey old stick didn't say a word. She gazed up at me from her wheelchair, silently inquiring, Do I know you? Are you here for me? She presented me with her card. Mrs. Elizabeth Booker, with the numbers for her room and phone. My next mistake was to address her as Mrs. Booker, prompting her to leap to the conclusion that I really was there for her.

"What's it like out?" she asked.

"Warm and sunny," I said.

"Just right for a stroll," she reckoned and asked me to take her out for a walk. I begged off, saying that Aunt Sarah was expecting me. Mrs. Booker said that next time I'd be obliged to wheel her out for a walk.

Over a series of visits, I proceeded to dig myself in even deeper by telling her my name, enabling her to introduce me to one of the care aides as her nephew, Max, and insist that I call her Aunt Elizabeth and asking, "How's your mother keeping?" Turned out that this new-found mother of mine was Mrs. Booker's sister, Henrietta who lived in Nanaimo. She was Mrs. Booker's only visitor, coming down to Victoria twice a month on the bus. Over the months during Aunt Sarah's time at Strathaven, I was on the lookout for Mrs. Booker and trying to avoid her. I liked her but I was getting too involved. It was complicated, having to nod along as her nephew and have her asking about that walk as if it was a promise made to her.

With Mrs. Booker's saddened gaze zapping me all over again, I ride up to the third floor and back down to the lobby to make amends, only to find that she's nowhere in sight. She probably caught the next elevator going up and passed me coming back down.

This is a stroke of luck. I don't know what came over me. A vacillating moment, remembering Aunt Sarah and Mrs. Booker. But I'm over it now and relieved after deciding that I won't be renewing acquaintance with Mrs. Booker. I won't allow myself to be drawn into this place. I want to stay focused on Kish and me. It's up to me to persuade her to come with me looking at condo apartments. I want her to keep an open mind about having us living together again.

16. Favourite wives

IT'S HAPPENING AGAIN. After that close call with Mrs. Booker, I should know better than to get involved with Nellie Kershaw after she calls out to me from her suite across the hall from Kish.

"Ah, there you are," she says while pressing the control button that raises the head of her bed. She's wearing a pale pink bed jacket and her hair looks newly coifed. She turns down the sound on the Cary Grant movie she has playing on her TV set.

"Please help me," she says.

I ask her if she wants me to call a care aide. She shakes her head and points to the bowl of oranges on her bedside stand.

What could be less demanding than a bowl of those easy-to-peel oranges? After I pick one up and present it to her, a trap of wrinkled hands springs shut around my right hand. The orange rolls onto the floor. She's holding on with all her quavery might. Smiling up at me, pleased with how artfully she has tricked me. Her cold fingers are interlocked and her knuckles are whitening. I could break her grip just by pulling away but I hold off on that.

My concern is that her old bones — like the rest of her, I'd guess, into their eighth decade — are about to crack and crumble. With her hands angled the way they are, I could sprain her wrist if I pull away. Reaching across with my left hand, I try to unscramble her grasp one finger at a time only to have her scowl at me and tighten her grip.

"No! Please, no!" she says in an urgent, scratchy whisper, as if she's hanging onto life itself.

I can see curly whiskers sprouting from her chin. She has a nasal drip going with a shiny bead at the end of her nose waiting to drop. I give up trying to extricate myself and take a tissue from the carton beside the fruit bowl for some left-hand daubing at the end of her nose. Fortunately the door to Kish's suite is open and she hears me calling to her across the hallway and joins me in Nellie's room.

"Ah Max, poor Max. The captive audience," she says and informs me that the same thing happened to her the other day. Nellie called her in to clean her eye glasses and the next thing Kish knew, she was taken prisoner. Nellie Kershaw was up to her old tricks, groping for human contact, clutching at life, what most of us do.

"Never mind, Nellie," Kish says, "help is on the way."

Nellie's husband Clancy, a punctual fellow and a dear man, according to Kish, will show up in five minutes. He'll arrive on time as he invariably does, three times a day, six days a week, so that he can spoon feed her breakfast, lunch, and dinner. One of their daughters takes over for him on Sundays. Clancy Kershaw? I know that name. A Clancy Kershaw was the manager at one of my father's lumberyards. The one in Sidney. I had a summer job there the year I started university.

While we're waiting for him to show up, Kish turns up the sound for the movie, *My Favourite Wife*, a screwball comedy, colourized from the black and white, but as old as Nellie herself. Her hands are warming up on me while Cary Grant strives to resolve his marital status. We don't get to find out

which wife he winds up with, owing to the arrival of Clancy
Kershaw. It's him all right, the guy who worked for my father.

"It's me, Nellie," he says.

She looks at him in bewilderment. All eyes for him. Smiling,
letting go of me and reaching out. Greedy for his left hand.
Kish introduces me to him. He's fat and benign with a rumpled
fedora, sloping bushy eyebrows, and kind, saddened eyes. I'd
say he's ten years younger than Nellie.

Now that Kish and I have parted company with Clancy and
Nellie, it's as if we need them as a buffer between us. Without
them, there's a silent chafing after I close the door to her suite
and start what little is left of my allotted half-hour. She's talking
non-stop, filling the void, saying that my encounter with Nellie
should serve as a reality check for me.

"She likes having everything done for her," Kish says. "You
should hear Clancy fussing over her and coaxing her along
at meal times. He has a patter going. 'Here you go,' he'll say.
'Come on. Just one more spoonful.'"

Kish draws a picture of Nellie. The baby bird in the nest,
mouth gaping, waiting to be fed. It's taking longer and longer
to feed her. She has difficulty swallowing and there are long
pauses between each spoonful. She'll accept a few spoon-loads
of the meat and potato puree on condition that he'll follow up
with a full serving of the sweet pudding. After dinner, the LPN
comes in with Nellie's evening meds and Clancy starts another
one of the old movies and watches it with her until she goes to
sleep.

Kish introduces me to a gem of terminology from Nellie's
world. The shit storm. The care aides used it to describe what
happened yesterday after Nellie had been constipated for three

days and the nurse gave her a potent laxative. Shit happened. What a stink. Nellie's room was cordoned off.

What's this about? Kish trying to shock me with geriatric horror stories? Persuading me that she's a Nellie Kershaw in waiting? As if it's a matter of months before she'll be forgetting what I look like. This is new, all this looking at the dark side. I liked it better when she was flirting with Alzheimer's Lite and staying above it all in the Mañana Treehouse. I suggest that she's getting ahead of herself; she's only forty-nine and yet comparing herself with a woman in her eighties who may have Alzheimer's but who is also simply getting old the way we're all getting old.

"She's not getting old the way you're getting old," Kish says. "She's getting old the way I'm getting old. Our brains are ageing faster than your brain."

Turns out that Nellie is much younger than she looks. Not in her eighties, she's in her sixties. What I'm seeing is the destructive wear and tear of Alzheimer's. She was diagnosed twenty years ago and she's been in care at Strathaven for seventeen years.

"When you're looking at Nellie, you're looking at me in a few years," Kish says.

Stretching it now, she's parleying her occasional lapses of memory into late-stage Alzheimer's while I take it the other way, prompting her about the treehouse and the sixty-second rule. Not only that, I remind her that with rare exceptions, she's quite clear and coherent about what's going on. But Kish responds as if she hasn't heard a word of it.

"You'll have to be a saint to put up with me," she says. "I'll be like Nellie, drawing a blank when I look at you but thinking there's something familiar about the sound of your voice. I'll grow a little goatee beard and lie there stroking it the way

110

Nellie does. I've seen her, off in another world, fondling her whiskers and watching Cary Grant."

"Well, Kish, if and when that happens, it would be okay with me. The two of us watching old movies together and I'll be fantasizing that I'm Cary Grant while he's romancing Rita Hayworth."

"If only I'd be able to react that way to Cary Grant," Kish says. "But alas, instead of hankering for a man in my bed, I'll be hankering for the bed itself. You should have seen Nellie a few days ago. They're getting her out of bed for a few hours every day. She was parked there in her wheelchair near the bed and trying to use a pillow to support her head. But the back of the chair wasn't high enough to prop up the pillow and it kept sliding onto the floor. What Nellie wanted desperately was to lie down and rest her head. Poor dear, she sat there all afternoon, longing for them to put her back to bed."

"Well, Kish, one thing that's clear to me is that Nellie and Clancy are still in love and they're still lovely to each other."

Kish finds this unsettling and tells me that the way things are between them has nothing to do with us. I'm reluctant to ask her what she means by that. Over the past several weeks, it's been one rebuff after another. One minute she's pretending to want me to get into bed with her, then it's the cold shoulder, brushing me off. While her rejection has been gathering momentum, I've been trying to keep things in perspective. I shouldn't take it personally by rising to the bait and getting angry. I should see it as her way of coping with the dementia.

We can hear the rumbling approach of the big stainless-steel wagon loaded with dinners for the residents on the ninth floor. It's close to five o'clock, dinnertime. She dismisses me once again.

"I'm late," she says. "I can't be late. They're expecting me."

She knows she's a couple of minutes late when the meal wagon comes trundling along the hall toward the dining room. I've seen where it all starts on the main floor. It's quite an event, like a chuckwagon race at the Calgary Stampede, starting a few minutes before mealtime, ten lumbering wagons loaded up with meals for some four-hundred residents at Strathaven, one wagon for each of the residential floors and the meal servers supplying the horsepower as they rumble and rattle from the kitchen at the far end of the main floor hallway toward the elevators.

"It's time for you to run along," Kish says dismissively.

If only she left it at that, allowing me to make my exit short and sweet. Instead, she's impatiently hustling me to the elevator. We're passing a slumping old man who has stopped to rest with both hands on the hallway railing to support himself. There's no belt on his trousers and they're drooping down to expose the top half of his buttocks.

Kish calls over to him. "Hello, John. Are you all right? Do you need any help getting to the dining room?"

"Thanks for asking. Just taking a breather here. I can manage by myself."

Then, realizing how uncovered he is, he turns his back to the wall and leans back and uses both hands to yank his pants up to waist level.

"Oh me, oh my," he says with a look of utter defeat. "This is embarrassing. Don't look at me. You go along to the dining room. I'm going back to my room to get my belt. And my cane. Can't go forgetting that cane, now can I? Now stop looking at me and please accept my apologies."

"Hey, John. There's no harm done and nothing for you to apologize for," she says.

While Kish and I are waiting at the elevator, Clancy comes along the hall. He's on his way out as well and it's a relief to have him there filling up the silence and thanking us for fussing over Nellie.

"She likes both of you," he says. "She's a good judge of character and she's very fussy about who she holds hands with."

The elevator doors open and I turn and Kish faces me for an awkward kiss. This is the parting gesture that's expected of us. It's a relief when I'm on the elevator and the doors are closing between us. Just at that moment another resident steps into the elevator.

Clancy hits the button to reopen the doors. "Where you off to, Bob?"

It's Bob Jones, one of Kish's dining room friends, trying to hitch a ride with Clancy and me. Bob wouldn't have the elevator door code that's been set up to prevent confused residents from leaving the floor they live on.

"Where you off to?" Clancy says.

"Nowhere in particular," Bob says. "Just thought I'd take a ride."

"Do you think you should be doing this?" Clancy says. "Belinda will be wondering where you are. Why don't we go to the dining room? It's dinnertime and she'll be wondering where you are."

"That's right," Bob says in full compliance, agreeing with Clancy that he can't have Belinda worrying about him.

"It's okay," he says. "You don't have to walk me to the dining room. I know where it is."

"Good man," Clancy says.

"You too," says Bob.

Going down in the elevator with Clancy, I tell him about my summer job at the lumberyard in Sidney. He's all smiles, saying, sure, he remembers me but I don't think he does. "Right," he says. "That would have been when I was the

113

manager." He remembers my father. A good guy to work for. A straight shooter. He wants to know how Kish is settling in at Strathaven. I'm off-hand about it, saying it would be difficult for any newcomer to a care facility.

"Yes, it can be difficult settling in," he says. "We could talk about it if you like." He explains that he's a volunteer at Strathaven and can show me the ropes. I don't know this guy well enough to trust him with personal matters and yet I'm allowing him to take charge. He leads me over to a row of chairs on the other side of the main floor lobby and invites me to take a seat near a fountain with a soothing of water sounds coming from the bronze casting of an oval basin with three frogs sitting in raised clamshells with streams of water spouting from their gullets.

Waiting for Clancy to say whatever it is that he's got to say, I'm communing with the frogs and letting the water sounds wash over me, only to have this reverie interrupted by the approach of Mr. Mundy, an elderly gent turned out in a white shirt, tie, and Harris tweed jacket. He's agitated and so shaky on his feet that Clancy persuades him to sit with us. He has lost his cane. Clancy asks him where he might have left it. Has he been outside? No, not for a long time. He does all his walking indoors at Strathaven. So it's in the building. Any chance he can remember where he last had the cane in his possession?

"I would have had it when I left my suite," Mr. Mundy says. "I never go anywhere without it."

"You're on the sixth floor, am I right? Did you stop anywhere?"

"No, I went straight to the elevator and came down here to start my walk. It's what I do every night after dinner. Getting my exercise, walking this floor then two of the other floors along the hallways all the way from one end to the other."

114

Does he remember sitting down anywhere? In the solarium on the other side of the lobby? Mr. Mundy lights up, saying that could be it. Sometimes he goes there to sit down.

"Let's take a look," Clancy says.

"Good idea," Mr. Mundy says.

Now rested, he walks away briskly, trying to persuade Clancy that he doesn't really need the cane. It's just that he started using it after he sprained his ankle and hasn't been able to kick the habit. They don't need me tagging along into the solarium. A minute later, they return without the cane. Where else could it be? The men's room on the other side of the elevators? They go there and return with the cane, having found it in a corner near the biffy. Mr. Mundy shows the cane to me. It's made out of a yellow wood with dark veins in it.

"It's zebra wood, from Africa," he says.

Off he goes, walking taller with the cane. He knows that we're watching him as he hits his stride with the swaggering flourish of the boulevardier, swinging the cane forward and back, momentarily planting it, imperceptibly pushing off then swinging it forward again on his way over to the elevator.

I'm dubious about Clancy's willingness to help Mr. Mundy. It's contrary to my strategy of trying not to get involved with anybody here. Clancy picks up on my disdain and asks me about it.

"If you really want to know, I just don't see getting involved in that way. I would have sent him over to Inga at the reception desk. She was right there taking it all in."

"Yes, I could have done that," Clancy says. "But Inga wouldn't have been able to leave the reception desk to help him. She would have called up to the sixth floor to get one of the care aides to come down."

He reminds me that it's bedtime at Strathaven and for the next couple of hours the residents will be waiting their turn for the help they need getting to bed. The care aides have all they can handle looking after them. Clancy wants me to understand how he was drawn into everyday life at Strathaven. Coming here three times a day, it didn't take long for him to be become such a familiar figure that some of the residents thought he was a care aide. He couldn't say no to them, within reason of course.

"I didn't step up and volunteer for anything," Clancy says. "It just happened. I started helping out where I can, doing some of the little things that the staff don't have time for. They're rushed off their feet because of all the government cutbacks. For this we can thank Gordon Campbell, the honourable premier who tore up the union contracts covering the care aides. The result was that this place and a number of other long-term facilities were privatized and the wages went down by something like thirty percent and the staffing levels were cut to the bone.

"I don't know all the ins and outs of government funding for care facilities. But I know this much. Before all the cost-cutting, Nellie got a bath every day under the care plan we could afford. But under the new deal, it would cost us $7.50 more for her bath. That's $7.50 a day more! Two hundred and twenty-five bucks a month. We couldn't come up with the money. So Nellie and many more like her were cut back to one bath a week. On the other days, they get a once-over-lightly at bedtime."

Residents know that they can find Clancy here at the fountain most days for an hour or so around six o'clock.

"Part of the deal," he says, "is my Lost and Found Department. Helping Mr. Mundy find his cane. Yesterday, it was Peter Simpson, looking for his helmet. They call him Crash Simpson. Oh boy let me tell you, his balance is so shaky that even with a walker, he falls down. He needs the helmet for protection. Turned out he'd left it in his suite and we found it on his bed."

Clancy thinks I'll catch the volunteer bug after I've been coming here for a while. Maybe it's already happened, he says, referring to the way I was with Nellie this afternoon, Well, let Clancy think what he wants. What choice did I have with Nellie? I'll know better next time. I won't allow myself to be drawn into this place. I'm not the Good Samaritan type. I won't be getting involved with anybody except Kish.

It's depressing to see what can go wrong in old age. Bob Jones yearning to go home. Nellie living out her life dozing in a wheelchair. And that old fellow with his bare butt showing while he hangs onto the railing. And numerous other sad sights at Strathaven Place. It's not that I'm indifferent. They have my sympathy. But I can't make life better for them, not in any substantial way. But I can make a difference in Kish's life. And that's what my life is all about. I have to think to myself, Wrong again, Clancy, when he says he knows what I'm going through.

"It can be tough when your wife doesn't want to be here," he says. "It'll take a while for her to get used to this place. But you'll see. She'll come round. I know Nellie did. It wasn't long before she felt safer at Strathaven than she did at home."

He's assuming that it was my decision to place Kish at Strathaven and that she came here under protest. After I straighten him out on that point, I tell him about her Alzheimer's Lite. But I stop short of telling him about the treehouse. I don't know him well enough for that. He speculates that Alzheimer's Lite won't stay light for very long.

Clancy, it turns out, has a university degree, a bachelor of commerce, and forty years in the lumber business. So what does he know about Alzheimer's? Hardly anything about the disease itself. But having lived with it for twenty years, he knows a thing or two about coping as the caregiver husband. As such, he says, there are two ways I can go. I can get involved with the care of my wife and become a regular. That's what the staff at Strathaven call him — a regular. Day by day, going the distance and becoming a bitter-ender.

"Or you can play it safe," he says. "You know, keep your distance. You can be one those guys who thinks there's something wrong with a man who helps to look after a woman and decides that the best he can do is to drop in on Sunday afternoon with a bouquet of flowers."

He mentions the few who have their spouses placed in extended care and then abandon them altogether. "That's what happened to John Gunderson up on the ninth floor," Clancy says. "His wife dropped him off here two years ago. She lives just a couple of miles away but I'm told that she hasn't come to see him. Not once. But he hasn't given up on her. He stopped me a couple of weeks ago and said that when his wife comes looking for him, I was to tell her that he'd be waiting for her in the activities room on the ninth floor."

This leaves me asking Clancy what you do if you want to be a regular but your wife sees you as the Sunday-afternoon husband.

"Well, if you really want to be more than that, you'll say to yourself, enough of the sweet nothings, you know, the easy stuff, the flowers and the chocolates, and you'll come up with more tangible sweet somethings. Take her for a stroll on the boardwalk. Or for Sunday brunch at the restaurant along there or to a movie or whatever it was that you did together when she was at home."

"I've been trying. But she won't go anywhere with me."

"Give her time," Clancy says. "And when she gets touchy and confused about something, make allowances for the Alzheimer's. In the first year or so with Nellie, when we'd disagree about something, I'd think that I could straighten her out by reasoning with her and explaining things. But when I did that, Nellie would just go blank. She'd shut me out entirely. I learned to take my time, the way you do on the highway when you see that sign saying slow down, congestion ahead. I wouldn't ask if she remembered something. I'd just mention the thing. Wasn't it great or wasn't it awful, without asking her to remember it. If she couldn't remember it, she'd be upset and think that she should."

"Sure Clancy, but Connie isn't there yet."

"What you really need to do is convince her that she's essential in your life. Make her feel worthwhile. That she has value. I think that when you get older, love is that basic. Mutual need. Being needed by somebody you care about. She may be letting on that she can manage on her own and maybe she can for now. But inevitably, she'll be needing your support and relying on you more and more."

Clancy wants to tell somebody about his darling Nellie. And I'm it.

"So we're at home, at the kitchen table," he says. "Before Strathaven. Having coffee after breakfast. She asks me a couple of times what day it is. And each time, I say it's Thursday. And the third time, before I can answer, she brightens up and remembers asking the first two times and says it's kind of me to be humouring her. And then she's crying. And I start crying. We're holding hands and crying across the table to each other. And Nellie puts her hands over her heart and tells me that she is still in there and I say I know that. Do you understand what I'm saying?"

"I think so, Clancy. I see it once in a while in Kish. Like a shadow passing over her when she realizes what's happening to her."

"You got that right. Nellie knew what was happening to her. One of the worst things was when she couldn't sew or knit anymore. She was a genius with a needle and thread or a sewing machine. Made all her own clothes. Looked fabulous in them. And oh boy, could she knit. You should have seen her. Fiddling away with her knitting needles."

The way Clancy tells it, knitting a scarf is as easy as it gets. Nothing fancy. Pretty much straight ahead, row after row. But Nellie's fingers failed her before she could finish the scarf.

"One of the few times I saw her get really angry over what was happing to her," Clancy says. "She had her teeth clenched, using the scissors, slicing up that half-knit scarf into little pieces. She really lost it and threw that cut-up wool, the knitting needles, all of it, into the garbage under the kitchen sink . . .

"Then she turned to me and apologized. She said, 'I'm not angry with you Clancy. You know that don't you?' And I said I knew that and that we were both angry at the same thing. And she had to spell it out. 'Yes,' she said. 'It's the Alzheimer's, isn't it?'"

Clancy draws my attention to the grey cardigan he's wearing. A Nellie creation, now heavily darned at the elbows with wool that's a shade darker than the sweater itself. "This sweater was the last knitting she was able to finish. That was twenty years ago. I've been darning it myself. Keeping it going. And now I'm getting carried away here. I should know better than to talk about this. She's getting weaker and weaker all the time."

Clancy is tearing up. He's a crier. It takes one to know one. And he's like Kish, with enough aplomb to be able to cry and talk clearly at the same time. It's either that or he's had a lot of practice.

17. Saving Nellie's whiskers

THE NEXT DAY, after my all-too-brief half-hour with Kish, I'm on my way out through the lobby when Clancy invites me to join him at the frog fountain. The moment I sit down, I notice that he's overly relaxed. Almost nodding off. Eyes slightly closed. Jowls and shoulders sagging. I catch the sour pong of whiskey on his breath. He's drunk and unsteady on his feet when he stands up and steps in front of me.

"So, how ya doing there, Maxwell," he says. "Now will ya do me a favour. Hold out your hands for me."

I extend them and he holds them for a moment. "Ah, that's just great there, Maxwell," he says. "They're good and steady."

There's no point in telling him it's Maximilian not Maxwell. It takes a moment for it to dawn on me that he's telling me that my steady hand is what's required to deal with Nellie's whiskers. He informs me that they started sprouting a few years ago after she could no longer remove them herself. Stubbornly possessive, she balked at having them removed by her hairdresser. Clancy was okay with that until Mrs. Dundee in Suite 936 started making fun of Nellie and her whiskers, saying that she should shave them off or sign up as the bearded lady in a circus freak show. Nellie is benignly unaware of it but Clancy takes it personally and worries that people will think that he isn't looking after her properly.

"I can't have that," he says. "I can't have people go round thinkin' that I'm neglectin' her. I need ya to help me out."

He's dead serious, informing me that he has tried to cope by prowling up to her bed at night with tweezers and a flashlight. He would have me believe that he managed to pluck out two whiskers. As he was about to try for a third, the flashlight strayed from her chin up to her eyes and woke her up. He let on to her that he was there to tuck her into bed. According to Clancy, she could sleep through the stinging tweaks from having two whiskers yanked out but a stray flashlight beam would wake her up.

Drawing me into the scheme of things, Clancy holds out his hands, showing me how wobbly they are. He wants me as the steady-handed tweezer guy. Without disturbing Nellie's slumbers, I'm to pluck out some of those whiskers. Clancy will hold the flashlight.

"We'll start tonight," he says. "We'll go in while she's asleep and see if we can remove two or three of 'em and leave the rest of 'em for a later date."

Clancy's kind and sozzled eyes make it hard for me to flat out say no. Fortunately, he wants to wait half an hour or so to give Nellie time to settle into a sound sleep. This leaves enough time for me to talk him out of it. I ask him if he's considered snipping off Nellie's whiskers with scissors. It would be less likely to wake her up than plucking them out. His thinking is that cutting whiskers off would have them growing back more bristly than before. Whereas, with roots-and-all removal, they would stop growing altogether.

Would I do it to Kish? Of course not. If she didn't want the hair dresser removing her whiskers, I'd say let them be. I'm coaxing Clancy around, asking if he has noticed how Nellie goes off into another world, fondling her little beard while watching her Cary Grant movies. If she's okay with those whiskers, who are we to object? Wouldn't it be disrespectful? It's a revelation to him. His jaw drops.

"Well I'm thankin' ya very, very much for straightenin' me out," he says. "You're right ya know. You're absolutely right there, Maxwell. Nellie would be lost without her whiskers. And do you know what? The next time Mrs. Dundee says anything, I'll tell her to go eat beans."

18. Flat out passively resisting

KISH PHONES ME AT HOME just as I'm clipping on Flora's leash. We're on the way out for our afternoon walk and I trust that I can speak for both us when I say that we wish Kish could be going with us.

"Well, I can be there in spirit," Kish says. "We can talk while you're walking. She won't mind."

As surprising as it would seem to Kish and probably to Flora herself, I'm throwing in with the dog, identifying with her by asking Kish if she would like to say hello to her.

"On the phone?" she asks in dismay. "Of course not. Not only would it be too maudlin for words. She'd be confused by it."

"She knows that it's you I'm talking to."

"You're going to tell her, is that it?"

"I don't have to. She already knows. She can tell from the sound of my voice."

As Flora and I are proceeding down the front steps, Kish mentions her list. This is a tipoff that she has the clipboard in front of her.

"Now let me get to my list," she says. "I've been wondering why you've been so on edge lately. Do you think it's because you're spending too much time at Strathaven?"

"What? Two or three hours a week? That's hardly too much."

I'm persevering, flat out passively resisting. I won't grumble about the way she's been shutting me out or tell her that this would contribute just a smidgeon to putting me on edge. Does she know this? In a calculated way I mean. Or has the Alzheimer's left her numbly unaware? It corrupts everything and has me holding back and measuring everything I say. I'm on guard against hurting her feelings and apprehensive about provoking her into rejecting me even more than she already has.

"Well," she goes on, "I can only imagine what a depressing place Strathaven must be for somebody as healthy and vigorous as you are. You need other activities. If you're not going back to your job as a school principal, you should think about volunteer work. For a worthwhile charity. What about teaching English as a second language? You'd be good at that."

I agree to look into it. I can see her in my mind's eye, ticking off that item on the clipboard, then scanning down to her suggestion that I get back to riding Lizzie on a regular basis. The idea of riding a bicycle built for two by myself, with that empty rear seat behind me, sticking out like a sore thumb, would be pathetically the same as dining alone in a restaurant. I doubt that Flora would tag along for a Lizzie ride without Kish. My empathizing with this dog extends to knowing that she wouldn't feel safe in her trailer with me steering the bicycle because Kish has always looked after that.

Flora and I are crossing the road over to Beacon Hill Park with the lilies in bloom. Still on the phone, I stay clear of waxing nostalgically about the tree where we first met while she was smoking marijuana and listening to a chickadee. She has become quite jaded about things like that. I am wondering if she would get Our Tree mixed up with her Mañana Treehouse.

She's back attending to her notes, saying again that I'm spending too much time at Strathaven. She wants me to be more out in the world.

"Have you sold the house yet?" she asks.

"Not yet. It was just an idea."

"You should get moving on it. Talk to Anita."

I'm trying to keep up with her agenda. When was it, she asks, that Conrad and you were talking about buying another sailboat? She wants me to get back to sailing with him. In our twenties, Conrad and I had a small sloop, the *Ozzie* — registered owners, the Osborne brothers — and sailed her out in the Strait of Juan de Fuca. We were afflicted with two-footitis. There's a plague of it among sailboat owners. In our case, as owners of that humble twenty-two footer with narrow bunks and cabin headroom of five-foot-eight, both of us six-foot-two, crouching like trolls in a cave, we were lusting after a bigger boat. Also on our wish list was a spinnaker foresail, an inboard diesel engine instead of our sputtering ten-horsepower outboard motor, and a flush toilet in place of the porta-potty. Rather than go on coveting just about every boat we'd see out in the strait, we sold the Ozzie and gave up sailing.

Kish thinks that I should buy Anita's sail boat, the *Summer Wind*. She has it up for sale, asking price, $49,000. It's a classy sloop with nice lines; in the photograph it's running with the wind with a crest of white water at the bow and a glorious blue-and-white-striped spinnaker billowing out.

"You could afford to buy it yourself," Kish says. "Or with Conrad."

An intriguing idea. Conrad and I buying it together. It would probably be financially difficult for him now that he's going through his third divorce. Even so, that thirty-six-foot sloop is a tantalizing proposition. Conrad would be as keen as I am over the 20 hp. diesel engine, the master bedroom and two smaller cabins and, this above all, six-foot-four headroom. It's a couple of years ago now that Anita took Kish and me out for an afternoon of sailing on the *Summer Wind*, an exhilarating time for me, at any rate. For Kish, not so much. After getting uproariously seasick, she avowed that she'd never go sailing again.

Kish is working all the angles, suggesting that if I can't see my way clear to buying the *Summer Wind*, I should approach Anita about purchasing a half interest in the boat and work out a time-sharing schedule and split what it costs for insurance on the boat and for moorage out at the marina in Sidney.

"Or why don't you and Anita just go sailing together?"

"She hasn't said anything about it."

"Well she should. Sailing is something you two have in common."

"Well, I can't invite myself, now can I?"

"You could hint around about it."

Where to next on Kish's agenda? Here she is again, urging me to sell the house, to talk to Anita, get it listed, and start looking for a new place. It's entirely my choice, she says, giving me free rein to spend every dime of what we would get for the house if that's what it takes. She wants to know if I've thought about Sidney and nudges me off in that direction. A condo on the waterfront with a view of the ocean and, wouldn't you know, overlooking the marina where Anita keeps her boat. Anita's name keeps coming up.

19. Building up scar tissue

SITTING IN A CHAIR in the doorway to her suite, Mabel Dundee is able to chat with people who are coming and going in the hallway. She likes to engage in hushed little bouts of gossip mongering. This afternoon, Clancy Kershaw is her target, leading me to suspect that he really did tell her to go eat beans.

"Have you heard the latest about Mr. Kershaw?" she inquires. "Well, I've been reliably informed that he has two women on the go. He has Nellie and a lady-in-waiting, so to speak. Her name is Gertie and he's been carrying on with her for quite some time."

Now I have an urge to tell her to go eat beans. But what I say to her is that she's mistaken about Clancy and that he's a devoted husband to Nellie.

Going into Kish's suite, I follow the boudoir protocol, knocking softly on the door and waiting for the all clear. We're so far apart that there's little in the way of friendly chit-chat, no It's good to see you or How was your day? We're in a state of mutual toleration, and I'm left asking her about the gossip about Clancy and Gertie.

"Oh that," she says. "Well let me tell you something about Mrs. Dundee and her wagging tongue. You know, don't you, that Alzheimer's can go after anybody with a brain and that leaves her in the clear."

Kish heard that on TV and asks if she told it properly and I reassure her that she did and that it was a good one about Mrs. Dundee. Kish knows about the ninth-floor gossip. Somebody saw Clancy holding hands with another woman at the Mayfair Shopping Centre and that somebody told somebody else who passed it along to Mrs. Dundee.

I'm on Clancy's side. He's devoted to Nellie. I've heard him crying over her. I've seen it in the way he takes her hand when he comes into her suite. Kish doesn't question Clancy's caring about Nellie but thinks I'm mistaken about the hand holding. The way Kish sees it, they aren't really hands. She's not holding Clancy's hand. She's clutching at the manual device that feeds her three times a day.

"She spends hours with her Cary Grant movies," Kish says. "More time with him than with Clancy. You saw the way she is. Stroking away at that little beard of hers. It's as close as she can get to any sensual gratification."

According to Kish, Nellie and Clancy haven't been in love for a long time but he's still devoted to her and doing everything he can for her.

"Another woman?" Kish says. "Another man? There should be more of it around here. The more the merrier."

As she would have it, there isn't, in the words of Jerry Lee Lewis, "a whole lotta shakin' goin' on". But it's been known to happen and there should be more of it. She's talking about women with husbands who no longer know who they are reaching out to men who are in the same boat with their wives in extended care. Kish still knows who I am and I hope it means that she isn't reaching out for somebody else. As for Clancy, Kish wouldn't begrudge some companionship and the comforts of home to a man who has devoted the last twenty years of his life to caring for an ailing wife.

20. Buying booze by the bottle

CLANCY CHOOSES NOT TO GO that easy on himself. He's telling me about it at the Tipperary, a pub that's a few minutes' walk from Strathaven. "I'm buying," he said when he invited me here for drinks. We're sitting outside under a heat lamp in beige wicker chairs near a stone fountain, splashing and sparkling in the sun, trying to brighten up our afternoon. Clancy is having a Happy Hour Highball and I'm sipping at a tall glass of lager. He sets me straight when I say how convenient it is for him to have a watering hole so close to Strathaven.

"Watering hole?" he says. "Hell no! I've never been here before. I can't afford to hang out in bars and buy my whiskey by the glass. I buy it by the bottle. The large economy size. But I'm having this fizzy drink because it's a special occasion. It's my coming out as the two-timing husband. I have to tell somebody and you're it, Max, now that Mrs. Dundee has been blabbing about me."

It's not that Clancy minds the gossip all that much. It was bound to come out sooner or later. His complaint is that if Mrs. Dundee is going to blab it around, the least she could do is get the other woman's name right. Her name isn't Gertie. It's Carole. Turns out that Clancy and Carole have been together for three months. But he wants me to know that Nellie still comes first and that Carole understands this. She went through it as the caregiver for her husband until he died at Strathaven. It's tighter than ever for Clancy paying the bills for Nellie's care.

"That's why I'm living in a dump and why I'm the caretaker in our building to cover half of the rent. And I take her laundry — everything except the bed sheets — and do it at home to save a few bucks."

He'll have me know that he's not whining for sympathy. But it sounds like whining to me. It's also a mirror held up in front of me. I see myself at times coming across that way to Kish. Still the woebegone worrywart and realizing that if I keep it up, I'll run the risk of having her turn away from me altogether. But this is about Clancy. What he needs is a shoulder to whine on and somebody to listen to him worrying about how the gossip will affect his reputation at Strathaven.

"I'm supposed to be the good guy volunteer," he says. "But now, people are going to think twice about that."

"I don't think so, Clancy. We've all seen how devoted you are to Nellie." I'm raising my glass in a toast. "Here's to Clancy Kershaw. A good husband and a good man to boot."

He wants me to understand what happened between him and Nellie going back to when she forgot his name a couple of years ago. It became apparent that she didn't know who he was. She may have had some deep-down awareness but there was no evidence of it in the way she related to him. This dawned on him two years ago while he was in hospital for surgery on his gall bladder.

"My daughter Susan brings Nellie in to see me," he recalls. "I'm in a room with three other guys. This was before she had to go into the wheelchair. She comes walking up in my direction but goes sailing right on past me to the guy in the next bed. She grabs his hands and tries to kiss him and he's all upset and pushing her away. Susan takes over and leads Nellie back to me and she's peering at me, trying to figure out who I am. The only thing she knows is that I'm teed off about something and that upsets her and she backs away from me. I admit that I was angry because she embarrassed me in front of the other men in the room. And then I tried apologizing to her but it just didn't register with her. We weren't really married anymore."

Clancy gave up trying to compete with Nellie's other life with Cary Grant. I've come round to sympathizing with him. He was building up scar tissue because he was going to need it as Nellie became increasingly remote. There isn't so much as a kiss on the cheek or a hug. She turns away and looks confused. Kish was right. There is no warmth in Nellie's holding hands with him. It's more desperation than affection.

"But it's not as bad as I'm making out," Clancy says. "The weird thing about it is that Nellie and I are getting comfortable with our new situation, still close together but leading separate lives."

Without asking, he hails a waitress and orders another beer for me. With his highball glass still half full, he's settling for that and telling me that one drink is his limit for the afternoon. "You probably think that I drink too much," he says. "And you'd be right. But I ration myself during the day so that I'm sober when I show up for Nellie at meal time. It's the least I can do . . .

"And I want you to know, Max, that if anybody had told me even a year ago that I'd be cheating on her, I'd've said, no way, absolutely no way. But look at me now . . . And another thing. I've been making it sound as if Nellie is at fault in some way. Well nothing could be further from the truth. She tried her level best, as long as she was able to. It was the Alzheimer's that came between us. She never complained when she was going through the early stage of it . . .

"The absolute worst time, when she was still aware enough to know what was happening to her. I've read about this somewhere. Some guy saying that it was like having two diseases. One of them is the Alzheimer's itself. The other one, just as bad, is the disease of knowing you have Alzheimer's and knowing what it's going to do to you. I wondered at the time, hoping is a better word for it I guess, that Nellie would recover from that second disease and find relief from the pain and uncertainty about what was happening to her. There were times when I could see her all worked up and angry and not knowing what she was angry about."

I'm off to the side, thinking that Kish is approximately where Nellie was twenty years ago, just starting out with Alzheimer's. Kish, however, is in a singular place, not worrying and angry the way Nellie was, but up there in the Mañana Treehouse, in remission and holding out with her diversionary tactics. She's still alert and capable most of the time but, at another level, in the throes of that second disease. Like Clancy, I can only hope that it will become easier for her as the dementia progresses and she becomes less and less aware of what's happening to her.

Clancy looks at his watch. "Four thirty," he says. "Time for me to head back to Strathaven Place. It's getting close to Nellie's dinnertime."

"Sure Clancy, I'll walk with you."

"Right," he says, "I'm forgetting. You've got Connie to think about. And I've got Nellie. We both have responsibilities. We're the bitter-enders."

I'm wondering what difference if would make to Nellie if Clancy didn't walk back with me to Strathaven and simply quit going there and bailed out on her the way John Gunderson's wife dumped him. My hunch is that at first, Nellie would be a little edgy having a care aide feeding her but she'd soon get used to it and forget about Clancy altogether and leave him to get on with his new life with Carole. But this guy Clancy Kershaw, the one that I'm getting to know, would never abandon Nellie, not in million years.

21. Don't forget the baking soda

THE NEXT DAY, CLANCY AND I are sitting in our usual spot near the frog fountain. He gestures toward the elevators, one of them with the door sliding open and a woman getting off.

"It's Mrs. Buckingham," he says. "She's comin' over here to see me. She phoned me this morning. She wants my help with somethin' or other. But I just can't. Not now. I'm bushed. Would you be a pal and help me out?"

Mrs. Buckingham comes over to sit with us at the fountain. She's wearing a brown dress with long sleeves and all muffled up with a rib-knit scarf coiled around her neck. Clancy tells her that he's sorry but he has another appointment. He introduces us and then leaves.

"But I don't know you from Adam," she says.

We're back and forth. I tell her about my wife, Connie Kish, and that she's a resident at Strathaven. Mrs. Buckingham informs me that she's a widow and insists that she's not to be confused with her late husband. She remembers him as Mr. Bunkingham because he was so full of bunk. She wants to know what floor Kish is on.

"The ninth floor."

"Well then, I definitely don't know her and I don't know you. I have to be sure that you're not a masher."

At this point, Inga Bumpus, the receptionist, calls over to us from the front desk. "Mrs. Buckingham. I know Mr. Osborne and I can vouch for him. He's not a masher."

This character reference leaves me in consultation with Mrs. Buckingham. She has a bald spot on top of her auburn-tinted hair and her eyes are magnified by thick spectacles. She's holding a three-ring loose-leaf binder and opens it to an old recipe for tomato soup. Over the years, the page has been fussed over with those round linen reinforcements that glue over the loose-leaf holes. There's a strip of yellowed and brittle Scotch tape mending a tear on the lower corner.

"It was one of my grandmother's recipes," Mrs. Buckingham says. "She got it out of the *Farmer's Almanac*. I should explain that I was raised on a farm. On the Prairies. Near Hazel Dell, Saskatchewan. That's why the soup is made with canned tomatoes. We never grew our own tomatoes on the farm. I don't know why. All we had was canned tomatoes."

She wants to give this recipe to her granddaughter, Cynthia. There are a couple of changes written in and the old dear is having trouble reading parts of it. This is where I come in. She wants me to double check the quantities and write the recipe out on another sheet of paper. I start at the top, reading the ingredients out to her as I transcribe them.

"Okay, we've got three cups of canned tomatoes, drained."

"Yes, write that in. Three cups. It's the same as one large can of tomatoes."

Working down the list, one pint of milk, salt and pepper, one half-cup of fried chopped onions, and one teaspoon of baking soda.

"Underline the baking soda," she says. "It's important. It stops the acid in the tomatoes from curdling the milk."

"I have to say, Mrs. Buckingham. I know this would be a really good soup. My mother used to make it this way. She'd serve it with a dab of butter melting on top."

Beaming her appreciation, she has me write in the suggestion for the dab of butter because it will make the soup more savoury.

"There's a note here about making your own croutons. Do you want to go over it too?"

"No we can skip that. Cynthia is a good cook. She'll know how to make her own croutons if she wants them."

If only Kish could see me now, getting involved, making a bit of a difference, as I wrap it up for Mrs. Buckingham by reviewing the cooking instructions: "In large saucepan, bring tomatoes to a boil. Add baking soda, salt and pepper, fried onions. Reduce heat. Add milk and heat through but do not boil. Enough for six servings."

Having had her way with me and thanked me, Mrs. Buckingham departs, heading for the elevator. Inga comes over to the fountain to tell me that Clancy would approve of the way I handled things.

"That was a nice touch," Inga says. "Saying that your mother used that recipe. Mrs. Buckingham felt really good about it."

She goes on to say that if I behave myself and play my cards right, she'll allow me to become one of her unpaid assistants. She has me on probation as a volunteer at Strathaven Place.

22. Miss me but let me go

BACK ON DUTY as the ninth floor yenta, Mrs. Dundee is sitting in the chair in her doorway and waiting for me. She wants to be the one to tell me that Nellie died this afternoon.

"It must have been all of a sudden," Mrs. Dundee says. "Because when they know it's coming, they move you into the dying room down on the third floor. They like to call it the quiet room. But Nellie had a surprise for them. She had just had her bath and they had her back in her own bed and she passed away without going to the quiet room."

My thoughts go out to Clancy and I ask Mrs. Dundee if he's been around this afternoon. "Oh yes," she says. "He's in there with Nellie and the head nurse."

The door to Kish's suite is open for a change and she calls out, inviting me in. She knows about Nellie.

"I'm going to miss looking in on her every morning," Kish says. "She had me calling her Aunt Nellie. And she wanted me to be somebody named Liz. I was her niece and she was my Aunt Nellie."

Kish, feeling sorrier for herself than for Nellie, speculates that Nellie would have been ready to go. She had been finding it harder and harder to swallow. There's a name for it. Progressive dysphagia. Forgetting how to swallow after it ceases to be automatic, you reach the stage where you have to think about it and consciously start the swallowing process.

"Clancy was so patient with her," Kish says. "Feeding her and allowing her to take her time. She enjoyed having him feed her. It was a different kind of spooning for her . . . And now I don't want you to be worrying about me. I'll be fine."

Meaning of course that she's not at all fine. But that she'll get over it, and would I be a nice guy and run along? It's almost dinnertime and she'll be going to the dining room. On my way along the hall toward the elevator, Mrs. Dundee informs me that Clancy is still with the head nurse in Nellie's suite.

I'm parked in a chair at the fountain, waiting for Clancy. He shows up just before six, tiddly on rye whiskey and bleary-eyed with a file folder under his arm. I'm ill-at-ease, saying to him that Nellie Kershaw was quite a lady and will be missed.

"Of course you're gonna miss her," he says. "There was somethin' goin' on between you and my Nellie. Holdin' hands the way you did."

"And here I thought it was our little secret."

"No, Max. I've been wise to ya all along and I've been meanin' to call ya on it."

"Yes, of course. You'll want the satisfaction of a duel. Pistols at dawn? Or I could drive you home. You sound all tuckered out. Do you think you should be driving tonight?"

"Well I guess you owe me for carryin' on with my lady the way you did. You could give me a lift home."

Then he changes his mind and asks if I'd drive him out to Clover Point. "Just to get some fresh air. That okay?"

On our way out to the car, Clancy pauses and opens his jacket to show me that he's wearing the grey cardigan that Nellie knit for him some twenty years ago.

"Aw shit, Maxell!" he says. "I was gonna show it to her before dinner. Ya know, kinda pose in it for her. Let her see me wearing it and hope that maybe she'd remember knitting it for me and — aw shit — just maybe, just for a couple of seconds, a little light would go on and she'd remember the way it was for us all those years ago."

I can see that he's tearing up and it's a relief to me when he turns away and walks around to the other side of the car.

On our way to Clover Point, he says it was real nice that she had her weekly bath a few hours before she passed away. "You know that sayin', 'cleanliness is next to godliness'? Well that was Nellie all the way. One of her little worries was 'dyin' foul,' as she put it. She had a way of holdin' her nose to ask me if I could detect any body odour and I'd reassure her by shakin' my head."

By way of convincing me that he's had numerous belts of whiskey this afternoon, Clancy informs me that when they were first married, Nellie introduced him to the Dutch oven, throwing the covers over his head and holding him under after she farted in bed. "And ya know, her poots didn't smell all that bad," he says.

Well, it takes all kinds now, doesn't it? Kish has a different take on a stunt like that. Once and only once, after several glasses of wine, I pulled a Dutch oven on her. She came on like Lady Baltimore, haughtily scorning it as grounds for divorce and as a degrading activity fit only for dung beetles.

We're parked as far out as we can get on Clover Point and rolling down our windows. We can't see much but we can hear the waves rolling out of the darkness onto the rocky shoreline.

"I've got a mickey of rye here," he says, taking the bottle out of his jacket pocket, screwing off the cap and taking a swallow.

"Come on, let's drink to Nellie," he says. "Yeah, a toast to Ellen April Rennie. That's what's on her birth certificate. I once looked up the Ellen part of it. If I remember right, it comes from a Greek name that means shining light.

"Yeah, that's what she was," he adds, taking another swig before passing the bottle to me."

"Sure, Clancy, I'll drink to that."

I take a small sip and cringe at the sensation of straight whiskey burning its way down and souring my empty stomach.

"Ya know, Nellie really liked it here on Clover Point," Clancy says. "We'd come out here for dinner. She liked it way better than goin' to a restaurant. That was a big, big hassle for both of us. Ya know. Gettin' her out of her wheelchair and into the car. Foldin' up the wheelchair and puttin' it into the trunk. Then, at the restaurant. Getting' the wheelchair out of the trunk and helpin' Nellie into it. And after dinner. Helpin' her out of the wheelchair and back into the car. Stowin' the damn thing back into the trunk and so forth. Back at Strathaven. Same deal. Gettin' the wheelchair out of the trunk. Helpin' Nellie back into the wheelchair. What a hassle it was. All that jockeyin' around with the wheelchair."

I get the picture. It would have been a lot easier for him having take-out dinner at Clover Point so that Nellie could remain in the car. Fried chicken or hamburgers and fries or a pizza and they'd listen to the six o'clock news on CBC radio, watching the seagulls while they were watching in case somebody happened to toss a French fry out the window.

"There wasn't much in the way of actual conversation," he says. "Ya know what I mean? And somethin' else. I want ya to tell Connie that Nellie liked havin' her drop in for a chat the way she did. It was good for Nellie just knowin' that Connie was there, right across the hall."

"What about you, Clancy?"

141

"Oh, I'll be okay. We've got four kids. Three boys and the daughter Susan who's still here in Victoria and three daughters-in-law and the son-in-law and the five grandchildren. Two of the boys in Vancouver. The other one in Seattle. I was on the phone to them this afternoon. We'll all be together the day after tomorrow. Fourteen of us. Fifteen countin' Nellie. We're gonna have a church funeral. I hope you and Connie will see your way clear to come. They also want to have a service for her in the chapel, ya know, at Strathaven. They always do it after somebody passes away. And I just can't bring myself to tell Inga that I won't be there. You're probably thinkin' that it's hard-hearted of me to be sayin' that."

"No, Clancy, with what you're going through right now, I can see where you're coming from."

"Right. I've had it up to here with that place. Twenty years of it. And done my bit as a volunteer. I'll never go back there. Never ever. And I'll let ya in on a little secret. I've had a belly full of Inga Bumpus. I know she means well but she can be such a bossy pain in the ass. So I'm takin' the coward's way out here. Askin' ya to tell her that I won't be there for the service for Nellie and maybe they'll decide to call it off . . .

"One last thing about Nellie," he says. "I want you to know how kind and loving and big-hearted she was."

He takes a mauve-coloured card out of the file folder and passes it over to me.

"Read it," he says. "It's about Nellie and me but it could be about Connie and you."

He's choking up and about to cry and says he needs a breath of air and another drink. A gust of cold wind bursts into the car when he opens the door and steps out onto the parking lot and disappears into the darkness. Under the dome light, I read the card. It starts with a poem.

Miss me a little
but not too long
And not with your head bowed low.
Remember the love that once we shared.
Miss me but let me go.

Sounds like something you'd find in a note from the grave. "Dearest Clancy," Nellie had written below the poem.

"The time will come when I'll want to say to you, Miss me but let me go. But when that time comes, I may not be able to find the words or have the awareness that they should be said. But you will know when it's time. And that's what you must do. Start a new life for yourself and if it's with somebody else, so be it. I'll want you to do that. I'll want you to miss me and let me go.

"Truly and sincerely and with all my love, Nellie."

I'd been going along with Clancy, sympathizing with him. But the moment he drew Kish and me into it, hinting at the possibility of another woman in my life, I felt betrayed. Just as we're driving away from Clover Point, he says he'll be back here in a few days with his family and Nellie's remains in an urn full of ashes for the scattering ceremony. Kish and I are invited.

"The sad thing is that Carole is gonna have to stay with her sister while I'm with the rest of the family," he says. "They don't know about Carole. Now just ain't the time to tell them."

Of course, Carole should be with him. He'll need her support and I know that he's earned it. I can think these thoughts and at the same time insist to myself that no matter what, there'll never be another woman in my life.

143

23. Gourmet ice cream sundaes

SHORTLY BEFORE FIVE, Kish is walking with me to the elevators before heading off to the dining room. Instead of going home as usual, I'm trying to manoeuvre my way into her Sunday evening by asking if we could spend part it together having dessert in her suite when she returns from the dining room.

"Oh well, I guess we could do that," she says. "If you want to. Dessert? Do you want me to ask them for two servings of whatever's on tonight's menu?"

Her response is just a shade less than overwhelmingly enthusiastic. Is it the Alzheimer's that has her so down in the mouth? She sounds the way I've felt for a while now, thinking that it's just as depressing to be together as it is to be apart. I'm trying not to sound desperate. It's brave-front time, stiff upper lip, best foot forward.

"Come on now, Kish. I can do better than Jell-o or chocolate pudding. Do they serve it with Reddi-Wip?"

"I think so," she says. "With that godawful spelling."

"Definitely, Kish. There'll be no Jell-o or chocolate pudding and most definitely no Reddi-Wip."

In that way, it's agreed that we have a date for dessert together at six o'clock.

I rush home and start in the mahogany box for silverware, two dessert spoons and a serving spoon. From the Grandmamma's crystal ware, a platter and two serving bowls and liqueur glasses and the bottle of Kahlua from our liquor cabinet and a thermos filled with ice cubes to chill it down.

Then it's a quick round of shopping at the supermarket for the dessert ingredients and, even quicker, my dinner at the Mayfair mall food mart — a drumstick and a couple of wings with fries in a red paper box on a lonely little brown tray. Moving along now to the kiosk where they sell quality ice cream. The server complains she can't spare the time it would take to work the scoops of the French vanilla ice cream into the narrow neck of the thermos. She offers to put the ice cream into a carton. I'm trying to look fretful and worried, telling her that the ice cream is for my dear wife who had open heart surgery yesterday and now has a craving for ice cream and that if I take it to her in a carton, it would melt away before I got back to her bedside in the intensive care unit.

The ice cream scooper, with Sally on her name tag, now has all the time in the world, taking smaller scoops so that they'll slide into the thermos while she tells me about her Aunt Sally,

"She's the one I was named after," Sally says. "And she'd be a good twenty years older than your wife and she had triple-bypass surgery and made a full recovery. It gave her a new lease on life. So don't go worrying about your wife. She'll be just fine."

It's a five-minute drive from Mayfair back to Strathaven. Kish is still in the dining room. I have time to go into her suite to set up a folding table with the bowls and glasses and to mound up the segmented crystal tray with the ingredients for our dessert the way she served it for dinner guests at home, with a dash of trivia about the origins of ice cream, how in

145

China some twenty-three-hundred years ago, a mixture of milk and sweetened rice was frozen by packing it in snow. When she comes into the suite, I'm standing next to the table, waiter-style with a linen serviette over my arm.

"Good evening, Madame. My name is Maximillian and I'll be your server for tonight."

She looks at me and then up at the ceiling. She's confused and I realize that I'm overpowering her with my obliging waiter schtick. I should have greeted her with a simple Hi Kish and kissed her but she's been shying away when I do that. She sits at the table and I sit across from her while she's taking it all in.

"Now what have we here on the toppings platter?" I ask. "Crushed pineapple, chocolate-coated raisins, white chocolate chips, mint chips, rainbow and chocolate sprinkles and at the centre, a mound of miniature chocolate chip cookies."

"This looks familiar," she says. "Our gourmet ice cream sundaes," sounding the T at the end of gourmet, a deliberate mispronunciation, the way she does. As the topping for her bowl of the ice cream, she opts for the pineapple with white chocolate chips and one of the cookies. I go for the pineapple with mint chips and the sprinkles and two cookies. I'm extolling what would have been her choice of Kahlua as the perfect liqueur for the occasion with its hint of vanilla beans carrying over into the vanilla ice cream.

I'm smiling to myself, thinking that it's mutually comforting, just being here, sitting close, over the small table, enjoying all the textures and the sweetness melting on our palettes. But I have to turn away slightly when she raises her bowl, laps into it, licking at the traces of ice cream and circling the bowl to get all of it. After she sets the bowl back on the table, she has an inkling of what she has done. But she's not sure.

"Did I just do what I think I did?" she asks and picks up the bowl for a close look at it. "Yes, I can see the lick marks. Now you know what's happening to me."

It's sad and funny. While I'm trying not to crack a smile, she starts grinning sheepishly and it's a relief to see that she's getting over it.

"It's so hard trying to think of everything . . . Sometimes I'm okay but I know it's not going to last. Have I told you that Bob Jones sits there in the dining room, waiting for Belinda to put the spoon in his hand? Then he'll finish his chocolate pudding by licking the bowl . . . And there's something else you should know. Licking the bowl runs in my family. My father did it toward the end. He'd lick out his soup bowl and then put it upside down on the table."

"It's nothing to worry about, Kish. You're forgetting the sixty-second rule, not to mention the Mañana Treehouse."

With that, the stresses and strains between us fade away. We're warmly engaged in a soirée for two. There's enough ice cream left in the thermos for sundae seconds. After a couple more splashes of the liqueur, Kish tells me it's bedtime. But it's not, as I would have thought, my cue to go home. I would have been okay with that. But she's asking me to wait outside while the care aide helps her to get ready for bed. Then I'm to come back for a Kahlua nightcap. It's a few more minutes of her evening and I'll take it.

Sitting close to the bed for the nightcap, I'm ogling her pale shoulders and the décolletage and weighing my chances. This Kahlua nightcap was her idea. Maybe she's also thinking about an interlude in bed. There's a rush of hormones. I'm surprised at how little it took to have me stirring. But my poor showing in response to her earlier overtures has me hemming and hawing about what to do next. Alas, an interlude is furthest from her mind. She sounds tired. Her voice has lost its sultry resonance. Almost imperceptibly, she's holding back a yawn by way of saying, Not tonight, dear. And I'm going along with it, thinking to myself, It's okay, my love. Some other time, perhaps.

There's always tomorrow and she goes along with my suggestion that we have a Monday brunch at a nearby restaurant. Now I'm getting somewhere. I have another date with Kish for ten thirty in the morning. Not only that. She wants me to leave the Kahlua and the glasses on the shelf under the TV set. For future nightcaps.

Just after I arrive home, Kish is on the phone, apologizing that she'd forgotten that her cousin Hilary will be coming over from Vancouver tomorrow and that they'll spend the morning together.

"I'm sorry Max," she says. "Sorry for being such a ditsy dame and forgetting that Hilary called yesterday and we made plans."

I know that she's saying just the two of them but I try to work my way into it by offering to pick Hilary up at the seaplane terminal. Thank you, but no. She'll be pressed for time. She has a case in court in Victoria in the afternoon and afterwards, she'll be flying back to Vancouver. Kish hopes I won't mind. She hasn't seen Hilary for several weeks and they're close cousins after all, with much to talk about. Girl talk.

"And she's going to be coming regularly," Kish says. "Just to see me. Isn't that great?"

So that's it for me for tomorrow, slotted into her schedule for my assigned thirty minutes of her time.

24. Happy Hobbling

SHE'S ON THE PHONE, telling me about her sprained left ankle. "They've got it all cuddled up in an air splint," she says. "And you know, it feels good. Like bubble wrap."

As she goes on to relate what happened, it turns into an hectic afternoon, starting downtown on Pandora Street in front of the sushi restaurant where she and Hilary were going to have lunch.

"I sprained my ankle," she says. "Well, I didn't do it to myself. I didn't just wrench it around on the spur of the moment . . . Well, you know what I mean to say. It was an accident . . . I was just stepping out of the taxi and the ankle collapsed on me and down I went. And gosh! Did it hurt! But don't worry. It's all been looked after and I'm taking something for the pain."

She tells me what it was like, there on the sidewalk with people gawking during the wait for an ambulance. Lucky for her, the taxi driver is a trained first-aid man. In the trunk of the cab, he has a first-aid kit and quickly has the ankle immobilized with padded aluminum splints. With Hilary's help, he gets her into the back seat of the taxi. Introductions are exchanged during the ride to the hospital. Connie Kish! The driver knows her as a children's storyteller from when he was a boy. It's lovely. Hilary and Carl — a tall, thin fellow — and Kish singing the

Barney Google song in the cab. At a red light, he turns around, leaning back to show her how he can still go cross-eyed.

The way Kish tells it, her good luck holds in the hospital emergency ward, meaning that she didn't break her ankle. Her take on it is that it's nothing more than a sprained ankle. However, according to the X-rays, it's a Grade 3 sprain with a full tear of the ankle ligament. My consultation with Dr. Google informs me that she wasn't all that lucky. With the support of an ankle brace, the torn ligament can take as long as three months to heal which is a little longer than it would take a fracture to mend.

When I arrive at her suite, she's not as I expected, hobbling around on crutches. She's in a wheelchair with the splint around her left ankle and the leg supported by the footrest. They gave her a tryout on crutches at the hospital. "I was okay on them, at least I thought I was," she says. "But the occupational therapist said that I didn't look secure on them. I think she had my medical records and knew about the Alzheimer's and went leaping to conclusions and decided that I was too far gone for crutches. So here I am, in this wheelchair. It's a fun thing. Scooting around in it."

It's a loaner with Royal Jubilee Hospital branded in white letters on the back of the seat. Sitting there, she looks frail and vulnerable. This is a diminished Connie Kish, taken down a peg and looking up at me. On her feet, she's tall. Five-foot-nine. Sitting down, she loses altitude. She's all legs — that's how she has described herself — and thus from the waist up, comparatively short in stature.

She wants to go out for a wheelchair ride on the boardwalk that skirts along the Gorge, an inner reach of Victoria harbour so that she can see the Christmas lights across the water. She puts on a green woollen toque with a pompom and a quilted, silver jacket. I'm chuffed at the thought of actually doing something for her, as trifling as it is, having taken a blanket off her bed and putting it on her lap, then pushing her in the wheelchair. It's high tide under the boardwalk. We can hear the sloshing high up on the pilings. In a perfect world, the boardwalk planks would go longways for a smooth wheelchair ride. It's bumpy going for Kish and the wheelchair over the gaps between the crossways planking.

There's a wind coming up, prompting me to ask her if she's warm enough. It's my mother-hen reflex, thinking that sitting in a wheelchair, you're never quite warm enough. Aunt Sarah was that way, frail and in her eighties with poor circulation in her legs and chronically cold and complaining about it. I'd be the solicitous nephew, getting a blanket for her. She revelled in my attention to her comfort. Kish on the other hand thinks I'm a fuss-budget.

"Am I warm enough! Oh Max, please. I'm just fine. I have the blanket over my knees. And this is Victoria after all. Yes, I'm warm enough."

Halfway along the boardwalk, we're passing a bench with a man stretched out with a rumpled, wide-brimmed fedora over his face. Parked close by he has a four-wheeled walker with a safety helmet in the front basket.

"Is that you, John?" Kish says.

"It sure enough is," he says, taking the hat off his face, putting it on while sitting up. She initiates the introductions. "Max," she says, "This is my friend, John Gunderson. And John, this is my husband, Max."

"Well, thanks there, Connie," John says. "We've already met. My pants were falling down at the time."

"Are you all right?" she asks. "Are you warm enough?"

"Sure I am," he says.

"Well, it's getting close to bedtime. Shouldn't you be heading home?"

"Home? Is that what you call it?"

"Come on, old man, you know what I mean. It's getting close to your bedtime and your care aide will be waiting for you."

"I haven't forgotten about that. My legs are shot but my brain still works."

"Better than mine I think."

"I doubt that, Connie. I doubt that very much. And I don't want you worrying about me. I'll be heading back in a few minutes. What I need right now is a little more time here, lying back and listening to the waves splashing around the pilings. I put this hat over my face, closing me in so that the waves are kind of washing over me. I like to come here and flake out and listen to the seagulls. I used to be a deep-sea diver and I like it here. Particularly when the tide is up."

"Would it be okay with you if Max sat down on the bench? We could hang out for a while and then go back together?"

"But that's not where you were headed. You were going the other way."

"What's wrong with me spending a little time with my favourite old man?"

"Ah come on. You and your husband have got better things to do than stand around worrying about me. There's no need for it. No need at all. I can get back on my own. I've got my walker and my helmet. Did you notice that, Connie? I've been reassessed. I've gone from needing a cane to needing a walker as well as a helmet in case I fall down. Now that's real progress, wouldn't you say?"

John catches himself, whining and whimpering as he describes it, and apologizes for it.

"Nothing to apologize for, John," Kish says. "That wasn't whining and whimpering. That was a nice touch of irony, talking about the great progress you're making. Ever onward and upward."

"Is that what it was?"

"I'm just wondering, John, shouldn't you have that helmet on your head where it belongs?"

"I look goofy and retarded wearing that thing. Don't you think I look a lot better wearing my fedora at this jaunty angle? I'm irresistible. I'm Clark Gable. And something else about that helmet. I know where it is at all times and I'm a really quick thinker and fast with my hands. So if I start falling down, I'll take off my hat and grab the helmet and put it on before I hit the ground."

"Just like that," Kish says. "The funny man with his whining and whimpering."

"You got me, there, Connie. Keeping up a brave front."

"Aren't we all?"

"Well, that's about as far as I can go with it for now," John says. "I hate having to say it, but all this conversation has tired me out. I'm just too pooped to get back under my own steam. Could you phone the nurse on our floor and have her send somebody to help me get back?"

He is visibly fading, as if his vitality has suddenly drained out of him. He looks so frail and worn-out that I'm surprised that he could make it this far away from Strathaven on a walker.

"No John," Kish says. "That would take too long. We'd be waiting around here half the night."

She takes charge the way she can when holding forth from the vantage point of the Mañana Treehouse. "What we're going to do is this. I'm going to get out of this wheelchair and sit where you're sitting. You're going to get into the wheelchair and Max is going to wheel you back. Okey-doke?"

"What? And leave you here all alone?"

"Not to worry, John. You're not the only one who likes communing with the waves and seagulls. I'll be fine. I've got this blanket to keep me warm. Max will come right back for me."

"What about my walker?"

It's agreed that I can't manage the walker and push the wheelchair at the same time. Kish suggests that John hold the walker on his lap.

"Could you do that?"

"Sure I could. I'm still pretty strong with my arms."

That's how we handle it. I have John in the wheelchair holding the walker, wheels pointing sideways from his lap as I push him along to the end of the boardwalk, up a winding pathway that takes us onto the sidewalk leading along the street to Strathaven Place.

"This is my first time in a wheelchair," he says, turning back to me. "I guess that's what's next for me. Going from a walker to a wheelchair. And then even more progress, they'll be putting me to bed and leaving me there."

He faces front and there's a change in his tone of voice. He's not talking to me. It's a soliloquy in a flat monotone, matter of fact, lamenting the way his life is going and making it more palatable by referring to himself in the third person.

"Get a load of the old fart," he says. "Sitting in his wheelchair holding a walker on his lap. You'd never know it from looking at him now but he once played lacrosse, semi-pro, with the Victoria Shamrocks. And then he was a deep-sea diver. For thirty-five years. With the big round helmet with the face plate, the air lines and the weighted shoes. He was the man on the job site, respected, the guy looking out through the face plate, the man going into the water, a hundred feet straight down. Well, he isn't the man any more, now is he? He's a sad sack of a man."

In the lobby at Strathaven, waiting at the elevator, John tells me that he'll get up to the ninth floor on his own so that I can hurry back to Kish on the boardwalk. I help him out of the wheelchair and onto the walker. He steadies himself, shifting his weight from one leg to the other. Before hitting the button for the ninth floor, he looks out at me. "Thanks for the buggy ride and thanks for listening to my little story."

John left out part of it. Clancy has told me the rest of it, the chapter where his wife abandoned him here two years ago and that he has no visitors. He couldn't go that far in telling me about himself. He settled for remembering that he was once a lacrosse player and a deep-sea diver. That made him somebody. Now he's trying not to be a nobody, holding out against being a lonely old man in a care home. Just as I'm holding out against my loneliness. I'm turning away with the empty wheelchair when the elevator doors reopen and John calls after me.

"We shouldn't have left Connie out there alone in the middle of winter," he says. "Don't you go wasting any time getting back to her."

TWO

25. Divorce Lite, a friendly parting of the ways

IT COMES WITHOUT WARNING. I'm flabbergasted, caught off guard, listening to her discreetly inquire as to whether or not it would be a good idea for us to get a divorce. What's utterly disarming is the way she sends it up like a trial balloon. She has it floating there as harmoniously as can be, waiting for me to deal with it. She has no complaints about anything. No explicit grounds for divorcing me, at least none that she's willing to tell me about. It's apparently unprovoked and as if she's forgotten about our ice cream sundaes and the warmth of the Kahlua the other night.

She had arranged for us to meet for a little talk in the solarium at four thirty. It's a glassed-in, humid little jungle with vinyl foliage and a fake brook, a few gallons of water wearily circulating through a pump and bedded with white gravel and a hokey wooden bridge going over it. There's a bench under a column of swallows' nests with round, swallow-sized holes but no swallows.

I catch sight of her coming off the elevator. She's still confined to that wheelchair and likely to be there for a few more weeks because she reinjured her ankle while trying to stand up in the dining room and help Belinda Jones straighten up in her wheelchair. Now that Kish has come wheeling energetically into the solarium, I'm wondering what's up. With her shoulders squared back, she cranks around to face me, bidding me to park myself on the bench. She wheels close and starts in, proceeding with the benefit of her clipboard as a memory prompter.

"I've been wondering," she says. "Do you think it would be a good idea for us to get a divorce?"

I'm trying to stay calm and collected. "What's this about? Something I've done?"

"No, Max. No. You're not to start blaming yourself and don't be upset. Divorce is a difficult word, I know. But in our case, it would be more of a friendly parting of the ways. Try to think of it that way."

She's not as vague and airy-fairy as she was at first. I think she was softening me up with that. Now she has turned the rheostat down a couple of notches, becoming frosty and aloof, looking at her notes and saying that what we need more than anything is flexibility and letting on that I'm not flexible enough. She's not saying outright that this in itself would be grounds for divorce. The closest thing to a transgression on my part is that I'm coming on too strong as the caregiver. The hovering husband.

"Come on, Kish. You know very well that I don't mean caregiver in the nursemaid sense of it. What I do mean is caring and wanting us to go through this together. I'm as flexible as I can be about having us go for walks and going out for dinner and to movies and concerts."

With the sun streaming in, it's muggy in here and I take off my jacket. Cooling off, I get back on track, trying to persuade her that I'm flexible enough to be selling the house and buying a condo where we could make a fresh start and live together again.

"Where was it we lived?" she asks. "Is it the house on Clarence Street?"

"No my dear. It's the house on Medana Street."

The house on Clarence was home for her for the first twenty-five years of her life with her parents and Grandmamma Constanze. Just a couple of blocks away, the house on Medana Street was home for Kish and me for twenty-three years.

"It's strange," she says. "Feeling vague about where home is."

"Maybe I can help you with that. Not now. But soon, in the new condo."

"How could I forget. Our house. Our home with the flagstone pathway and that lovely stained glass around the front door."

How hit and miss the Alzheimered memory can be. There it is again. A mix-up over street names. She forgets the name of the street where she lived for more than half of her life. I take dubious satisfaction in thinking that if she's confused about that, she's probably hazy about getting a divorce and that it will blow over.

The sixty-second rule kicks in again. Having got past her confusion, she sounds sure of herself, trying to convince me that by selling our house and moving into a condo, I'm in the process of divorcing her.

"And that's okay," she says. "We don't need to be married. We didn't get married for ourselves. Not really. We went through it to please my mother and grandmamma and your mother. Also the school trustees. They would have taken a dim view of you as a vice-principal shacking up with one of the teachers."

"Is that what you want for us now? Marital status, shacking up."

"I'd go along with that. Don't you see what I'm driving at?"

It's all too painfully unclear to me. Pry as I may, when I ask her what I've done or haven't done, she tells me not to think of it that way.

160

"You're blaming yourself. And you shouldn't be doing that. You should be trying to think of it as a no-fault divorce. That's the way it'll work for us. It's not your fault and it's not mine."

What bothers me is that it's all so vague. We're talking in circles. I suggest that we get some counselling to help us with this.

"Definitely not," she says. "We don't need outsiders getting involved and complicating things . . ."

"Yes, here it is," she says, glancing at her clipboard. "'Honest thinking.' That's what we need, both of us. I've been doing it and you should do the same. You should think about what you've said about me being too young for Alzheimer's. Do you remember me reminding you that you're only two years older than I am? That makes you much too young and much too alive to be the husband of a woman with Alzheimer's. You should be protecting yourself."

She has forgotten that we've talked about this before. Here I am again asking, "Protecting myself against what?"

"You should be thinking ahead to when I won't be who I am and protecting yourself against that. You should also ask yourself why you're so unhappy about things. Why you look so woebegone, right this minute. What you may need is some honest thinking about how you feel about us. Not how you should feel but how you really feel."

Then she eases off, wanting me to know that there is no rush for us to be getting a divorce. She's thinking about it and I should do the same, think about where we are and where we are going and realize that everything has changed. It's time for a new life for me and a new life for her, and just let it all percolate without fretting about it. She looks at her watch. Almost quarter to five. Time for her to go wheeling off to the dining room on the ninth floor. She wants to show up early to

161

rearrange the seating for the growing number of residents who want to sit at her table. They're calling it Connie's Corner.

"They've added another table for our little group," Kish says. "We've got some newcomers joining us. There's Arturo who is a very interesting man. He'll be sitting next to Mrs. Dundee."

I'm seeing Kish off at the elevator on the main floor. What's to be done? Do I bend down to wheelchair level to kiss the would-be divorcee or do I shake hands with her? What transpires is a feckless excuse for a kiss, another peck, owing to the fact that I don't know who I'm dealing with. Now that she's on her way up to the ninth floor, it dawns on me that I should have made it clear that for us to be thinking about divorce is to be thinking the unthinkable. I want to say that to her. I'm jabbing away at the elevator button, intending to go after her.

In the time it takes for one of the elevators to come back, I'm having second thoughts. She'd be in the dining room by now and I'd find myself barging into Connie's Corner, the centre of the new life she's been talking about. She feels safe up there. She and the others can be themselves, coping with their disabilities without me invading their comfort zone.

I'm on my own, with that word — *divorce* — nagging at me. What's hard for me to swallow is the prospect of being without her in my life. And goddammit, where does she get off with that vague nit-picking about flexibility. Whatever it is that she has in mind, she's not in a rush to proceed with it. That will give me time to reason with her and work my way around it. I'll also work on myself, on my woebegone disposition. It's not enough for me to have the crying under control. I'll have to stop looking like I'm about to give in to it. She has complained about that more than once.

My brother Conrad is a veteran of the marital wars. He's twice divorced and going down for the third time. Growing up, I looked up to him. I wanted to be as sure of myself with women as he seemed to be and to have as many girlfriends as he did, even after he was married. Later on, I became aware of the anguish that goes hand in hand with infidelity. I saw it in my mother's eyes, a long-suffering hurt and feeling betrayed over the years' putting up with my father's dalliances. I also heard about it from Shirley, Conrad's first wife, humiliated and desperate, when she phoned, asking me for advice about winning him back.

When I talked to Conrad about this, he said that he was truly sorry about hurting Shirley but that he couldn't help himself. His craving for other women was hard-wired into his brain, the amygdala, I think he said. I gave him my one-dame man lecture, saying that we're hard-wired for other primitive responses but we don't give in to them. Conrad has the higher cortical authority to pause and think about the cost of getting his jollies in terms of how much Shirley would be tormented by his infidelity.

I leave it at that. Conrad may have shortcomings as a husband but as a brother, he's solid. I'm on the phone to him tonight. After hearing my woeful going on about the divorce, he wants to come right over.

"I'll be there in twenty minutes," he says. "I'll bring a pizza, the one you like with anchovies. And some beer. And I've got some really good weed. We could get wasted together."

This leaves me explaining that the way things are, marijuana would only make it worse and that all I need is a brotherly voice on the phone.

"I hear ya," he says. "You've been through the mill. I've been there. You're blaming yourself. You're all stressed out. You know what they say. Stress kills, and it can at our age. So first thing tomorrow you should make an appointment with your doctor and level with him about what's going on. He'll probably put you on Trazadone and recommend some counselling."

I should have expected Conrad to take it one step further by telling me what the doctor wouldn't prescribe. "What you probably need as much as anything is to get your ashes hauled," he says. "You know. Get laid. Connie doesn't have to know. How long has it been?"

He may be right, physiologically speaking. But I have no idea who I could get to do the hauling. I'd also like to know who I can get to scratch my back. The way things are, I can no longer ask Kish to attend to those pesky little itches that are out of reach in the middle of my back. For now, I've acquired a chrome-plated back-scratcher. It has a little rake that telescopes out far enough to give me access to any itches back there. It's not natural for me to be doing that. What nature intended is that, like chimpanzees, we should all be paired up with a mate who'll scratch our backs.

"And one more thing," Conrad says. "I hope you won't take this the wrong way but it needs to be said. You're trying too hard. You've always been that way. I remember you telling me how you got a charge out of the way Connie would say 'Oh Max' and I said that's great, having the Oh Max Factor, turning you on. You got all huffy with me and said it was a different kind of turn on and how special Connie is. She's got you sounding desperate. Trying to see everything from her point of view. You shouldn't be taking that approach. And whatever you do, don't grovel. If you don't respect yourself, she won't either."

He goes on to say that if Kish is serious about divorcing me, she'll be lawyering up and so should I if only to get some advice about my situation.

"But I'd be jumping the gun, going to a lawyer when I'm not sure that she's really serious about divorcing me."

"I know, Max. She's a great lady and everything. But you're going too far with thinking it's all about her because it's not. Not entirely. It's terrible what's happening to her. The problem is that for you, this is a lose-lose situation. If she's divorcing you, you're the dumpee, the one on the receiving end. You come out of it looking bad. What have we got here? A woman with Alzheimer's who needs her husband more than ever. So what's she doing? She's divorcing him, raising questions about what kind of a dirty, rotten s.o.b. husband he must be. Going the other way, if he's the dumper, divorcing her, he's still the dirty rotten s.o.b. who's abandoning his wife in her time of need."

That night, regretting that I had called Conrad in the first place, I'm tossing and turning and fretting. Kish is so vague about things and then so certain. It's the Alzheimer's and the frailty and vulnerability that goes with it. Conrad doesn't understand. It's so much more than the lack-a-nookie. It's the sleeping alone and the waking up alone. Here it is, dawn. The sheet and blanket are knotted up around me. I'm clutching my side of the bed in the chill of waking up without her. I'm wondering if the divorce talk ties in with her latest get together with Hilary a few days ago. Hilary is a lawyer. They confide in each other. Join the dots.

When I get up, if I time it right, I can talk to Hilary on the phone after she gets her sons off to school and before she drives to her office in Vancouver. But then she's on the phone to me while I'm sipping coffee, waiting to call her.

There's some pussyfooting back and forth about the neurologist and the level of care and so on before I put the question to her. "You're not by any chance acting as her lawyer are you?"

"Why would I be?"

"She's talking about divorce."

"No. I'm not her lawyer. I'm her cousin. She's my closest friend."

"Do you think she's serious about this?"

"I have no idea. Is there any reason for her to be serious about it? What have you been up to? Have you been a bad boy? Fooling around?"

Part of me wants to deepen my voice and say, Well, not lately, hinting that it's a struggle but I'm managing to control my surging bad-boy tendencies. Instead of that, as if I'm outing myself and owning up to a character flaw, I tell Hilary that it just ain't so. I've never thought of it as being faithful to Kish. It's simply that I've been a good boy because I haven't had the opportunity to be a bad boy. Occasionally, I've been attracted to other women, Anita Stokes next door for example, but never urgently enough for me to try to start anything with her, even after her husband died.

Before Kish and I were married, Hilary confided in me that Kish, normally given to understatement, had gone over the top, raving about me to the extent that Hilary wanted my assurance that I wouldn't take advantage of her. Now, twenty-five years later, Hilary wants to know if the Alzheimer's is putting my fidelity to the test.

"It happens," she says. "The roving eye. More so with men I would think. They just can't cope with dementia."

"So I've heard."

"Yes, even if you haven't said anything but you were feeling that way and Connie picked up on it, she's just contrary enough to think, well, Max, two can play at that game."

"Bailing out on her has never occurred to me. Not for a minute. If anything, I've been overdoing it as caregiver. More than that, I've been hanging onto her for dear life while she's pushing me away. I can't figure out why she's doing this. Did she say anything to you?"

"I don't have any answers for you," Hilary says. "All I can tell you is that she's thinking about a divorce. I asked her why and she said it was a good idea. I think it's more than a passing fancy. It's very much on her mind."

The issue of Kish's competence comes up again. According to Hilary, a divorce lawyer would have to establish that she is legally competent to proceed. She would have to go back to Dr. Winkler the way she did before she signed that lease at Strathaven.

"If she gets as far as going to a lawyer," Hilary says, "she would have to have an opinion from her doctor saying yea or nay about her competence. If it's yea, then the lawyer could proceed. If it's nay, there would have to be a court hearing to determine her competence."

I need Hilary's reassurance about a falling out that Kish and I had seven years ago. Heaven knows, back then she had grounds for doubting me as a caregiver. I realize now how wrong I was by not coming through for her when she had breast cancer. She was booked for daily radiation treatments in May and June, and I was to drive her to the cancer clinic and be with her. I asked her if the treatment could be postponed into the summer months. As if her cancer cells would go into remission to accommodate me, the VIP, the Very Important Principal. In fact, I was the Very Insecure Principal, telling Kish that May and June were hectic months at the school.

Kish agreed, saying my work was important. She would have Anita Stokes go with her for the radiation treatments. I was okay with that until Hilary called me out on it, saying that I should be there for Kish. I mentioned my obligations at the school. Hilary jumped all over me. "Come off it! You have two vice-principals," she said. "And you can't delegate some of your work to them and take a few mornings off?"

That shamed me into asking Kish to let me get involved. But she declined. She and Anita would get along just fine. The tacit without me kicker was left hanging there.

"That's right," Hilary says. "You were a self-centred bastard. It was the only time that I saw Connie angry with you. But she got over it."

"Okay. So how do I deal with Kish wanting to get a divorce?"

"Let her talk it out," Hilary says. "Just listen to her. Try not to get upset. And tell her that you love her before somebody else does."

It comes blurting out of me: "Has she mentioned somebody else?"

"Oh no. Telling her you love her before somebody else does is something I heard last night in a jeweller's TV commercial. Diamonds for Valentine's Day. All I meant was that she needs reassuring."

That afternoon, Kish is at her wry and whimsical best, telling me that we should think about divorce as a Valentine's Day gift we could give to each other. We've always made a point of ignoring Valentine's as a hollow affair that has little to do with love and everything to do with marketing chocolate, sexy lingerie and greeting cards. Can she be serious now? A divorce petition as a Valentine's present?

She has me mounting the barricades with our battle cry — Alzheimer's Schmaltzheimers, Forget about it! I'm persuading her to join me on February 14 for a strictly non-Valentine's Day dinner.

"You're not going to go all mushy on me, are you? You know, 'Roses are red, violets are blue, sugar is sweet' and blah blah blah."

"Who me? Not a chance."

Listen to us. Making light of divorce. In my case, it's landing with a heavy thud, hurting even more when I laugh; but nonetheless, I try to laugh it off. Kish can't say no to my quirky dinner invitation. Make the reservation for seven o'clock, she says. That way, she can be with her friends in Connie's Corner in the dining room at five and then go out with me. She's making a note to herself to get her hair done.

26. Lawyering up, lawyering down

THERE'S A COUPLE OUR AGE at the next table. They're cooing away to each other. She calls him Barry. They're exchanging Valentine's cards and unwrapping gifts. A glittery broach for her and for him, a pocket-sized Ussies photo album with two hearts on the cover. Kish, captivating in her platinum pantsuit, is in good form as she looks over at them with that bemused expression, the one with the Gallic shrug and cocked left eyebrow, a tipoff that her Valentine's Day *boo-ul shee-it* detector has just kicked in.

We're drinking martinis. I like the way she holds the glass, blatantly putting on the dog, letting on that she was weaned on gin and vermouth. I'm not to-the-manner-born but I'd drink martinis with her anytime just to watch her pulling it off. She's got the hands for it. They have such flair, be it for strumming a guitar, cracking an egg into a frying pan, or cradling a martini glass while she drinks her cocktail a lick at a time. Then she checks the level of her sobriety by resting the empty glass on her lower lip and blowing into it.

She has explained the aerodynamics of it to me. The gust of air scoops down into the glass, changes direction and vents softly up the other side onto her forehead. If she can't feel the air on her forehead because of a numbness there, then the martini had the requisite jigger of gin and she must be slightly sozzled. If she can feel the gust of air, the bartender has slipped her a watered-down martini. I can tell from the look on her face that this one is up to snuff.

She orders a small steak with a cognac cream sauce. I'm having the baked sockeye salmon with a dill sauce, rice, and asparagus. The salmon is hearty enough to go with a red wine. That way, we imbibe from the same carafe of an Australian merlot. She wants to order a litre of it. But that would be more than a skin-full for the two of us and I persuade her to settle for half that much in the carafe.

She takes charge of the pouring. "Even Steven," she says, holding the glass up, looking at me through it and sizing me up.

"What a handsome devil you are," she says.

"You're not seeing straight there, Kish."

I raise my glass and offer a toast with a twist, adding a question mark — "To us?" Catching my drift, she raises her glass and puts the same spin on it. "To us?" She leans over the table. "Have you thought about it? You know, about getting a divorce?"

"What I've thought about with all my heart is not getting a divorce."

She empathizes, saying that this stage of it is the hard part.

"My lawyer says that we're in the detox stage. We're getting the marriage habit out of our systems. And we're halfway there. We're living apart."

What was that? *My lawyer?* Has it come to such a pass?

"Well, not quite," she says. "I haven't actually seen her. But I've talked to her on the phone. I have an appointment with her next week."

As Kish lays it out, she'll be the petitioner, the one who initiates the proceedings and I'll be the respondent. Ah yes, the dumper and the dumpee. While she's raising a fork-load

171

of roast potatoes, I'm thinking how I would handle the role of the dumpee, telling her that while she's lawyering up, I'll be lawyering down. I won't be going to a lawyer. Sounding coldly rational, she says it makes sense for her to be the petitioner.

"For appearances sake. That's the way it should work. I'm the one with Alzheimer's."

I fail to see any logic in that but if she's going to get all legalistic about things, I suggest that she should be asking her lawyer to represent her in the sale of our house.

"Why would I do that?"

"To see that your interests are protected."

"Oh Max, I trust you to do that."

She hasn't said anything about the issue of her competence to engage in divorce proceedings. Either the lawyer has mentioned it to her and she'll be seeing Dr. Winkler about it or the lawyer doesn't know about the Alzheimer's and it has yet to come up. I'll wait and see.

She orders a second carafe of wine. And later, even after four glasses of the merlot to my one, she's still not ready to call it a night. She wants a liqueur, a Kahlua, to go with the cheesecake. This is new for us. We don't normally have dessert or a liqueur when dining out. I'm okay with splitting an almond amaretto cheesecake but dubious about anything more to drink. I'm the party-pooper, abstaining from the Kahlua. This is also new for us. Usually, she's the careful one while I drink more than I should and she winds up driving us home.

She has difficulty steering her way out of the restaurant. The side of the wheelchair scuffs against a table, knocking over two glasses of wine. And then a footrest bumps into a busboy and he tips a tray-load of dishes onto the floor. While she's making her apologies, one of the waiters takes over, curtly stepping behind the wheelchair and steering it over to the exit. Another waiter holds the door open. They don't say a word but it's clear that we're getting the bum's rush out onto the street.

She decides against going straight back to Strathaven. It's almost eight thirty. Already half an hour late for her scheduled bedtime, she's rebelliously declaring that the night is young and that Sophie the care aide can wait. She can wait for another half-hour, an hour for that matter, to help her to bed. What difference can it make to Sophie who's on shift until eleven?

Kish wants to show me the weeping willow trees she found the other day while wheeling around the neighbourhood. This takes us to the south end of the boardwalk and along a gravelled pathway under a grove of seven weeping willows. This is seven too many for my liking. They may look luxuriant and inviting on a calendar. But stand under one of them and you're in a place where the sun can't shine and nothing much grows. I can't see very much in the darkness but I know that the grass is pale and sparse and that even hardy dandelions know better than to try their luck under a weeping willow. Seven of them at night? It can't get any darker or spookier than this.

Kish is unfazed. Opening her purse, she has just what's required to dispel the gloom. From her purse, to my surprise, she produces the wherewithal for toking up — cigarette papers, a lighter and a plastic vial with enough marijuana for a couple of joints. She informs me that it's Arctic Moon, an esteemed variety of BC Bud and that Hilary gave it to her.

She invites me to sit on a low stone wall under the trees. She pours some of the marijuana onto a cigarette paper and proceeds to roll a joint. Believing as I do that she hasn't done this since she gave up marijuana in favour of storytelling before we were married, I'm impressed with how deft her fingers are, twisting, coaxing, then licking the glue edge of the paper and sealing it up.

"Hey Kish. Just like riding a bicycle. You never forget."

"Not quite," she says. "I've been keeping my hand in, so to speak."

It's true confession time. Over the years, she's been toking up once in a while with Hilary, the way they did as teenagers climbing that tree in Beacon Hill Park.

Why not with me?

"Because I didn't want to get back to doing it regularly and risk having it affect my work as a storyteller. Something else, Max. Things were so good between us that we didn't need it."

"Well, I've also been keeping my hand in. With Conrad. Once in a while."

"I thought so," she says.

We're huddled close together. How beautiful she is with the flare from the doobie lighter illuminating her face the way candlelight does. We're passing the joint back and forth, creating a warm spot under the willows. In the gloom, she can't see that I'm not inhaling. I'm guided by the premise that it would be highly derelict of the caregiver to be getting stoned along with the care recipient. Another consideration is that marijuana makes me weepy and I can't start tearing up in front of her. Just when I would expect that she's mellow enough to have any thoughts about divorce going up in marijuana smoke, she broaches the subject again.

"Oh Max," she says. "We could still toke up together after we're divorced."

And then, as if she's having a change of heart, she suggests that we stay here all night and offers to share her wheelchair blanket with me. Well maybe not all night. But we stay until the night is not as young as it was an hour ago. On the way back along the boardwalk, she finds that it's too hard for her to keep the wheelchair moving over the rough planking.

"Max, if you please, will you push me? It's past my bedtime and I'm tired and I want to go home."

Home? It's no longer our house on Medana Street.

She's drunk on alcohol, squiffy on the THC and a touch poetic. "What's that saying, 'home is where they have to take you in' It's Robert Frost isn't it. Yeah, it is. And d'ya know where they have to take me in? What's it called? Yeah, Strathaven Place."

Thus, I'm bidden and willing to oblige as wheelchair pusher to the other end of the boardwalk and up the pathway onto Waterfront Crescent where it's smoother going on the concrete sidewalk. We can hear a skateboarder coming up behind us with little pulses of speed each time he pushes off the pavement. After he goes scooting past us, Kish comes alive. Bolt upright, she starts pushing down on the wheels. She wants to make a race out of it.

"Come on, Max. Push harder," she says, turning back to me in a whisper so that the skateboarder won't hear her.

He's a lanky teenager, as poised as a ballet dancer on the deck of his skateboard and smoothly pushing off with his right foot. We're closing the gap and he hears us coming. He kicks into a higher gear and starts pulling away from us in front of an apartment building that's under construction next to Strathaven Place. With Kish urging me on, we're into the homestretch under the street lights and catching up to the skateboarder. What's he got? A motor on that thing? It's effortless the way he races along in a soft whirring of polyurethane wheels.

But Kish won't surrender. With our quarry in sight, she's shouting, "Tally ho!" I'm giving it my all, head down, running behind the wheelchair. Looking up, I can see the outline of the cherry top light bar on the roof of the parked police car. And just as I'm easing off on the wheelchair, the car headlights flash on. Blinking squarely into them, I'm blinded just long enough for the wheelchair to angle off the sidewalk, flip over sideways and send Kish tumbling onto the grass.

Kneeling beside her, asking if she's all right, I take off my jacket and fold it as a pillow under her head. She's laughing and telling me that she's okay.

"Oh Max, am I drunk? Are we drunk? Are we as drunk as a skunk. Or are we drunker than two skunks."

I want to say there's only one skunk involved and it's the one she's as drunk as and that I'm stone cold sober now that the policeman is getting out of his car. He introduces himself as Constable Del Vecchio.

"Are you hurt, ma'am?" he asks.

"I'm as drunk as two skunks," she says. "But I'm not hurt. Do you think you could help Max get me back into the wheelchair?"

"Are you sure?" he says, shining the flashlight over her. "Maybe we shouldn't be moving you. Do you have a broken leg under that splint you have on?"

"No, it's only a sprained ankle."

"I don't think we should move you," he says. "We should call an ambulance so that you can be checked out in hospital."

Kish sidles down into her cajoling, sugary contralto and asks him his first name. Frank, he says.

"Please, Frank," she says. "My name is Connie and I'm okay. I don't hurt anywhere. Just help me back into the wheelchair. I want to get back to Strathaven Place. It's right there. Do you see it, rising like the face of a cliff. I'm one of the swallows with a nest up there."

"Well, Connie," he says. "You're not the best judge of whether you should be moved or not. Neither am I. So I'm going to call the shift sergeant. He's got a first-aid ticket. He can be here in a couple of minutes."

He goes back to the squad car and returns with a blanket. I work it in around Kish, getting her to roll sideways so that I can tuck it in underneath her. The shift sergeant is none other than the avuncular Sergeant Angus MacAskill, a member of the Connie Kish fan club. He's been briefed by the constable and he's stooping down.

"Well, Connie Kish! Fancy meeting you here."

"Sergeant Angus!" she says.

"Give me a moment," he says to her and turns to Constable Del Vecchio and tells him to put in the call for an ambulance, then turns back to Kish. "We're going to make sure that you're properly looked after. This is too complicated for us to be taking any chances."

The complicating factor is that Sergeant MacAskill knows about the Alzheimer's. While she tells him how she landed in the wheelchair, also what a wonderful time she and I had going out for dinner, he has Constable Del Vecchio burying her with blankets from the police cars while we wait for the ambulance.

"But Sergeant, please, there's no need for me to go to hospital," Kish says.

"We can't take any chances, not with that cast on your leg," he says. He's in charge, ordering the paramedics to transfer her onto a stretcher. He takes me aside. He's angry with a muffled intensity that makes it even more intimidating than if he'd been bellowing at me.

"I have to ask you," he says. "How could you allow this to happen to her? You're her husband. You're the responsible party. You let her drink too much and you drink too much. You should be ashamed of yourself."

177

What more is there to say. He's right. I'm the irresponsible party. Trying to be the good-time Charlie. I don't think it would cut any ice with the sergeant if I told him that I had abstained from the Kahlua.

Seeing the ambulance doors opening is a sobering sight for Kish. She's in fine form while she reasons with the sergeant. "Please," she says, looking up at him. "There is no need for this . . . Do you know that song, 'Show me the way to go home'? Well that's me . . . I had a little drink about an hour ago. And it's gone right to my head and I'm tired and I want to go to bed. So please, have them put me back in my wheelchair. I'm really tired and I want to go to bed."

The sergeant relents in his fatherly concern for her and the paramedics put her into the wheelchair. I go with her into Strathaven and up to the ninth floor where Sophie is waiting to help her into bed.

27. Catching up with the scuttlebutt

APPARENTLY, I'M THE ONLY ONE who sees that chasing after the teenager on the skateboard for what it was. A lark. Seems that everybody at Strathaven wants to puff it up into a calamity of some kind. It starts the next day with Inga Bumpus after she calls me over to the reception desk. "Really, Max," she says. "Racing in a wheelchair? I'm told that it was rough and tumble for Connie out there on the street last night."

Inga then informs me that Margaret wants to see me. That would be Margaret MacDonald, the nurse in charge of all the nurses at Strathaven Place. The way I heard it from Clancy, she's a tough cookie, ruling the roost over several other registered nurses, the licensed practical nurses, and the rank-and-file of care aides.

Her glass-fronted office is on the other side of the lobby just past the elevators. The lights are always on in there with the blinds closed. She's a ghost. You can't tell if she's at her desk or elsewhere in the building and that's the way she wants it. I'm edgy at the doorway, knocking softly, waiting for her to invite me in. If I was wearing a hat, I'd doff it deferentially. While she lolls back in a plush, tilting executive chair, she has me sitting on a hard, wooden chair set squarely in front of her desk. She wears two watches, one on her wrist and the other one, a gold lapel watch with the dial hanging upside down, on her chest.

Even though she puts us on a first name basis, I want to call her Mrs. MacDonald.

Without further ado, I'm facing the music over what happened last night. Turns out that Sergeant MacAskill has been sleuthing way as if major criminal activity was afoot. Nurse Margaret has his report, including a copy of the restaurant tab with a record of the alcohol intake — two martinis, two carafes of wine and the glass of Kahlua.

"Of course," she says, "You realize, Max, that's far too much alcohol for a woman with dementia. And as her husband, it was up to you to see that she drank responsibly."

Now we come to the highlight of the evening. She's reading what Constable Del Vecchio had to say in his report. "The guy had his head down, going flat out, pushing the lady in the wheelchair along the sidewalk as fast as he could. She was just sitting there. She informed me that she and her husband were, in her words, 'as drunk as two skunks.' But she must have been terrified and he lost control and the wheelchair tipped over and the poor lady fell out onto the grass."

There's no point in telling Margaret, Well, you had to be there, chasing after that guy on the skateboard with Kish enjoying herself in ways I haven't seen for quite some time. I take my lumps all over again. Mea culpa. But Margaret is past the events of last evening.

"What I'm saying to you, Max, is that if Connie has a history of alcohol abuse, I need to know about it."

"That's not it, Margaret. In all our years together, I've never known her to go overboard the way she did last night. She'll get a bit squiffy once in a while but she usually holds back, keeping some control in reserve."

"What do you think went wrong last night?"

Darned if I can explain it. I'm not about to say anything about the divorce. Kish may be as uptight about it as I am and was trying to drown her sorrows in alcohol. And I'm not going to risk Margaret's greater wrath by telling her that Kish and I were toking up under the weeping willows. Margaret strikes me as one of those Scotch whisky imbibers who, while righteously abusing their livers with alcohol, think that marijuana is the devil's weed.

To my surprise, she knows that divorce may be in the offing for Kish and me. She wants an explanation regarding the scuttlebutt about it on the ninth floor. Kish may have said something to one of the care aides. And now they're gunning for me as the dirty rotten s.o.b. who's bailing out on her.

"Is it true Max? Are you divorcing her?"

"Absolutely not."

"Well, what is the situation between you and Connie? It came up at a staff meeting. They asked me to speak to you about it."

So what now? Do I straighten Margaret out by telling her the way things are? Or is it none of her business? I decide that I owe her the explanation that it's Kish who's wants the divorce and that she'll be seeing a lawyer about it next week. Before I level with Margaret, I get her assurance that she won't be talking to Kish about it and have us getting into a 'he says, she says' back and forth. It wouldn't help.

Later on with Kish in her suite, first thing before I say a word about our carousing, she confronts it herself, complaining about her hangover. She recalls chasing after the skateboarder. "I was so excited," she says. "Wasn't it a blast! I'm not blaming you for my falling out of the wheelchair. I remember egging you on. I also remember drinking too much and smoking pot.

I felt rotten this morning. Nauseous with a terrible headache. I was in a foul mood with my friends in the dining room. I felt so guilty about it that I flushed the rest of the marijuana down the toilet. That's it! Never again!"

I'm with her all the way. I'm going to phone Hilary and ask her to refrain from supplying her cousin with any more Arctic Moon.

28. The soaps

KISH AND I need an escape from the divorce doldrums and intrigues. I have just the ticket for it. By way of helping us to lighten up, I suggest to her that we imagine the divorce scuttlebutt for what it is. Soap opera. I'm cooking up a heart-wrenching daytime serial on TV with *Strathaven Place* as the title. The main setting for it would be the ninth floor. That would keep it true to life, depicting real people and actual events. Our Valentine's Day adventure is tailor-made for a separate episode.

To my surprise, Kish is lukewarm about it. I'm wondering what has happened to her offbeat sense of humour.

"Well, Max," she says, "If you want to spice it up, to dramatize things, I guess it would be all right. As long as it helps you to see that I'm right."

Well, never mind. This soap opera has a practical spinoff as a survival tactic, an escape hatch from my agonizing over the prospect of a divorce. It's the watcher in me, stepping back, once removed, and sketching in the storyline for an episode about Mable Dundee. This is reality TV. She's visiting her husband in a scene at Victoria General Hospital where he's recovering from hip-replacement surgery. There are complications and an infection keeping him there. The episode cuts from VGH to a table in the dining room on the ninth floor where the flirtatious

Mrs. Dundee is carrying on with the darkly handsome Arturo Hebb. She's furtively holding hands with him.

Inevitably, I become a character in *Strathaven Place* as the long-suffering Max Osborne falsely portrayed as the dirty rotten s.o.b who's abandoning the charming, albeit dementia-stricken Connie Kish. In today's episode, the TV camera follows doleful Max along the ninth floor hallway on his way to visit Connie Kish. The camera pans over to Mrs. Dundee in the chair planted in the doorway to her suite. Max knocks on Connie's door.

"She not there," says Mrs. Dundee. "She's with Arturo in his suite. They're quite the couple, don't you know?"

There's a close-up of Mrs. Dundee's face revealing how devilishly delighted she is to be informing Max that he'll find Connie and Arturo Hebb in Suite 915. Now that Arturo has lost interest in Mrs. Dundee, dumped her in fact, she's the woman scorned. Hell hath no fury to match her scheming.

Max, riled up with jealousy, strides grimly down the hall. He raps softly on the door of Suite 915. The door opens. It's Arturo. He looks like an Arturo, dark-eyed with a trim moustache.

"I'm looking for my wife, Connie Kish," Max says.

Yes, she's here," Arturo replies. "We're having a cup of tea."

Connie comes to the door in her wheelchair. "Max, how nice to see you."

Max catches a whiff of marijuana smoke. Wait a minute! Turn off the cameras! It's one thing for Connie and Arturo to be sipping tea. It's another thing entirely for them to be toking up together. The aroma of it is so faint that Max can't be sure. However, even the possibility of it is no laughing matter.

It's the breaking point. So much for the soap opera. The joke's on me. I'm back as narrator, relating that Arturo and Kish invite me in for a cup of tea. I decline and say that I'll be waiting for Kish in her suite. I turn away in a huff, going back down the hall. All I can think about is that they were toking up together. Convinced of it now, I'm counting the minutes on what's left of my half-hour with Kish. I showed up on time at four fifteen.

Goddammit, I'm the chump, sitting alone in her suite. It's nearly quarter to five. Dinner will be served in fifteen minutes and she'll be saying, Off you go. Here she is now and I'm confronting her about Arturo.

"What's going on with that guy?"

"We were having a cup of tea."

"Why did you have the door closed?"

"I don't know. But it's not because there's anything *going on* as you put it."

"Does he sit next to you in the dining room?"

"Well, yes he does but it's not because I want it. One of the care aides looks after the seating arrangements."

"Is that why you don't want me there? I've asked, what is it, two or three times, to let me have dinner with you there. And you always make it abundantly clear that I'm not welcome in the dining room."

"Oh Max. It's not that you're not welcome. I'm doing you a favour. You're just too young and too alive to be sitting down with us. You'd be bored to death."

Kish doesn't understand or maybe she's pretending not to understand why I'm upset about Arturo. She wants me to know that he's had a stroke. Before that he was a structural engineer.

"That's what Conrad is, isn't he?" she asks. "He probably knows Arturo. He's been all over the world, building bridges. He's an interesting man and that's all there is to it. There's no reason for you to be jealous of him."

"Not jealous of him but jealous of the time you're spending with him. This half-hour is supposed to be our time together."

"I'd forgotten. Max, I'm sorry. But you've got to understand that I need something different in my life and that's what Arturo is."

She can't remember toking up with Arturo and sincerely doubts that it happened. He's too straight-laced for it. He wears slippers all day and that sets him apart from me. I shouldn't be waiting around for her. I should have better things to do. Her afternoons are a little more crowded now that she's going to a hotel spa for a bath. One of her few complaints about Strathaven is that under the care plan she signed up for, she's limited to one bath a week. She doesn't think it would be worth it to pay extra for a bath every day because there's something wrong with the heating in the tub room on the ninth floor and it's too cold for a leisurely bath. She chooses to bathe three or four times a week at a hotel spa where she can soak and luxuriate. I'm thinking, go for it Kish. Soak and luxuriate to your heart's content.

Kish, up in her treehouse and under the spell of it, sweeps me along.

"Sunday would be so much better for us," she says. "Saturday too if you want. We could go for a drive. We could have brunch."

Figuratively on bended knee, trying to reason with her, I'm under the gun, waiting for that second divorce shoe to hit the floor. It's been a week since Margaret MacDonald broached the subject and the gossip spun out of control. Since then, Kish has said very little about it. Even so, I'm taking a stand.

"We're Connie Kish and Max Osborne. We've been married for twenty-five years. Remember the vows we made? I can't remember anything about it being a weekend marriage."

"Well, we're lucky having had twenty-five good years together," she says.

"Why can't we have another twenty-five years, sticking together through thick and thin as we promised we would?"

"When we're young and healthy, we don't think through the promises we make."

She looks at her watch. It's dinnertime and I know the drill. We're in the hall. She's seeing me off at the elevator. We wait for the doors to open. Then there's what passes for a kiss. "Have a nice evening," she says. Why not have a nice week? Mercifully the elevator doors roll shut. She'll be heading off toward the dining room to join Arturo and the rest of her clique of friends at their row of tables with Mrs. Dundee glaring over at them from another table.

It's early evening at home when a woman named Pamela Shaw phones on behalf of the local Alzheimer's Society, informing me that Strathaven Place has given my name to her. She wants to know if there's anything the society can provide in the way of help for me as a husband and caregiver.

And in that regard, "How is it going?" Ms. Shaw inquires.

She catches me twisting in the wind as the husband hanging on for dear life and prone to opening up to a stranger at the other end of a telephone connection.

"My wife says she's leaving me."

"Let me assure you, Mr. Osborne. Alzheimer's patients sometimes talk that way. They go through stages. They may even have innocent flirtations."

I'm spilling my guts to a stranger on the phone and feeling pathetic in the process but spilling nonetheless. Ms. Shaw might as well know the rest of it. I find myself telling her that my wife has a divorce lawyer and I'm troubled about her liaison with an interesting man by the name of Arturo Hebb.

"Really!" says Ms. Shaw. "She's divorcing you!"

A familiar refrain. That was Hilary's reaction at first. I also heard it from Nurse Margaret and from Conrad in his inimitable way, summing up my lose-lose, dumpee situation. That's what the staff on the ninth floor must be wondering about. It's lose-lose all over again in my dealings with Ms. Shaw, making me aware that it's entirely possible to have somebody peering along a telephone line and looking askance at you. She doesn't come right out and say, There, there, now, Mr. Osborne. But I can hear it in the tone of her voice, suggesting that I sit in on the weekly sessions of the society's self-help group.

"It's a small gathering, six or eight people," she says. "Most of them like yourself, people who are learning to cope with having a spouse with Alzheimer's."

I'm old-school, out of step with the times and with the new attitudes toward group therapy. I imagine troubled souls, sitting around in a circle with a moderator encouraging them to bare their souls, holding hands, hugging and even crying, the ultimate in letting it all hang out in front of strangers. Ms. Shaw would be the moderator. I can hear her asking me if there's anything I'd like to talk about. She'd coax me along. She's already been pretty good at drawing me out. Before you know it, she'd have me blathering away that Kish is divorcing me and taking up with Arturo. What else am I to think? And I'd be sitting there in the circle, the centre of attention and exposed as the sad-sack Alzheimer's cuckold. It's too much.

"Our next meeting is next Wednesday at seven thirty," Mrs. Shaw says.

"Let me check," I say, letting on that I'm reviewing my activities calendar. "No, I've got something else on. Let me get back to you about it for the following week."

29. Groucho, you naughty boy!

INGA BUMPUS KNOWS what's going on at Strathaven Place. With her office right across from the main floor entrance, she's part sentry, part receptionist and part paper pusher. She looks stylish in a navy-blue blazer and long grey hair with a swath of it coming close to her left eye as she scoots around on her wheeled office chair, shoving off from the reception desk to the photocopier to the filing cabinets, then rolling back to the reception desk, answering the phone and keeping tabs on who's coming and going through the lobby.

Coming in, it's as if I have an Inga Bumpus detector in my pocket beeping away, telling me that she has me under surveillance. Recruiting me as a volunteer, she wants me to help Mary Oliver find one of her dogs. Mary is sitting over by the frog fountain with a baby stroller. Seems that one of Mary's three dogs — Groucho, Chico and Harpo — has gone astray. They're not real dogs. They're stuffed, little doll dogs. Mary fusses over them, chatting away and it's understood that they yip and yammer back to her. They go everywhere with Mary as a cuddly trio under their blanket in the baby stroller with its faded blue canopy. At night, Mary tucks them into bed with her.

The crisis for Mary is that Groucho vanished earlier this morning. This is where I come in.

"We can't leave Mary worried sick about Groucho, now can we?" Inga says.

All that's required of me is to pay attention to Mary, to take her seriously. Inga has the search for Groucho narrowed down to the laundry department on the main floor. That makes sense after what happened when Mary and her brood were getting up this morning. Apparently Groucho was playing hide and seek under the bed sheets and Mary didn't notice the care aide rolling them up with Groucho hidden away and tossing them into the hamper which was then wheeled down to the laundry department.

Mary looks up at me with her stroller wheels squeaking sluggishly, carrying Chico and Harpo along the hall to the laundry. When we get there, Jean, the attendant, informs us that Groucho had a narrow escape. When she found him buried in the sour confines of the laundry hamper, the bedding was about to be dumped, Groucho and all, into the scalding torment of a washing machine. She sprays Groucho with a deodorant and presents him to Mary.

"Oh Groucho! You naughty boy!" she says, giving him a hug and a kiss and nestling him into the stroller between Chico and Harpo. The stroller wheels squeak merrily back along the hall. I wish Kish could see me now, helping out, getting involved. Mary is crying in relief. I've got to get away from her or she'll have me going in a minute.

Telling me a little more about Mary, Inga establishes that the tough-cookie head nurse Margaret MacDonald can also be a caring cookie, bending the rules the way she did when Mary first came to Strathaven. She had a bottle of gin in her suitcase so that she could pour herself a gin and tonic before dinner every night.

Mary complained bitterly, even threatened a hunger strike, after the gin was confiscated. Nurse Margaret calmed her down with an assurance that she would get her gin and tonic every evening. The fridge at the nursing station on the fifth floor would be stocked with tonic water and the bottle of gin with Mary's name on it. Margaret made sure that the staff would come through with a gin and tonic for Mary every evening before dinner without telling her that it would be tamed down with a light splash of gin instead of a couple of ounces of it.

30. The ubiquitous Arturo Hebb

KISH IS HUMOURING ME. SHE lets on that she wants to go for a drive without much enthusiasm for it. She doesn't care where we go. Just a drive around town, she says. I'll keep any ruffling of feathers to a minimum by lying back, reading the signs and wondering how often she'll look at her watch while waiting for this Saturday morning with me to come to an end.

We're on our way out to the car and she's wheeling off ahead of me across the main floor lobby. She's bright-eyed and riding high. Maybe she's always like this at ten o'clock in the morning. I wouldn't know about that because I don't normally get to see her at this time of day. She's wearing her oversized sunglasses and the green jacket. I'm hoping she wants to be outdoors and taking Flora for a walk. We discussed it but she was iffy about it. She may be in the process of divorcing Flora as well.

"Your car has a sunroof doesn't it," she says. "It's such a nice day. We can have it open and let the sun shine in on us. Trusty John will enjoy it as well."

If she believes that Trusty John will be there in the back seat, that's good enough for me. With any luck, he'll watch over her while she transfers herself from the wheelchair into the car. I'm apprehensive about her falling in the process. She seems to know what she's doing. She has the wheel locks on and the wheelchair lined up just behind the open door. She flips up the footrests. Even while favouring her right ankle, she's able to get up onto her feet and stand up and turn to face away from the car so that she can lower herself onto the front seat. It's left to me to put the wheelchair into the trunk.

On the drive up Jutland Road, she faces up into the sunshine coming in through the roof opening. Decidedly not in the mood for lolling back, she gets down to business with the clipboard on her lap. She seems to have it with her all the time. I'm wondering if the subject of divorce is on her list. Not for the moment at least. She has Flora on the top of the agenda and wants my assurance that the new condo will be dog friendly and big enough for her to have a space of her own.

"Off course," I say. "That's exactly what Anita is looking for. A place with two bedrooms and a den with room enough for Flora's mattress."

Kish lets me know that she's now clear about which house we are selling. The one on Medana Street. She has it written down as a memory prompt. When she asks for a progress report on the sale of the house, I tell her that we're close to signing off on a deal to sell the place for nine hundred and fifty thousand. She isn't concerned about the price. She wants to know what's to be done with her wheelbarrow.

That's Kish for you, talking about a wheelbarrow as if it's part of her last will and testament. She doesn't want me selling it with the rest of her gardening tools. She wants me to give it to Anita who'll remember to call it Barry and to coddle him with encouraging words. Another item that's not to be sold off is the umbrella stand, an 1890s piece, hand-forged iron with a bronze trim, that Grandmamma Constanze brought over from Marseilles. Kish has me promise that the stand will be part of the move into the new condo.

Luther the crow also has a place on the list. Kish is deadpan, wanting to know what I'm going to do about him. I explain that there'd be no point in giving Luther our new address because Anita has adopted him even though he's pushing his luck by harassing her cats. The cross-eyed one, Ms. Jones I think it is, has become a nervous wreck since Luther started swooping down on her, cutting close enough to brush her back with a wing tip.

We're a block away from the house on Medana Street when I mention that Flora is going to be very pleased to see her.

"What do you mean?"

"We talked about it. Taking Flora for a walk in the park."

"No. I don't want to do that. Just keep driving. I don't want her seeing me in the wheelchair. She wouldn't understand."

"She's still wondering where you are. She makes the rounds every morning, looking for you all over the house, in your studio, in our bedroom."

"You can explain it to her Max, now that you've taken up talking to her. Tell her that I'll be back to walking very soon and that then we'll be going for our walks."

After I turn into the drive-in on Douglas Street, she changes her mind about having lunch there. Normally, we'd be acting out a little skit, going back to where we first met, just across the road in the park. Part of me wants to reminisce and wonder whatever happened to the mystery girl listening to the chickadees while smoking marijuana up in the treetops. But I'm halfhearted about it and so is she. We're not in the mood for any traipsing down memory lane.

She looks at her watch. It's eleven thirty. We're heading back down Finlayson, then Jutland Road on our return to Strathaven where she has that overriding obligation to have lunch with her dining room coterie, including Arturo, the interesting new man in her life. I wonder if she has told him about the Mañana Treehouse.

There's just no getting away from the ubiquitous Arturo Hebb. He's at her table for breakfast and lunch. Then they're toking up and drinking tea in his suite. And then it's dinner and so forth into the evening. What it amounts to is some eight hours of togetherness over the course of the day. This is way out of whack in comparison to my allotted half-hour on weekday afternoons and going out for a drive on Saturday morning. Looking for a bright side, I'm taking note that during this time together, there wasn't a word said about the divorce. I accept that as a small mercy.

Arturo's name comes up again when Kish phones me at home in the afternoon about our arrangement to go for brunch tomorrow at the restaurant where we commemorated Valentine's Day.

"Now about that bruncheon date, Max." Well you see, she'd forgotten about another commitment. Arturo likes to have her go with him to the Sunday morning prayer service at 11:00 AM in the chapel at Strathaven. Would it be okay if she scheduled me in for nine thirty for coffee and toast in the dining room? There would be time for us to do the weekend crossword puzzle. Sunday morning is a busy time for her, what with breakfast in the dining room with Arturo and her other friends, the chapel service at eleven and lunch at noon, again with Arturo in the dining room.

Taking a little dig, I ask her about going to the chapel when she isn't the least bit religious.

"It works out just fine," she says. "Arturo is religious enough for both of us."

31. Divorce ducks all in a row

WE'RE ALONE in the ninth-floor dining room for our Sunday brunch. Sitting at a table with a centrepiece of plastic flowers. Having coffee and toast from a sideboard they have for between-meal snacks. That's what this is for her. A nibble between the breakfast she had here two hours ago with Arturo and the lunch they'll have together later on this morning.

Working on the crossword puzzle is a far cry from doing it at home, chummy, sitting side by side in the breakfast nook. Here, we are exposed and conspicuous in the bright lighting and the wide, white maze of tables. It's difficult to read her frame of mind. She's wearing sunglasses and her navy sheath dress with a pink jacket. I'm leery of the puzzle, fearing as I do that she's lost a step in her fluency with words. Not only that. She may have had a sleepless night. Or is it another hangover? She sounds hoarse and tired. Now that she's taken off the sunglasses, she's bleary-eyed as she frets over the crossword clue asking for Chopin's middle name. She's tapping impatiently on the table, taking a sip of coffee, waiting for the name to come to her. I'm no help on this one. I think his first name is Frederic but I can't be sure even of that much.

"I know it," she says. "I know it as well as I know my own name."

Instead of leaving it for later and moving on to another clue, she's staring out into the hallway, confused and slipping a little further away.

"What are we doing here anyway?"

"It's the crossword puzzle."

"What's a crossword puzzle? Where do you cross the words out?"

I don't know what's happening. Is it the hangover closing in on her? Or is it the Alzheimer's?

"This is ridiculous," she says. "Who gives a damn anyway. Arturo doesn't put a lot of pressure on me, expecting me to do a crossword puzzle."

She's stiff and controlled, tearing down the newspaper fold line to remove the puzzle page. She crumples it into a ball, pressing hard and placing it on the table beside the plastic flowers. I lean toward her to put an arm around her shoulders. But she shrugs me off. All I can do is hope that it will pass. These cognitive lapses are becoming more frequent. The sixty-second rule won't apply this time. It's been several minutes since she lost her way.

"I don't like it in here," she says, sounding desperate. "Let's go into the lounge."

I'm walking beside her wheelchair down the hallway toward the lounge. Halfway there, looking back and forth, she changes her mind and heads off in the other direction toward her suite. She calms down, inviting me to sit in one of the chairs. Taking off her sunglasses, she wheels to the sink in her kitchenette and fills a blue plastic jug, a perky little thing with a long curving spout, to water the plants on her window sill. I know what they are — a blooming hibiscus and a pair of pale yellow calla lilies. She asked me to buy them for her a couple of days ago. This after telling me when she moved in not to bother with houseplants because she couldn't be relied upon to water them.

It's gratifying to have her emerge from the hangover if that's what it was. More likely, it was a cognitive daze. And now, coming out of it, she's buoyed up and pleased with herself as she informs me that it's François as in Frédéric François Chopin. Still fighting the good fight, up in the treehouse, she's clear-eyed and wheeling off into her bedroom alcove. She turns toward the mirror on the dresser, brushes her hair and comes back with two manila envelopes. She opens one of them, from her lawyer she says, and presents me with a document.

"This will make it easier for you when you sell the house," she says. "I've signed over power of attorney to you. Complete control over everything. Title to the house. Everything."

Making it easier for me? That singular thought is a switch turning on the idea light bulb, the one you see in the comics, blinking over the head of the genius inventor. But I'm no genius. I'm the dullard and this is a delayed-action light bulb. It blinks with the notion that she's being completely selfless and wants to make it easier for me by releasing me from the burden of a wife with Alzheimer's.

"It's just occurred to me, Kish. The reason you've been talking about divorce is that you want to give me an out."

"An out from what?"

"From our marriage and from the Alzheimer's. I should have seen it before this. You want to clear the way for me to start a new life for myself."

"I'm disappointed in you, Max. You've got me mixed up with somebody else. I'm not the wilting, handmaiden type."

"Please, Kish, let me finish. I don't mean for better or worse in the sense that I think you've become a burden to me. I don't see it that way at all. I'm being entirely selfish about this. I want us to stay together for my sake. I'd be lost without you. So you see, you wouldn't be doing me any favour by divorcing me."

"Oh Max, you're patronizing me. I'm not the humble, self-sacrificing woman who thinks she has outlived her usefulness."

"Is it patronizing of me to say that I want to be with you in this?"

"Are you sure that's where you want to be?"

"Quite sure. I'm with you. Believe that."

I can't remember her ever taking such a hard line and stopping just short of saying that I'm domineering. I'll ask Hilary if Kish thinks I'm heavy-handed. Maybe I really am like some men I know, Conrad for example, who used to refer to himself as a male chauvinist pig without seeing all that much wrong with it. Yesterday, he came across to me that way, telling me to go along with the divorce so that I can get out while the getting's good.

I'm reading the document giving me power of attorney. It's all there, dated two days ago.

"Did your lawyer advise you to do this?"

"No. It's what I wanted. Come on. You know it's the right thing to do. The right thing for both of us. If I can't trust you, who can I trust?"

"You may as well know right now that I've taken up with a sweet young thing and we're going to steal away to Costa Rica with all the money."

"Oh Max! If only you would do something like that. Something for yourself."

The second envelope looks fatter than the first one. As I will discover, it's fat with my copies of all the documents required to proceed with the divorce.

"No need to open it now," she says. "Wait until you get home and you can take your time going through it."

She tells me not to worry because there are no big surprises and just one of the documents needing my prompt attention. It's the separation agreement covering the property settlement. She's not asking for spousal support. What she proposes is a fifty-fifty arrangement, divvying up our assets. If we can get that resolved, we'll have it all wrapped up in three months. She sounds sure of herself, informing me that the divorce proceedings are under way. Her lawyer has all but one of the required documents ready to file with the court registry. All that's needed for her to proceed is the separation agreement. That's where I come in. Just sign on the dotted line, have it witnessed and we'll be divorced in three months. If I don't sign up for it, then it becomes a contested divorce and that would take about twelve months.

"Don't look at me that way," she says. "It's not the end of the world."

I'm speechless, defenceless and sternly dry-eyed while she insists that either way, contested or uncontested, it's going to happen.

"Why not simply get it over with," she says, sounding sweetly reasonable. "You'll come to see that it's for the best."

She informs me that there's one more thing I should read. It's a copy of a letter from Dr. Winkler. I'll find it in the envelope with the other documents. Kish wants me to be fully aware of her situation. I'm curious. Is it the letter that enabled her to sign the lease for this suite without involving me?

"No," she says. "It's another letter." There isn't time for me to read it now. But then I don't need to. I know what it says.

Time's up. The chapel service starts in ten minutes and Arturo will be waiting for her. We're parting at the elevators.

Hers, going up to the eleventh floor, comes first and she steps onto it. Wearing that sheath dress. Looking just great for Arturo. Okay, fine. If she wasn't in such a big hurry, I would tell her that I won't be signing the separation agreement. Whenever she asks about it, I'll smile and nod along, putting her off while I stall around.

When I get on the elevator going down, there's an old fellow standing at the control panel and taking charge, pushing the door-close button and talking in just above a whisper, asking me what floor I want and telling me that his name is Ben.

"Ben for Benjamin," he says.

I'm looking straight ahead, trying to ignore him. He wants to share his peanut brittle. He has a small white cardboard box of it and offers me a piece with the assurance that it's sanitary. He hasn't touched it. His daughter brought it in for him and it's still in the box the way it came from the candy store. He's so persistent that I take a chunk of it.

"You have to be careful when you eat peanut brittle," he says. "Don't bite down on it. Just leave it in your mouth and suck on it and let the brittle part melt away leaving just the peanuts. Then you can take your time chewing them. If you bite down on the brittle part, it'll stick to your teeth."

I should have waited for that advice before chomping down on the peanut brittle. He's right. It's gumming up my back teeth, clamping them together. He asks me if I have a car and wonders if I could drive him home. I'm trying to clear my molars and smiling in a non-committal way. Arriving on the main floor, I want to get away from him but I can't offend him by turning away while he's still talking to me.

"It's all right," he says. "I understand. You can't drive me home because they've taken away your driver's licence. Those bastards took away my driver's licence too. They think I'm too old. Well I'm not. I haven't been in an accident for thirty years but they wouldn't listen and my daughter Peggy has my car and is driving it around. I'm a much better driver than she is. She'll tell you that herself."

He wants my advice about going home. There in front of the elevators, he has me thinking, okay there, Ben for Benjamin, how should I know? I ask him if he has a home to go to. Have arrangements been made for him to go there? Well, sure. His house on Cadboro Bay Road. He lived there for eighteen years and thinks that he still owns the place. He wants to make sure they're looking after his dog, a beagle named Arthur. But then he isn't sure if there would be anybody at the house to be with him. It's dawning on him that there wouldn't be. He comes round to that with no input from me. He's feeling a little better about Strathaven Place.

"It's not all the bad here," he says. "There's roast beef, my favourite thing, for dinner tonight. They have the menu on display at the nursing station on the eighth floor. Nice of them to do that. Gives us something to look forward to."

After dinner, he says, there'll be *I Love Lucy* on TV until the care aide comes in and helps him to bed. Tomorrow, he thinks it is, Peggy will come visiting.

It's a relief to get away from him and sit sucking on a second piece of the peanut brittle while communing with the three frogs at the fountain. What a sad-eyed crew they are. I tune in to the water sounds, trying to settle down so that I can deal with the letter from Dr. Winkler. It reads much the same as the one enabling Kish to sign the lease for her suite. The doctor had her take the mental status test again. This time, she scored only slightly lower, twenty-four out of a total of thirty, but still high enough to remain in the Alzheimer's Lite range.

"In conclusion," the doctor says in the letter, "I consider Ms. Kish to be fully capable of looking after her affairs. This would include making changes in her marital status and understanding the consequences."

I've been hoping that she wouldn't be able to establish her competence to proceed with the divorce and that would put an end to it. Now that lifeline has been yanked away. Kish has been vague and iffy at times but now she's got all her ducks in a row.

She phones me at home that afternoon.

"Just calling to remind you about the separation agreement," she says, sounding smug about it. "I hope that you're going to sign it and get it back to me. It makes no sense to let this thing drag out, now does it? So please, Max, do the right thing and we'll have it all wrapped up in a couple of months."

I promise to think about it on condition that we have one of our beer and pizza chow downs in her suite. I'm wheedling my way in with plans for a pizza night the way we used to, in the breakfast nook, stuffing ourselves, drinking beer, belching and gorging on saturated fat and sodium with leftover pizza for breakfast the next morning, cold and rubbery, straight out of the fridge. She says okey-doke in her good way, letting me know that she's amenable to a pizza night. Sometime soon, she says, putting me off when I try to pin her down to a date. But she can be specific about the time. At six o'clock, allowing her to have dinner at five in the dining room with Arturo and the rest of them.

I'm hanging in there. I won't be taking Conrad's advice about going to a lawyer. And I won't be signing the separation agreement. I'll let it play out, allowing the case to go to court where I'll speak for myself and never mind the adage that a man who acts as his own lawyer has a fool for a client. As a substitute for any more of this whimpering, I'm cooking up another soap opera episode set in the courtroom.

The TV camera pans over to Connie Kish, the petitioner, sitting with her lawyer. Alone at another table, there's Max Osborne, the despondent respondent and devoted caregiver. He takes his place in the witness box. He pleads his case, telling the judge how much he loves the petitioner. Fade to black with Max throwing himself on the mercy of the court.

We'll have to tune in tomorrow to find out if the judge has enough romance in his soul to dismiss the divorce petition out of hand.

32. Togetherness in separate beds

ONCE AGAIN, INGA BUMPUS is prevailing upon me as the replacement for Clancy Kershaw. With nowhere to go and nobody to go there with me, I'm the willing volunteer. I don't mind at all that Inga has Janica Brodsky waiting for me on the other side of the lobby. I've seen her around Strathaven. A big woman with broad shoulders. She's patrolling back and forth around the lobby in her wheelchair as if it's a workout, doing laps. She's also calling out the number, "Six-twenty-three!"

"It's a call for help," Inga says. "Six-twenty-three is her suite number and she wants somebody to take her there. Would you mind, Max, taking her up to the sixth floor?"

Inga also informs me that Mrs. Brodsky hasn't seen her husband for several days. Since breaking his hip in a fall, he's been in a rehab unit learning how to get around in a wheelchair. When I approach her, Mrs. Brodsky asks if I'm one of the attendants. She's tense and rigidly square-shouldered while we sort out who I am. She asks about Kish. On the ninth floor? That's three floors up from where she is. Mrs. Brodsky knows where that is. On the sixth floor.

"Suite 623," she says. She may be uncertain about where she is at the moment. But she's sure of herself in the wheelchair. One push on the wheels and she's over at the elevators and another push and she's coasting into one of them.

We're on the sixth floor and Mrs. Brodsky has her bearings and is pleased with herself.

"Ah yes," she says with a sigh of relief. "Here we are. We're down this way."

Now quite at home, she's showing me around, pointing out the dining room, the nurses' station, and an activities room where she's been working on a jigsaw puzzle and where she goes to the exercise classes every Tuesday and Friday. The last stop on the tour is Suite 623.

"Do you see?" she says. "They have our names, Boris and Janica, on that little plate beside our door."

Kish has told me about the couples' suites. Bob and Belinda Jones live in one of them on the ninth floor. The regrettable thing, according to Kish, is that although Belinda and Bob are sharing a suite, they are in separate beds. What Kish wants for the couples' suites is a hospital bed built for two. Such a contrivance, with all the requisite levers and controls accommodating two people, wouldn't be feasible. Kish, believing devoutly in togetherness in a hospital bed, says that it's not entirely a lost cause. There is a model that can be bolted up to a second bed, like twin beds pushed together for couples who want to be within easy reach of each other.

Mrs. Brodsky isn't concerned about the sleeping arrangements for her and Boris. There are beds on either side of the suite with a small refrigerator, a microwave, toaster oven, and coffee maker.

"I'm not helpless," she says. "I'm able to get out of bed on my own and dress myself."

She tells me about her plans for when Boris returns to their suite. She'll be making coffee for him and he'll have it in bed the way he likes it. And one of their daughters will bake a

Ukrainian honey cake for them. And Mrs. Brodsky will warm it up in the toaster oven and they'll have it on Sunday morning.

I'm trying to imagine Kish and me in a setup like this with one of those bolt-together beds. If I were to mention this to her, I know she'd say it's pathetic of me to be jumping the gun on myself by twenty or thirty years. Barring accidents, it will take that long for me to need an extended-care facility. Still, it's oddly agreeable to picture Kish and me as old folks in a suite like this. I know she'd think it's soppy of me. Still, I like to imagine that one of us would be hale enough to get out of bed, make the coffee and warm up some blueberry breakfast cake for us on a Sunday morning.

Mrs. Brodsky wants to know if I can think of anything more she could do for Boris. My answer is that he'll be a lucky man to have her serving the coffee and the honey cake. That pleases her and she's beaming away. She turns her wheelchair around to accompany me back along the hall and see me off at the elevator. Listening to her, so buoyant about sharing a suite with Boris, leaves me warily wondering where Kish and I will be when we're as old as Mr. and Mrs. Brodsky.

33. Free spirits

WAITING AT THE DOOR to Suite 932, I'm playing along, knocking a second time. Following up by testing the doorknob. What did she call it? Her boudoir, a sulking place, every woman's entitlement. Now with patience wearing thin, I'm thinking, come off it, Kish. *C'est le gros boo-ul-shee-it.* You know who it is at your door. Almost as if she has tuned into my silent protest, she calls out, giving me permission to come in.

"Hello Kish, my dear. How are you feeling this afternoon? Everything okay?"

"Why are you asking?"

"Because it's not like you to be lying on the bed at four fifteen in the afternoon. Are you coming down with the flu? There's a lot of it going around."

"Not around here. I just wanted to lie down for a while . . . Now, do you notice anything? Anything different about me."

"Yes. You're not wearing the ankle brace."

"I don't need it any more. They took it off this morning. I'm as good as new."

"How does the ankle feel?"

"Just a little on the stiff side. But I don't need the wheelchair any more. I can walk with hardly any limping. I was able to take a taxi this afternoon and go for my bath at the spa."

"That's great. You're making a comeback. You're a free spirit."

"A free spirit?" she says, puzzling over it. "Just a minute. I'm going to make a note of that."

She's holding the clipboard and writing the words down and giving them more emphasis than I intended. My calling her a free spirit was a throwaway line, something encouraging to say. She's finding a relevance that I didn't know was there.

"A free spirit!" she says. "Yes! I like the sound of it. Yes, that's what I want to be."

I'm egging her on, saying that she has always been a free spirit. That's what she was when she made her way up into the Mañana Treehouse and even before that.

"There's nothing new about you being a free spirit. You were a free spirit the first time I met you, sitting up in that tree in the park, smoking marijuana, and telling me it was a Turkish cigarette and that Oscar could come up and smoke with you if he wanted to but that I'd have to find my own tree. You remember that, don't you?"

"Of course I do but . . . "

Now off track as a free spirit, she's confused, groping for words and looking at her clipboard as if she'll find them there.

"Oh Max," she says with a sinking voice. "There's something else. When I got into the taxi this afternoon, I couldn't remember where I wanted to go. This is my curse, isn't it? Reliving these crushing moments. Remembering them. Sitting in the taxi. Feeling flustered and conspicuous. The driver asked me where I want to go. And I couldn't remember. I could see his expression change, giving me that look. Oh you poor thing. And that only made it worse."

She goes on, recalling that the driver went into Strathaven and came back out with Inga Bumpus. By that time, Kish remembered where she wanted to go. But the driver wouldn't take responsibility for her as a passenger.

"I was so embarrassed," she says. "But then Inga came to my rescue, asking me if I was good to go, then telling the driver that being a little forgetful once in a while is nothing to worry about and talked him into driving me to the hotel for my bath."

I agree with Inga and reassure Kish that her moment of forgetfulness in the taxi would be covered by her sixty-second rule. "Even more to the point, my dear, I wish I had a tape recorder so that you could hear for yourself how clear and analytical you are in the way you're talking about this."

"Well, that's not the way I'm hearing myself," Kish says.

I'm on my way out through the main-floor lobby when Inga informs me that Nurse Margaret wants to see me again. Going into her office and seeing her tilting back in her plush chair for the second time, I should be at ease. But I'm guarded — once on the carpet, always on the carpet. She tells me she's concerned about what happened to Kish in the taxi this afternoon. She intends to ask Kish's doctor to reconsider allowing her to come and go in a taxi without supervision.

Now that would be an absolute shame. I'm trying to persuade Margaret that Kish is a special case. That she's a free spirit. That's what I want for her and that's what Dr. Winkler wanted when he wrote that first letter saying that she can manage her own affairs, implying that she should be free to come and go at Strathaven.

Margaret has no quarrel with Dr. Winkler's assessment. "It doesn't surprise me," she says. "I know that she's functioning at a high level. But at the same time, I'm not sure that free spirits can be accommodated at Strathaven. The fact that she's here tells us that she needs a level of care."

I remind Margaret that there are limits on how far they should go in imposing care. They don't strap residents down because they might fall out of bed. They're not putting a lock on the chin-strap on John Gunderson's helmet to force him to wear it. There's also Barry Erickson, a ninth floor resident who's allowed to do his thing in the activities room in the evening when it's deserted.

He cruises around in his wheelchair shunting the furniture into the centre of the room. It's a compulsion of some kind. He starts with the tables and follows up with the chairs until he has all of them herded in together. Then he'll sit back looking with satisfaction at what he's done, murmuring that it's one big happy family. The staff put a stop to it by wheeling Barry out of the activities room and locking the door but that left him protesting in a loud voice and disturbing other residents.

The easier way out was to let him have his way. No harm done. It takes only a few minutes for the night janitor to put the room back in order after Barry has gone to bed.

"My point is that you have a permissive approach to patient care. When you need to, you bend the rules to accommodate individuals. I know about you, Margaret MacDonald. You're the tough-cookie head nurse who keeps tonic water and a bottle of gin in the fridge specially for Mary Oliver."

"Okay, Max, okay. I guess I can make *some* allowances for Connie. She's so well-liked on the ninth floor."

Margaret informs me that so many residents want to sit with Kish in the dining room that they've put three tables together in Connie's Corner. One of the beneficiaries is John Gunderson. A month ago, he was a short-tempered loner so reluctant to go to the dining room for his meals that he had to be escorted there. Now that Kish has befriended him, he's never late at mealtimes.

"Sometimes I think we should put Connie on the payroll," Margaret says. "She's a house mother and cheerleader at the exercise classes. She has residents humming along with her at our golden-oldie sing along."

211

34. Lady Baltimore travelling incognito

THIS AFTERNOON Sophie the care aide accosts me in the hallway on the ninth floor and leads me off into the lounge for a hushed conversation.

"I want you to know that I saw Connie smoking pot on the smoker's balcony," she says.

"Really! Are you sure about that?"

"As sure as I can be. It was this morning. She was off by herself, away from the other smokers. At the end of the balcony. I could see that what she was smoking wasn't a cigarette. I know a joint when I see one, Mr. Osborne . . . Not only that. She was acting very strangely, talking to a seagull while it was flying along past the balcony."

I have my doubts that Kish was actually engaged in conversation with a seagull. More likely, feeling warm and friendly the way she does when toking up, she would have been nodding to the bird as a courtesy as it went flying by.

"One more thing," Sophie says, barely above a whisper. "Mr. Osborne, I could lose my job by not reporting this. But if I did report it, they'd probably ask Connie to leave Strathaven. I'd hate like the dickens to see that. She'd be dearly missed around here."

"Well thanks, Sophie, for telling me. I'll speak to her about it. You're absolutely right. She shouldn't be smoking marijuana."

I go directly to Kish's suite and ease into telling her that Sophie had seen her toking up on the smoker's balcony.

"Oh that," Kish says.

"She could smell it in your hair."

"Oh dear, oh dear, I'm slipping. I've been neglecting my hygiene. The next time I toke up, I'll wear a shower cap over my hair and spray myself with cologne."

"No Kish. This is serious. You can't brush it off. If they catch you toking up again, they'll ask you to find another care facility."

I know better than to come right out and ask her to let me have her marijuana and the rolling papers that she probably has in her purse. When I ask her where she got the marijuana, she's up front, telling me that she bought it from a dealer who operates out of his fifth-floor suite. How convenient. A fellow named Chris who makes his weed-selling rounds with the merchandise stashed under the seat of his wheelchair. When Clancy introduced him to me in the lobby, he was slouched in his wheelchair, fat and stolid, wearing wrap-around sunglasses and a leather head band for his shoulder-length grey hair. I'll have to get in touch with Chris and let him know that if he sells so much as another sliver of cannabis to Connie Kish, I'll turn him in to the police.

She falls short of swearing off marijuana. The best she can do is assure me that she'll no longer be toking up alone. "That's right, Max," she says. "I want you to know that I don't like toking up alone."

For a moment, she's confused, dwindling down, fumbling for words and looking at her clipboard. Then she snaps out of it, looking up from the clipboard and keeping faith with the sixty-second rule. That flash of forgetfulness qualifies and she puts it behind her. She's back in her treehouse remission, clear-headed and enthusiastic. Her face lights up and so does mine after she explains that what she meant to say was that she wanted me toking up with her.

"That's right. The only time I enjoy toking up is when you're with me. Next time, I'll have you with me. On that balcony. With Jonathan Livingstone Seagull."

More urgently, she wants to go to my car and toke up with me there. "Now," she says. "It's exactly what Dr. Winkler would prescribe for me. For us."

I know that I shouldn't be going along her. But I'm doing just that in an effort to ingratiate myself with her. Before we leave, she looks at herself in the mirror on the closet door.

"Will you look at that! An old biddy. I've got to do something about my hair. It makes me look so old."

As a cover up, she puts on a pearl-grey hat with a narrow black band and a wide, dipping brim. She's also wearing her big, audacious sunglasses and a long, grey overcoat, an outfit that I haven't seen before.

"How do I look now?"

"Very mysterious. You're Lady Baltimore, travelling incognito."

The parking lot is deserted and we're sitting in the car. Kish takes the cigarette papers and marijuana out of her purse and rolls a joint for us.

"I'm not skimping," she says. "I want it big enough for both of us to get a good buzz going. What do they call it? A number? A fattie?"

In stoner parlance, the car becomes a hot box with the windows steaming up with marijuana smoke. There's an urgency in the way she's toking up. I go the other way, as the responsible party, pretending to inhale and coming out of it with a contact high but sufficiently in control of myself to be able to drive, at her request, to the Mayfair mall. Getting out of the car, she's giggling away. Her sunglasses are comically askew. She wants to go to the food fair so that she can deal with a pressing attack of the munchies with the THC having tricked her brain into thinking that she's ravenously hungry. We make the rounds at the food fair counters, then sit at a table while she tucks into a pasta salad. She also polishes off a tub of yogurt, half of my roast beef sandwich, a bottle of green tea, and a blueberry muffin.

She's oblivious to the people at nearby tables. Hiding out under the floppy hat and behind the sunglasses, she chortles away. "This muffin is so, so good." Then she's singing to herself.

Oh do you know the muffin man
The muffin man, the muffin man
Oh do you know the muffin man
Who lives in Drury Lane.

"Look," she says. "It's quarter to five. It'll be dinner at five in the dining room. I mustn't be late . . . On second thought, maybe I shouldn't go there tonight. Right? Who knows? They might be able to see that I'm high and know that I've been toking up again. We can't have that now, can we?"

"Certainly not, Kish. Why don't I phone the LPN on the ninth floor and tell her that we're going out for dinner and that you'll be back around seven?"

"That's a spectacular idea, Max. Spectacular! We'll stay here for a while and give me time to get my act together."

"What about dinner?"

"I don't know about you, Max. But I'm still hungry. What about Chinese food? Why don't you go and load up a tray for us. Some greens. A vegetable dish . . . And fish if they have any.

Seafood. See if they have the garlic crab with black bean sauce. No, they wouldn't have that. It's all ready-made here isn't it? Get something with shrimp as long as it's not deep fried. And don't forget the chopsticks."

We settle for a honey-garlic shrimp with red peppers, a mix of vegetables with cashew nuts, spring rolls and steamed rice. I pretend to be high myself, getting into the spirit of things while we peck away with our chopsticks, hanging out with nary a word about the impending divorce. My sense of it is that we are closer than we've been for months.

35. Scoring Brownie points

NURSE MARGARET PHONES to arrange for us to meet at the fountain in the lobby instead of her office. I'm thinking, What now, there Margaret? And who cares where we meet? I'm sorely in need of a day off from Strathaven Place. I've been coming here for two years. Visiting Kish day in, day out, barring two days off with the flu. I don't know what's come over me. I'm sick to death of this place. I have to hand it to Clancy, coming here for twenty years. A glutton for punishment.

At least I'm not in Margaret's office, hard-assing it on that chair in front of her desk. But this is the third time I've been summoned by the almighty head nurse. Here at the frog fountain, I'm submissively inquiring, "Well, what have we done this time."

"An interesting choice of words," she says. "The we being?"

I can't help editing myself. It's the English teacher in me wanting to be grammatically correct and say, Kish and I, but coincidentally trying to be one of the guys, I inform her flatly that the we equals Kish and me.

"I can see that you've got your dander up," she says. "Having a bad day, are we?"

Thus we arrive at the what now of it. She wants to know how I became involved in an abuse case involving a Strathaven resident named Dorothy Walton. Margaret has the file about it showing on her laptop.

My involvement started two nights ago on the elevator on my way down from the ninth floor. Mrs. Walton came on at the fifth floor, dressed in a green fleece dressing gown over a matching long nightie with knee-high woollen socks and slippers and yet hugging herself and shivering on a warm August evening. When we got off on the ground floor, she was so out of breath that she had to sit in one of the chairs across from the elevators.

"Why don't we go back to the fifth floor," I said.

"No, no, I can't go there. Morris is waiting for me. Please! I've got to hide."

I called over to Inga Bumpus at the reception desk and asked her to phone up to the fifth floor and have them send a care aide with a wheelchair down to the lobby.

"There's isn't time for that," Mrs. Walton said. "He'll be coming down looking for me. That's what he does. When I'm not in my room, he comes looking for me."

She wanted me to take her to the lady's room along the hall. "You could go in with me and sit with me," she said. When she saw me noticing the bruises on her arms, she overlapped them so that her hands covered up the dark patches. Just then, one of the elevators was coming to a stop at the main floor.

"It's him," Mrs. Walton said. "It's Morris."

She guessed right about the man stepping off the elevator. She was clearly afraid and shying away from his scowling. He wasn't showing any concern for her, not even looking at her. A little younger than she was, dressed more like a visitor than a resident, he was taking charge.

"I'll look after her," he said.

"No," I said. "We'll wait for the LPN to come down for her."

Summing up for Margaret, I informed her that I waited for the LPN to show up and help Mrs. Walton into a wheelchair and take her up to the fifth floor. And that was about it.

"There's a little more to it than that," Margaret says. "I have the LPN's report right in front of me. She's saying that the husband Morris was confrontational at which point you said one of two things was going to happen. Either Morris would leave her in the care of the LPN or you would call the police and have them look into the bruising on her arms."

The LPN was right about that. If Morris had persisted, I would have called the cops. At any rate, Margaret and the security people now have Mrs. Walton's situation in hand. It turns out she also has severe bruising on her thighs. For the time being at least, Morris will be allowed to visit his wife only when accompanied by one of their daughters. It's been left to them to decide whether or not the police should be called in.

"It goes without saying," Margaret says, "if you hadn't come to Mrs. Walton's defence, Morris might still be abusing her. I want to thank you on behalf of Strathaven and Mrs. Walton and her daughters, for standing up for her."

She wraps it up by handing me a loonie.

"You're our dollar-a-year man," she says. "This puts you on call as our volunteer good guy. It's all under the table with absolutely nothing in writing. Meaning that if you foul up and Strathaven is liable in some way and the lawyers come to me asking about it, I'll deny any knowledge of this arrangement. I'll be saying, 'Max Osborne? Never heard of him.' I had the same arrangement with Clancy Kershaw. We really miss that man. Not only for the countless hours he spent feeding Nellie and freeing up one of the care aides at meal times. There was also what he did as a volunteer. Did you ever notice what big feet he has? Size twelve, I'd say. Which means that taking his place Max, you've got a big pair of shoes to fill."

It could be asked, whatever happened to Max Osborne, the hard-case visitor, coming and going only to visit Kish? The guy who bailed out on Mrs. Booker when she approached him in the lobby? Sad to say, Mrs. Booker died two weeks ago. A letter from her lawyer informed me that she remembered me in her will with a bequest of twenty thousand dollars. Equally surprising was her gratitude for what she referred to as my courtesy and kindness while we chatted in the solarium. The lawyer's letter also said that Mrs. Booker thought it was kind of me to pretend that I was her nephew and she was my Aunt Elizabeth.

Over the course of a year or so visiting Aunt Sarah I had spent a couple of hours chatting with her. She'd be paying me in the order of ten thousand bucks an hour for my time. Seems a bit much. Too much considering that the last time I saw her approaching, I couldn't get away quickly enough. I've told Margaret about the bequest and we're going to use it to set up a fund, possibly for a few bus excursions to Beacon Hill Park and picnics there for the shut-ins. Calling them that sounds patronizing, I know. But that's the situation for residents like Mrs. Booker, having outlived family and friends.

When I help out where I can, there's another force at work besides the institution, Strathaven Place, asserting itself and drawing me in as a volunteer. It's not that I'm all that altruistic. There's an ulterior motive. I'm hoping to score a few brownie points with Kish. She always said I should take up volunteer work. Well this is it. I want Margaret to tell Kish what I'm doing. She would think more highly of me and realize that I'm not as far removed from her life at Strathaven as she thinks I am.

What's encouraging is that for several days now, she hasn't said a word about divorcing me. Every time I see that clipboard in her hands, I expect her to remind me about signing the separation agreement. Who knows? Either she's forgotten about it or she has changed her mind. She might realize that our lives are coming together at Strathaven Place now that we're both increasingly involved in the life of the place. I'm no longer just another visitor. Kish never was just another resident. Margaret is right. They should put her on the payroll in return for what she's doing as house mother in the dining room and for helping out as an activities coordinator.

Even though I'm excluded from that, I sense that we're closer than we've been for some time, particularly now that she's accepted my date invitation. Tomorrow night is pizza night and never mind that it took forever for her to agree to it. Just like old times in the breakfast nook, we'll be together, stuffing ourselves on pizza and beer and strawberry ice cream.

36. Humbled and humiliated

GOING ALL OUT, I'M PAYING fifty dollars for a pizza delivery bag. Professional grade, says the man at the counter in the food equipment store. He gives me this insider's tip, one pizza enthusiast to another. If I warm up the bag in the oven at home beforehand, I'll be assured of a delivered pizza that's almost too hot to handle. Later, at the pizza emporium, as a customer with a pre-warmed bag, I'm getting the respect that's due to a true aficionado, ordering our customary toppings, chicken, artichokes, and a mix of cheeses for Kish with anchovies instead of chicken on my side of it.

At 6:00 PM precisely, I'm Pizza Man, getting off the elevator and striding triumphantly along the hallway toward her suite, laden with a cooler for the six-pack of beer and a thermos full of the ice cream and strawberries. I have the day-glo orange pizza bag held out in front me like a festive serving tray. I'm gung-ho over the prospect of telling Kish about the condo that Anita Stokes has found for us. I want Kish to like the place and to see it as a home away from home. I've been waiting for the right moment to talk to her about this.

However, it won't be tonight. To my dismay, Kish has gone out. Arturo has gone with her. My informant is Mrs. Dundee, sitting in the doorway to her suite and beside herself with delight to be informing me that I just missed them.

"They left a couple of minutes ago and they were all dressed up," she says.

From the sign-out sheet on the counter at the nursing station, I affirm that they checked out together at 5:50 PM. Both names in Kish's handwriting. Connie Kish and Arturo Hebb, as if they're a couple. I'm in an angry daze, looking around, not sure for a moment where I am and trying to get my bearings.

It's no consolation to realize that I missed them by a couple of minutes. I'm trying to persuade myself that forgetting what Kish and I had arranged for this evening must have been one of her Alzheimer lapses. It's hard to believe it was deliberate and that she was cutting it so fine that if I'd shown up a couple of minutes earlier, I would have met Kish and Arturo coming out through the main-floor lobby. That's the last thing she would have wanted.

The Kish I know doesn't have the spite it would take to stand me up intentionally. But then it's not the Kish I know who wants to divorce me. This could be her way of provoking me into signing the separation agreement. Here I am left holding the pizza bag, standing at the nursing station, giving solemn consideration to plastering the door to her suite with her half of the hot pizza, then leaving a dire warning to Arturo Hebb by slapping a dribbling ooze of cheese and anchovies up against the door to Suite 915. That's too over the top for me and I chicken out on the idea. But never mind. It's perversely gratifying just to be scheming away to myself about it.

On the way down on the elevator, I'm getting past the anger. It's even worse feeling humbled and humiliated. I avoid Inga Bumpus at the reception desk by leaving through the exit to the parking lot even though I'm parked on the street. She'll see me ducking out but I won't have to face her. Even so, she will figure out what's going on. She would have seen Kish and Arturo on their way out and soon after that, me on my way in through the lobby.

The reception desk serves as Strathaven's gossip central, the clearing house for the divorce scuttlebutt and other choice tidbits. Connie and Arturo don't you know? Toking up together in his suite. Carrying on in ways that I'm clueless about. Inga probably knows where they've gone. She could well be thinking that I'm in hot pursuit of my wife and the new man in her life.

That very thought provides the wherewithal for another soap opera episode. We have the hapless Max Osborne and stirring melodrama when he tracks Kish and Arturo to their trysting place. Max shocks and confronts them, saying, "See here, Ms. Kish and Mr. Hebb! Just what am I supposed to with all this pizza and ice cream? And who's going to drink all this beer?"

It's a windy night and I'm sitting in the car parked on Waterfront Crescent. Looking up at Strathaven through the sunroof. Checking her window on the ninth floor. I have it counted off as the third one along from the south side of the building. Looking farther along the row of windows. Guessing where Arturo's suite would be. Knowing they aren't up there. *Ahhh Kish*, with him? He's way too old for you. While I consider noshing on a slice of the pizza, I check inside the insulated delivery bag. This pizza really is nice and hot. But I'm at rock bottom, unable to stomach even the thought of taking a bite of it.

I twist the cap of one the bottles of beer and take a few swigs. Not quite chug-a-lug but wasting no time in finishing the first bottle and opening the second one. There's no hurry to go home. Killing time. Wondering how things would have turned out if I'd been able to tell her about the new condo. Before I know it, I'm sipping away at the third bottle of beer and feeling just squiffy enough to realize that I should call a taxi instead of driving home. While I wait for the cab, the wind whips up against the Garry oak tree off to the side of the car.

There's a deluge of acorns. Ripe and ready to fall in late September. A bumper crop of mighty oak tree seeds. They're nattering away, scolding me as they come pelting down onto the hood and rattling on the roof. The taxi pulls up nearby. Just as I blearily suspect, the acorns are out to get me when I step out of the car onto a litter of them on the pavement. They're round and lumpy underfoot. My feet shoot out from under me and down I go into a soft landing flat on my butt. Embarrassed, unhurt as the taxi driver helps me back on my feet and I plead my case to him.

"I want you to know that I'm not drunk. I slipped on those goddamn acorns."

"Yeah I know," he says. "They'll get ya every time. It's like walking on marbles."

37. A toast to loneliness

I'LL BE ON SLIPPERY GROUND when I try to explain to Kish just how it came to pass that Anita and I had been on the verge of going to bed together. Even in my zealous, hot-to-trot condition, I knew that I'd be telling Kish about it. I'd have no choice. Flora had followed Anita and me into the guest bedroom. That steadfast, chaperoning dog was my conscience and would have me obliged to fess up to Kish. The gist of it would be that an irresistible, bad-boy lusting had seized control of me and something snapped. I can say quite truthfully that there are extenuating circumstances.

For one thing, Kish, it wouldn't have happened in our bed, that singular place. Anita and I were in the guest bedroom. Forging on with my confession, trying to explain what happened. Well, my dear, you had to have been there over the weeks it took for Anita to sell the house and turn up the new condo. She was so much more than just another realtor angling for a quick commission on the hurried sale of the house. On her advice, I rejected a couple of offers. She showed the place several more times and we finished up with a sale price that was ninety-five thousand dollars more than the original offers. I'm also indebted to her for finding the perfect condo apartment.

Even with that, I was the live-alone guy who didn't want to move in the first place. I was venting about Kish and Arturo · and convinced that she had taken him with her for a bath together at the hotel spa last night. The remedy for my sorrows was to have one last smoke-up. Where else but in the breakfast nook? With marijuana from a little cache that Conrad had given to me, I rolled a joint. Lighting up and lolling back, I inhaled down to the tip of my toes, mellowing out and going back over the sale of the house.

Just as I was thinking so generously about Anita, she was knocking at the back door. This is where friends and neighbours show up instead of presenting themselves more formally at the front door. She had gone beyond the customary bottle of wine that realtors give to clients to celebrate the purchase of a new abode. She came bearing the gift of a home-cooked dinner on a tray. Having just toked up, I was bedevilled by the munchies and thinking how fortuitous it was for Anita to show up laden with roast chicken, hot out of the oven.

There's no such thing as roast chicken for one. It should be shared along with the apple and sage stuffing and the roasted carrots and potatoes. She had the gravy in a Thermos flask and a bowl of fruit salad — raspberries, sliced peaches and white grapes with a splash of kirsch. She also had a bottle of chardonnay in her overcoat pocket. There was more than enough for the two us. She accepted my invitation to stay and make it dinner for two.

I opened the wine while Anita set the dining room table with dishes, silverware, and napkins from the good-china cabinet. We were a mismatched pair. Anita, chic in a navy-blue pantsuit with a ruffled grey blouse and me in blue jeans and a tartan shirt, better suited for pizza and beer. Having damask linen napkins folded beside the bone-china plates transformed it from a good meal to fine dining. We tucked into the roast chicken and sipped chardonnay. Still nicely afloat on the THC, I trotted out my quip about haute cuisine of the hautest order.

I can't remember much else of what was said, focused as I was on Anita as an alluring woman.

Like Kish, she's ditsy enough to be interesting, talking to the new plants in her garden and to her Manx cats. I've seen them, Mr. Flanders and the cross-eyed Ms. Jones on leashes strolling around the block with Anita. When she would chat with Kish over the back fence, I'd have a *ménage à trois* going with my ear for women's voices savouring the sounds they were making as if they were divas in a Mozart opera, with Kish a ten-out-of-ten as the honey-throated contralto. Anita in the mezzo range was also highly rated for being easy on the ears.

We had finished dinner, cleared the table, and loaded the dishwasher and Anita was about to go home.

"Thanks for everything," I said. "Thanks for being a friend in need."

We stepped toward each other in a wrapping of arms and back patting. It went from there to full-body contact with the cushioning of her breasts against me. I let her take charge, holding on somewhat longer than is customary for a neighbourly hug. Right this way friends, down the slippery slope.

I invited her to join me for a final glass of the chardonnay. We sat in the living room on the sofa. I did the pouring and passed a glass to her. She came sidling over into that vague zone, close enough to make me edgy but not intrusive enough for me to slide away from her. She raised her glass in a toast to the condo I'd be moving into in a couple of weeks.

"To a new home sweet home," she said.

"Yes, be it ever so humble," I said, clinking glasses with her.

Two sips into our wine and Anita was edging to her left, close enough for me to wonder about her perfume. She proposed a toast to loneliness.

"We both have it," she said. "You're living with it and it's been my lot for four years and I'm so hungry. I think that you are as well."

After taking the glass out of my hand and setting it on the table, she took my right hand and lowered it onto her knee. The preliminary necking and groping was underway. It was awkward, craning to kiss while sitting side by side. She upped the ante by kissing my ear and tonguing and blowing into it. This was something new. Kish and I aren't much for ear fondling. Anita was on intimate terms with every nook and cranny of my left ear. That's when something snapped. My blood knew what to do and went rushing into the vital vesicles. She had me by the hand and was leading me up the stairs to the guest bedroom. We would have made it all the way into bed if she hadn't been so solicitous about it.

"Connie won't mind," she said.

"Connie won't mind! What do you mean?"

"You're getting a divorce, aren't you?"

"Did she tell you that?"

"Well yes, she did," Anita said. "We went out for lunch on Friday. She seemed to think that you and I have potential. That I'm your type."

I can't resist asking what Kish had in mind for us.

"She wanted nature to take its course," Anita said. "After a glass or two of wine, we got to talking about men in general, then you in particular. Connie was growling away, imitating the way you lower your voice when you talk to me. She said it was your way of flirting with me. I said that I enjoyed it and that I found you attractive. And we agreed that I was a sophisticated woman with excellent taste in men and now that you were getting a divorce, I could have first dibs on you. Sounds bizarre, I know. I drank a toast to 'first dibs on Max Osborne.'"

This should have been my cue to rise up in protest against being shopped around as beef cake. I stopped short of asking Anita to elaborate on my attributes. But I confess. I was flattered. And it was news to me that I notched my voice down when I talked to Anita.

"This is so embarrassing," she said. "I feel like such a fool, showing up here uninvited, as if I could seduce you with roast chicken. Connie even gave me a list of things you like. One of them was Burnt Almond chocolate bars, as if I could sweeten you up with them. You must think I'm a prize idiot."

"No, Anita. Far from it. And I'm just as confused as you are. I don't know whether I'm coming or going. I just can't give up on Kish. She's pushing me away with all her might, and I'm hanging on to her for dear life."

"She's a lucky lady."

"Well, so am I. "

Anita anticipated that I was going to say that her interest in me was flattering and asked me not to go there. It was her cue to say, "Good night to you, Max. And please, not another word. I'm going home. I'll have a little chat with my cats."

Alone with Flora, I'm trying to mitigate my guilt. What really riles me is Kish's over-the-top manipulation, trying to set me up with Anita with that list of things that I like. Well, I could give her and Arturo my blessing by providing him with a list of things he should know about her. There's her favourite dessert, the gourmet ice cream sundaes. I take a spiteful delight in doubting that he could or would go to the trouble I did, serving them up in her suite. My list for Arturo is a work in progress. There must be other things I've done for Kish that he couldn't handle. And I'm not about to tell him that Kish is justifiably proud of her décolletage.

And I won't tell Arturo about the way Kish mispronounces the word pseudo. Somehow she's always had it jumbled in with the word suede with the result that pseudo passes her lips as swaydough. The first time, I couldn't bring myself to correct her. After that I couldn't set her straight and have her scold me for allowing her to go on mispronouncing the word.

Besides that, coming from Kish, I liked the sound of swaydough. I've considered writing to the word scholars at the O.E.D. and making the case for changing the pronunciation. But it would be endlessly complicated. Changing pseudonym to swaydonym, pseudomorophic to swaydomorphic and pseudology to swaydology and so forth and so on. So let it be. I can only hope that the word will come up between Kish and Arturo and that he'll fall into the trap and set her straight about the pronunciation and she'll be mortified.

There's one thing I'll never surrender to him. And that is my ironclad right to call her Kish. It belongs to me and me alone. And when you get down to it, why should I help him in any way at all. I don't owe him a goddamn thing. All I have to say to you, Arturo, is that you're on your own and you can take a flying leap and go to blazes.

38. A final decree on divorcing me

I SHOULD BE ON FAMILIAR TERMS with every nuance in her voice. Over the years, I've heard it every which way but never quite the way it's coming to me now with a timid softening over the phone at seven thirty on the morning after the night before.

"It's only me," she says.

Diffident, little old me. What gets my hopes up is the offhand way she talks about what almost happened in the guest bedroom last night. Having talked to Anita about it, Kish knows what didn't happen. She's asking me if I know what the word divertimento means.

"Is it a diversion of some kind?"

"It's Italian for a lighthearted musical composition. It also means a bit of fun. That's what I wanted for you last night. A divertimento."

There's a little more to it with that soap opera turn of events — Kish giving Anita first dibs on me. What a contrast for me. After falling into temptation last night, I felt as guilty as sin, but this morning I'm brimming with self-righteousness.

"I want to see you," she says, pausing and faltering. "Not right this minute. It's just that I need some time. Let's see. This is Sunday, isn't it? Yes. We could meet at eleven."

She's thinking out loud, planning the rest of her morning. She needs time to go shopping and buy the wherewithal for a wiener roast at French Beach.

"It'll be like a picnic," she says. "Picnics are so much fun."

Sounds familiar. I've heard her say that numerous times and the resonance of it only improves with repetition. That's what she wants. The way we did years ago, whiling away a couple of hours in folding chairs around a beach fire, cooking hotdogs on roasting forks on a sunny day. I'm not going to inquire about her Sunday morning dates with Arturo in the chapel. Maybe she's forgotten about them. Even better, she's breaking it off with him.

"We'll drive out there. To French Beach. Oh and another thing. I'm calling about the magic words."

"And what pray tell, what would they be?"

"Well, let me see now. Oh this is terrible. I can't remember. I have them written down. Oh and another thing. I've got a surprise for you. And don't worry. It's something good."

In an afterthought to her string of afterthoughts, she leads me to think that we're still in divorce mode. It feels like a decade ago that she first mentioned it. And here's the D word rearing up again. She asks me to bring my copies of the divorce papers. I guess that includes the separation agreement, the document still awaiting my signature.

Here we are at French Beach, a sandy and secluded ocean shoreline with access down a pathway from the parking lot. She looks robust and athletic, carrying a little table with fold-up legs and two beach chairs and her clipboard, leaving me with the picnic hamper, a pair of roasting forks, a toasting rack and a bundle of firewood. A breeze coming in off the Strait of Juan de Fuca greets us with a steady lapping of waves. We settle in halfway down the beach. Kish looks out over the ocean. She's proclaiming loudly into the wind.

"I'm Connie Kish! And this is Max Osborne! We are here together!"

She would have me believe that if we wait for a few moments, the wind will carry her words around the world and they'll come circling back to us. I'm the smarty pants gearing it up with science, speculating to myself that apparently her voice travels faster than the speed of sound and closer to the speed of light. Kish wants me listening closely so that I'll hear that her outcry has circled the planet and resounded back to us instantaneously.

Her authority for this goes back to our favourite newspaper comic strip, Richard Thompson's *Cul de Sac* and Kish having me read a memorable episode with the central character, a precocious four-year-old named Alice Otterloop, informing her friend Beni that it's a well-known fact that the wind carries their voices around the world and then the voices come back to them. As it is for little Alice, Kish's imagination is boundless in time and space. Anything can happen.

"We are truly back together," she says.

We have the beach all to ourselves. Lighting the fire becomes a team effort after my Boy Scout training in the craft of fire-lighting fizzles out into clouds of smoke with hardly a flicker of flame. Kish saves the day, applying her Girl Guide expertise with several squirts of an accelerant from her can of doobie lighter fluid. We have a good fire going. We're in our chairs and settling into the primal comfort of our Stone Age ancestors feeling secure with their faces lit up by a tribal fire.

"Can't you feel it?" Kish says. "Are you letting go?"

"I'm letting go as we speak. Ahhh."

"And can you feel it going down? You know, don't you? The thing that goes down when you're relaxed and shoots up when you're all stressed out?"

"Blood pressure?"

"Yes," she says. "The B.P. is going down. Down. Down."

But then my B.P. shoots up after she asks me if I have the divorce documents with me. These mixed signals are getting to me. In one breath, she's warm and fuzzy and then goes veering off on a tangent. She has me in retreat again.

"Yes, but I still haven't signed the separation agreement."

She says I won't need to and informs me that what we have in front of us is a bonfire and that the word is not, as commonly believed, of French derivation. It's not *bon* fire meaning good fire. And just when I think she's on the ball, she slips into forgetfulness.

"Oh Max, this is pathetic. I know what it isn't. But what is it? When I was thinking about this morning, I made a note about it. I have to write things down."

Leafing through her papers on the clipboard, she comes up with her note and then runs into difficulty reading what she has written.

"Well isn't that the limit," she says. "I can't read my own writing."

This is the disease of remembering by writing things down and then being unable to find the note you've made or being unable to read what you have written down. What we're looking at is the effect that Alzheimer's can have on handwriting. I've seen it on the website about Dr. Alzheimer's pioneer work in the field with Frau Auguste Deter. The case file has samples of her handwriting, a trembling scribble with the lines slanting haphazardly. Kish's handwriting, although not that muddled, has become more compressed and spidery. But

I can read it easily enough and it seems to me that if she wasn't so exasperated with herself, she could read it if I coax her into it, sounding out the first few words.

"It says 'Late Middle English.'"

She takes the note from me. Proceeding with the rest of it, she explains that the word bonfire comes from ye olde English for a big fire fueled with livestock bones — the bone fire — that was used for burning heretics or proscribed literature. She has relegated our divorce documents into the second category. She tugs her copies of them off the clipboard and has me producing mine from my jacket pocket. She starts tossing them, two or three sheets at a time, onto the fire and invites me to do the same. The pages are curling up and turning black with flimsy offshoots floating away. Her storyteller's magic goes to work. Poof! The divorce vanishes into the smoke. Even with her lapsing pauses, she's insightful about what she has done.

"What's that saying about justice?" she says. "You know, that justice must be done."

"And that it must also be seen to be done?"

"That's it," she says and explains that after what she has put me through, trying to divorce me and harassing me about it, she wants me to see justice being done. What an inventive woman she is. This is why we're having the wiener roast. She wanted this fire to dramatize the fact that she no longer wants to divorce me and that she never did, not really. It would then have occurred to her, well if we're going to have a fire, we'll also have a wiener roast. I have to hand it to her.

On the scale of one-to-ten, this surprise gets a lovely, big fat ten. I should have seen through this divorce business right from the start. But she was so convincingly relentless and hard-hearted, persuading me that I didn't fit into her life at Strathaven. She really wanted to give me the freedom to leave her — that was the simple truth — and wheels within wheels, all along she was hoping that I'd hang in there out of a sense of duty if nothing else. It was pretty cute the way she covered her tracks, persisting so that she could be sure that I didn't want out.

Now she's on again about the magic words and asks me if we've talked about them.

"Yes, but you haven't told me what they are."

"I haven't?"

"You said you had them written down."

"Yes, here it is," she says after leafing through the pages on the clipboard. "We can thank Anita for telling me what you said last night. The magic words. I had her repeat them so that I could write them down. You said I was pushing you away with all my might and that you were hanging on to me for dear life."

"It seems like ages ago now."

"No, no. It was last night. After what I put you through. Oh, Max, you dear man. I don't deserve you. I'm the one hanging on to you for dear life."

We turn toward each other in our chairs, intending to reach across and embrace only to have it cut short when one side of my chair starts sinking into the sand. We're waiting for the fire to sizzle down into the hot coals we need for cooking the hotdogs. Holding hands, we are warmed by the fire as it settles into a glow. Kish has the picnic hamper open. She takes out the plump deli frankfurters, the Alsatian sauerkraut, a spicy German mustard, and the sourdough buns. I have the frankfurters speared onto the roasting forks and the buns in the toasting rack. In a few minutes, we're eating our hot dogs. Kish is herself again, finding the words she wants.

"You'll never guess where I am," she says.

"But you're going to tell me."

"Yes. I'm over the moon. The moon I mean is the moon that the cow jumped over."

She thanks me for not asking about Arturo because it leaves her free to reassure me that nothing happened last evening. They shared a taxi. He paid half the fare and the driver dropped him off at his daughter's house. Kish went on to the hotel spa for a bath.

"Now I want to know, does it bother you that Arturo and I are friends?"

"I'm okay with it."

"It sounds as if you do mind. Is it because you don't like him?"

"We're not going to become bosom buddies if that's what you mean. He's your friend and I'll go along with that."

"You're not still jealous of him are you? Well if you are, just in case, let me tell you, truly, that Arturo and I are friends, nothing more."

Do I need anything more to be convinced that there's nothing to be jealous about? She'll have me know that in addition to her *gros bool-shee-it* detector, she's equipped with special radar that beeps at the most infinitesimally slight surging of male hormones within a range of fifty feet. But she hasn't been getting a flicker of interest from Arturo.

"He may be more interested in you than in me," she says.

"Is that so? I haven't picked up on that."

"Yes, if you were that way inclined, you would make an interesting couple."

"Don't you think he's too old for me?"

"Come to think of it, yes, he is."

"What matters is that I'm just right for you, Kish. I'm your one-dame man."

"And I'm your one-man dame."

"I'll hold you to that."

"And even if I was scouting around for another man, my prospects would be slim to none."

"You're selling yourself short."

"No. You're forgetting that men aren't scouting around for women with Alzheimer's."

She has given me the opening I need to get in a dig about Arturo and how she really had me going. "You had me convinced that you and Arturo were getting together. I'll be launching a formal complaint about you at the next meeting of the Society for the Prevention of Cruelty to Caregivers."

"And so you should," Kish says.

I want to believe what she's telling me about Arturo. Not entirely convinced, I lead her on, saying it was nice that they could toke up together and that it would have been good for her morale and likely helped her to get through a rough day.

"But we didn't toke up together," she says

"I thought you did. I noticed the smell of it while you were in his suite."

"I don't remember that."

"Well, it happened."

"There was the time. Maybe that was it. Arturo having to go to the dentist."

Kish has no clipboard notes to help her through this. She remembers Arturo fretting about having a root canal procedure. She rolled a joint for him to help him to relax.

"It was a waste of my BC bud," she says with the rest of it falling into place. "He was allergic to it. He started coughing and retching. I thought he was going to pass out and I called the nurse. But why am I telling you about this . . . How did we get onto this?"

She has me convinced about it now. With jealousy and suspicion having turned me into a conniving skunk, I'm ashamed of myself. But not enough to level with her about it. I let on to her that it was simply that she initiated it and wanted to tell me about her friend Arturo. She moves on, finding another page she wants on her clipboard.

"Here it is," she says, reading slowly. "'More flexible.' You're going to have be more flexible.'"

She describes the circle of friends she would have for us, starting with herself and Arturo as friends. She also wants to have Anita and me as another twosome. That's where the flexibility on my part comes in. Kish would expand the group even further by having Clancy and Carole coming to lunch with us.

"Have I met Carole?" Kish asks. "I think I have. I remember Nellie and Clancy. I'm not sure about Carole. But it doesn't matter. Clancy and Carole would be another twosome. That would add up to three twosomes. Making a sixsome. Sixsome? I wonder if it's a word. Well if it's not, it should be."

Listen to her. The same old Kish, playing with words. Even better, she's getting back to being inclusive, opening up to Clancy and Carole. He called me the other day to say that he wants to come back to Strathaven. "As a volunteer," he said. "Yeah, I'm a glutton for punishment. I miss having Inga Bumpus boss me around. I miss being part of that place. It's in my blood." What he has in mind is spelling me off with three or four evenings a week of volunteer duty at the frog fountain. I'm sure that Margaret would welcome him back. I know I will. What's that Humphrey Bogart movie quip to Claude Raines as they walk off into the night at the end of *Casablanca*? "I think this is the beginning of a beautiful friendship." Can't help seeing that ahead for Clancy and me. Once he was my boss and now we've been through a lot together.

Overall, for Kish and me, I can see that a bigger circle of friends would be good for both us. We wouldn't be relying entirely on each other. There'll be a widening of the circle now that Hilary will be coming over from Vancouver every two weeks. Susan Green and Helen Etherington, two other friends who go way back and who have been checking in with me regularly to ask about Kish, will also come into the fold as part of this support group. Kish now turns to stringing me along about a little adjustment to this arrangement.

"You can be right here for me," she says.

"That's where I want to be."

"Yes. You can also be over there for yourself."

She's back where she was a few days ago with her tenuous matchmaking. Holding onto me and letting go simultaneously.

"You and Anita," she says. "You have potential."

"What do you mean?"

"The right chemistry. For sailing together. You and Anita have it."

"Sailing together?"

"Yes. Didn't Anita tell you? I have bought half interest in the *Summer Wind* from her. She let me have it for twenty-four thousand bucks. It's a good deal. Less than half of her asking price of forty -nine thousand. I signed it over to you. Your name is on the title."

She's giving Anita and me her blessing all over again. She wants us out sailing together and tells me that *Summer Wind* has a waterbed.

"So don't forget the Gravol, okey-doke? We can't have you two getting seasick on that waterbed, now can we? Imagine! Making love on a waterbed. With two rhythms going at once.

241

The waterbed moving with the rocking of the boat. And lovers with a rhythm of their own and the waterbed moving with them instead of pushing back the way an ordinary mattress does."

She has me musing to myself, well thanks all the same there Kish, but I have a different arrangement in mind. First thing, I'll manoeuvre my way out of any entanglement with Anita. She wouldn't have it any other way. Then I'll sign my half interest in the *Summer Wind* over to Conrad, thus clearing the way for him and Anita to go sailing together. I'll be the matchmaker, persuading Kish to have Anita and Conrad as sailing companions and as another twosome in our circle of friends. They'll come to lunch with Kish and Arturo and Clancy and Carole. The more the merrier. I'll be fine-tuning the group into a sixsome plus yours truly. But I won't be the odd man out after I arrange to sit at the lunch table between Kish and Arturo.

Now that I have two more frankfurters roasted over the hot coals, I can stoke up the fire with the last few slabs of our firewood while Kish is at work on the little table, loading the frankfurters onto the toasted buns and spooning on the mustard and sauerkraut. We're munching away, sipping beer and looking into the fire flaring up again.

39. A tipping point

WE'RE BACK IN THE CAR and she's swaying sideways over the console, brushing up against me shoulder to shoulder, then settling into the upholstery. With the clipboard on her lap, she starts leafing through the pages.

"Okey-doke. We have it. We have everything we need . . . Everything except this darn clipboard. It's confusing me. Too many notes. I don't want it anymore."

She tosses it over her left shoulder and it falls onto the back seat and she turns to me, stuttering. "Oh . . . Oh . . . "

She falters there, failing to come up with my name. Her face darkens and she's horrified. She asks me to pull off the highway and stop the car. Squeezing her eyes shut with embarrassment, fists clenched in her lap, she goes into a ramble about backsliding.

"Oh Max, Max, Max! I forgot your name," she says. "And I know. I know. 'A rose by any other name would smell as sweet.'"

"Well now, there you go. Selling yourself short. The dotty and forgetful Connie Kish is clear-headed enough to be quoting Shakespeare. You're still the treehouse lady, proving my point. You haven't forgotten who I am."

"You have to accept that I'm becoming somebody else," she says. "What do I do? I need discipline. I can't allow myself to let go. Oh, what do I do?"

These are not idle questions. She's trying to be analytical and answer them. What stays the same is that, as she has all along, she's struggling hard to hold the line and to stay aware.

"I don't want you going easy on me," she says. "Don't write me off."

"I promise not to do that. And now that we've got that all settled, I'm waiting for Lady Baltimore to tell me want to do."

This goes back to a game we used to play in the car by imagining that it was a horse-drawn carriage. She would become the haughty Lady Baltimore and I'd be James, the liveried coachman, waiting for her to say, "Home, James and don't spare the horses." At which point, I would reply, "Your wish is my command, Madame." Silly stuff, I know, but we got a kick out of it. I ask her to remember it now and she takes up the challenge.

"By all means, home James, and don't spare the horses," she says quietly and as high up on her high horse as she can pretend to be.

And home James it is. I'm steering the car back onto the highway and we're heading home to Strathaven Place.

40. A space nearby

DR. WINKLER IS ON THE PHONE. Not the way it normally works, with a receptionist setting up the call. But the way he is, as much a friend as a doctor, he has dialed the number himself and he's on the line to me about Kish.

"I had her take another MMSE test yesterday," he says. "I wanted to let you know that since the last test, she's showing a decline of several points. There's a clear degree of impairment. Does that surprise you?"

"No it doesn't. She's becoming more forgetful. She forgot my name. Just for a moment."

"I wouldn't make too much of it."

"Of course not. I downplayed and ignored it as much as she'd let me. She found it very upsetting."

"I've been wondering about the treehouse. What has she been saying about it?"

"Hardly anything. I can't remember the last time she mentioned it. But then it's been her thing all along. I wasn't really part of it. You were more involved in it with her than I was. You cooked it up together."

"Cooked it up?"

"Bad choice of words. I didn't mean it was a plot of some kind."

"It was her idea," the doctor says. "Remember? I said she was doing well, up on a plateau, and she took it from there."

"I remember. She fantasized her way off your plateau and into her treehouse."

"What I'd like to know from you, Max, is how it has worked out for her as an imaginary retreat. A place of remission. How has it affected her attitude toward the dementia? I approached her about it yesterday and she looked away. She seemed to be at a loss for words. Or perhaps she didn't know what I was talking about."

The doctor agrees with me that trying to satisfy his clinical interest by asking her about the treehouse would probably confuse her. I don't want his questioning her to interfere with anything she has left in the way of an enchanted treehouse. She may not have it specifically in mind. But that doesn't mean that the potential of it no longer exists for her.

In her suite that afternoon, we're sitting in the blue armchairs with our arms nudging together. The chairs are warm and welcoming and we are attuned to them.

"I want to ask you something," she says. "What would you think if I said, 'Look up. Look waaay up!'"

"I'd think we were kids, back watching *The Friendly Giant* on CBC television. What was it? Forty? Fifty years ago?"

"Yes Max, with Friendly and the puppets, Rusty the chicken and Jerome the giraffe. But we don't have to go back all that time. I saw it on TV this morning. In a rerun."

I'm remembering it. A TV show for children age four to eighty-four and the way it starts, showing the shiny brown leather foot of a boot with Friendly saying, "Look up . . . look waaay up," while the camera moves up the leg of his giant's boot.

"It'll be on again tomorrow morning," Kish says. "At ten thirty. We could watch it together."

"It's a date. I'll be here."

"I'm making a note of it on my clipboard," she says.

It's encouraging to see this renewed faith in her clipboard. She has it on her lap with a top page of fresh notes to replace the muddle of jottings that were confusing her.

"There is whatchamacallit . . . And whoozit . . . And also what's-his-name . . . You know, I'll never forget what's-his-name . . . Maximillian Osborne . . . Yes, I have that written down . . . I've also got those new words written down because I'll be needing them."

"Well Kish, you're not the only one. Those weird words will also come in handy for yours truly. I've got a few more for your list. Such as doodads and thingamajigs and thingamabobs."

"Yes, by all means. I want to write them down."

She has me repeat them — doodads, thingamajigs, and thingamabobs — so that she can make a note of them. They may sound silly. But they're survival words.

"I've been writing things down," she says. "So that I can tell you what I'm thinking. There's something I want to tell you about the treehouse. And I don't want you looking at my notes. If you do that, you'll get ahead of me."

"I promise. No peeking."

"But you can ask questions or remind me of something."

"Yes, I'll try to do that."

"The first thing is about the guitar . . . I can't play it anymore . . . My fingers can't find the chords in it."

I don't want her to see how saddened I am to hear that. Reminds me of Clancy saying what an awful downer it was when Nellie's fingers forgot how to knit a scarf. I guess it's like that for Kish. She's been playing the guitar since she was six.

"And I won't be going to the singsongs in the chapel anymore," she says. "Oh well, not to worry. We have Dinah taking over for me."

That would be Dinah Harper who moved into Nellie Kershaw's suite across the hall. It's been a gradual process with Dinah taking over from Kish. What was Connie's Corner in the dining room is now Dinah's Corner. She has replaced Kish, coaching residents in the exercise classes. And it's Dinah playing the piano for the golden-oldie singsongs in the chapel.

"Ah well, it was bound to happen," she says with one of her Gallic shrugs.

It's a blessing from the treehouse that leaves her quietly resigned to it. There's not a whimper of complaint from her, the way she has been all along, with no show of anger about what's happening overall with the light of her intelligence flickering away. I'm more upset than she is. What a loss this must be for her. The activity, being involved, gave her a reason to get up in the morning.

"It was getting to be too much for me," she says.

"Well, that's all right. You've done your bit."

"Yes I guess I have, haven't I? I've done my bit . . . Do you know Dinah?"

"Yes, I've seen her around."

"I like her. And her name. It's like a cushion . . . And you should hear her playing the piano. She played a piece for me . . . Chopin . . . A nocturne. It sounded like a dream . . ."

After a long pause, I'm obliged to pitch in with a reminder. "You were saying, about the treehouse."

"I can't remember what I called it."

"Do you mean the Mañana Treehouse?"

"That's it. I like that word. Mañana. It's so rounded out and indefinite, going on forever . . . Now where was I?"

"You said you'd been thinking about the treehouse."

"That's it, Max," she says, glancing back at the clipboard. "I wanted to ask you about giving the treehouse to Dinah."

She might just as well wave a white flag of surrender and give up the ghost of her former self entirely. I look off to the side to avoid having her see me going into my woebegone Ahhh Kish look. The one that she finds so upsetting.

"What's wrong?" she asks.

"I'm all right. I have a headache. That's all."

"I have something for headaches," she says, getting up from her chair, going to her bathroom cabinet and returning with two little red tablets and half a glass of water.

"I like helping you," she says while I'm swallowing the tablets for my non-existent headache.

"Thanks, I feel better already."

"Oh Max, I don't get to do things for you anymore . . . Now let me find my place . . . The treehouse. Yes, I want to give it to Dinah. Do you think she would like to have it?"

I try to imagine Kish broaching the subject of the treehouse with Dinah. It's so vivid in Kish's imagination that it would come across to Dinah as an actual tree. Kish would elaborate and mention the rocking chair with the blue-and-white cushion. Given her overall decline, she wouldn't be able to convey the promise of remission or other magical aspects of the treehouse as a framework for the mythical tree of life, also the tree of love, the same thing. They're grafted together. I believe in it now, more than I ever did. From what I've heard about Dinah, she'd be kind and warmly receptive to what Kish was offering. Even with that, Dinah would be unable to give her a positive response and this would leave Kish feeling confused and rejected.

The point is that the Mañana Treehouse doesn't have a certificate of ownership, the kind that comes with a car so that it can be transferred over to somebody else. It started as gleam in Kish's eye and grew from within. It's her brainchild and so deeply rooted within her that it cannot be given away. Trying to steer her away from offering it to Dinah, I'm asking Kish to keep it for herself.

"Would you like to have it?" she asks.

"Not for myself but could we make it work for both of us?"

"Yes, we'll keep it together . . . A good thing . . . A good thing for both of us."

She starts in again, asking me not to go easy on her.

"Don't make excuses for me. And don't write me off. Don't let me become an old biddy saying the same thing over and over again."

"Connie Kish an old biddy? Ain't gonna happen. No way. No how."

"I like the sound of it. 'Old biddy'."

"It's much too soon for you to become an old biddy. You're going to have to wait until I become an old galoot."

"That's us. The old biddy and the old galoot. If I forget your name, I'll call you Old Galoot. And if you happen to forget my name, you can call me Old Biddy."

They're friendly words. Old Biddy. Old Galoot. Just right for us. Lest we forget that biddy rhymes with giddy. That's where we are. Giddy in this flighty back and forth between us.

I'm no longer indulging in any why-oh-why hankering for the way things were. I've come to terms with the Alzheimer's. Like Clancy, I've layered up some scar tissue. I'm going to get in touch with that woman from the Alzheimer's Society and see about getting involved with her self-help group. I've still got a lot to learn. But I've come far enough to be able to stop cursing the dementia. There'll be no more woebegone. Clancy said that for him, that kind of frustration settled into simply being there for Nellie. Doesn't sound like much. But that's what it boils down to. Staying as close to Kish as I can and going through this as well as I can. Occupying a space nearby in a world that's shrinking around her.

There will be days when she'll forget my name and days when she'll remember it. It will go back and forth that way and I'll try to be grateful that we have as much as we do. We don't bother with days of the week. It's always today. It's our secret handshake.

41. Still the storyteller

I'M DRIVING OFF THE PARKING LOT at Strathaven Place and she knows that we're going to the new apartment. I've told her that much and let on that I have a couple of surprises. As a distraction for her, I have a lesser surprise on the back seat. I reach around for a well-worn leather briefcase with her initials in gold on it.

"Where did you find this old thing," she says, fondling it.

"It was at the back of the shelf in the closet in your studio."

Her short-term memory may be failing but the long-term part of it is hitting on all cylinders.

"Grandmamma gave this to me," she says. "When I was six. For carrying my music to my piano lessons. I was so pleased with myself after I learned to play a little piece by Robert Schumann. It's called "The Happy Farmer". With the left hand playing the melody. And then I changed to guitar lessons because it was easier than learning how to play the piano."

"I thought you'd like to have it. You need a place to keep your clipboard."

"My clipboard? Yes, that's right," she says, sliding it into the case. "The leather is drying out. I'm going to give it a good going over with some brown shoe polish."

My strategy is working. Kish, preoccupied with the leather case, isn't paying attention to the streets I've been following. She doesn't know where we are when I turn down the ramp to the underground parking. When I touch the remote to open the gate, Kish twigs to where we are going.

"So this is your new abode," she says.

We're parked and exchanging smiles, walking to the elevator. We'll bypass the main-floor entrance and its whoop-de-doo of helium balloons and a billowing white banner that wants the world to know about the gala opening for this high-rise tower with its tinted glass, stainless steel, and charcoal brick. There's a slick, corporate feel to the place, with a security guy in a green blazer standing ready to open the slab of a glass front door for prospective condo buyers and say welcome to the Princess Cecilia.

Foregoing all that, Kish and I are riding the elevator to the tenth floor, hand in hand, taking it a step at a time with things I would have us learn all over again. At the end of the hallway, there's a warm glow of sunlight coming through an amber-tinted window. We're half way along the hall at Apartment 1012.

"So this is your big surprise!" Kish says.

I try to downplay it, asking her to wait and see and beginning to regret trying to psych her up with surprises. It's going to affect the way she reacts to the place. I want her to set the pace and warm up to it gradually. When I touch my key card to the lock, we hear the sound of a dog's paw raking against the other side of the door. Now Flora is in front of us with her rear end wobbling in synch with the wagging of her tail. Kish leans forward to stroke her head.

"Maggie!" she says. "What are you doing here?"

Maggie was the deerhound we had before Flora. She's attuned to the sound of a more familiar name. The tail wagging stops and she looks up to me for an explanation. Kish knows something's wrong and also turns to me. They seem to think that I have all the answers. I see now that I'm overwhelming Kish. I should have told her before we came up that Flora would be here.

"What's wrong with Maggie?" Kish asks.

"Well, her name is Flora."

"Oh Max . . . Now do you see what a dotty old thing I am, forgetting Flora's name. And wasn't I forgetting your name? You should have cut your losses when you had the chance."

"Well, we tried that didn't we? And it didn't work for either of us."

Flora follows us along the inner hall. I'm hoping that Kish will notice Grandmamma's umbrella stand near the door and on the kitchen wall the trio of Hummel figures we got as a wedding present. The kitchen opens onto a dining area with our table and chairs, the matching mahogany china cabinet and in the living room, the other furniture from home. I was hoping that those familiar things would be comforting for Kish. But they're not registering with her. Her eyes dart around, confused. I imagine that in her estimation, the apartment doesn't measure up against that rambling old house of ours. Both of us are haunted by the ghosts of her and me and the way we were at home with the breakfast nook and the stained-glass panels around the front door.

"I want you to know that we can rearrange the furniture any way you want."

"Why are you saying that?"

"I want you to feel at home here. We could change things around the next time you're here."

That's assuming there'll be a next time, which is not a sure thing. I want there to be a next time. I have a key card for her and I'm showing her the title to the apartment with her name as half owner.

"This place is yours as well as mine, Kish. You can come and go as you please."

She's turning back to our dog. "And you're Flora. I've got that straight now. Dear Flora. And you're Max. Dear Max."

This visit is going badly. But I have another card to play. Going back to when I was first moving in, the idea was to enable her to come here for a bath without having to go to the spa downtown. In a perfect world, it would be a walk-in bathtub built for two. Can't be done, the tub salesman said. Nothing like that in his catalogue. He agreed with me that there should be and said he would check around with manufacturers to see if one of them could build a one-off bathtub for two. A few days later, he got back to me. A tub manufacturer in Vancouver would take it on. They set the price at thirty thousand and asked for ten thousand in advance.

And here it is with the caulking barely dry. The plumbers installed it three days ago as one of my surprises. Gleaming white with chromium fixtures. I'm showing it off to Kish. Opening and closing the tub door. Listening to the little gasps of the door seals engaging. On with my spiel about the fast-fill taps for gushing bath water deep enough to come up to the chin should Lady Baltimore deign to slouch a little on the seat. There's also an array of jets providing a whirlpool massage of bubbling warm air. Kish is closing her eyes.

"Ahhh!" she murmurs, with a look telling me that her imagination has placed her in the tub and she's luxuriating and loosening up on that cushioned seat in a rising tide of warmth and relaxation.

When I ask if she's noticed how wide the seat is, she says, "Yes indeed, Max. Our tokuses should fit nicely on there."

I chime in, calling her Daisy, and singing:

And we'll look sweet upon the seat
of a ba-athtub built for two.

Piling luxury upon luxury, I mention that the seat is heated for the tokuses. There are also the towel warmers. As if one of them, drawing 450 watts, wasn't energy-squandering enough, I had two chrome-plated radiators installed. They're turned on, one of them warming a pair of aubergine bath towels and the other one for his-and-hers terrycloth dressing gowns.

I ask her if she's noticed that the towels are warm. I know she's catching my drift when she goes into the bedroom and remarks on the bedspread, her favourite, the one with pale red roses on it. She takes a moment to remake the top of the bed with diagonal folds of the top sheet and blanket on either side, coming to a point at the top, leaving the bed open and inviting on both sides.

I'm holding that thought while I lead her out past the sliding glass door and onto the deck. A few moments pass while she takes in the view. Looking down onto a familiar driveway circling at the entrance to the next building, then looking straight across in the sunlight to a particular window on the ninth floor. We're close enough to see the blooming hibiscus and the pair of pale yellow calla lilies on the window ledge.

"My lilies?" she says. "My lilies!"

It's a surprise all right. She turns toward me with a how-can-this-be look. "So close," she says. "Oh Max, you lovely man. You've been with me all day it seems."

Still sizing it up with her voice trailing off. "And now this. You live here. And I live over there. And we will have a zip line going back and forth."

Anticipating this moment, I had intended to explain to her how convenient it would be, going back and forth from her suite to this apartment. A space nearby. Should she have a craving for a leisurely hot bath, it would take her just under a minute on the elevator going down from the ninth floor, another minute or so walking over to this building, and a minute up on the elevator and here she would be. And vice versa for me to go over there. But I won't be telling her about any of this now that her treehouse magic comes into play, conjuring up a storybook way of going back and forth. It's the zip line and she's visualizing it for me.

"Do you see?" she says. "It goes from here to there. And from there back over here."

Warding off her confusion and still the storyteller, she has it all worked out, combining the slick technology of her zip line with the charm of Cinderella's coach carved from a pumpkin as our conveyance for riding back and forth in style.

"Oh Max. We're so close... I won't be afraid any more... It's not over for us, is it? We're not over."

She starts to cry and shrugs it off. Recovering, she says, "I don't cry. What is this anyway? It's because I'm tired."

"Well, so am I."

It's agreed that we're absolutely frazzled and that what we need more than anything else in the whole wide world is a nice long soak in our bathtub built for two. Yesterday has vanished and any thoughts about tomorrow are out of the question. It's today and we're getting somewhere with it.

Acknowledgements

Shortly before her passing, my wife, Pauline St-Pierre Dion, said that I should write a book about our struggle with her Alzheimer's. This story is the result of that urging. What kept me plugging away at the writing was the recall of her courage, wry wit, and dignity in the shadow of Alzheimer's. Going through it with her gave me authority to write about a brave woman facing up to the scourge of the disease. For a time, devastated by what was happening to her, I was on the receiving end of Pauline's caregiving when it should have been the other way round. This novel isn't biographical in any way. Pauline was the inspiration, the jumping off point for Connie Kish.

The family connection goes beyond Pauline to my three children, Nancy McLean, Andrew MacLean and Moira Chambers who helped along the way and have taught me so much. In addition, there was invaluable assistance from son-in law Paul Wohlstetter who designed the book cover. There was also my niece Barb Kollman and her husband Kim who let me tap into their long struggle with the Alzheimer's afflicting her mother, Lorraine (Lo) McLean.

And where would I be without Thistledown Press, the publisher of this opus? I'd be nowhere as a would-be novelist and has-been newspaper reporter. I'll be forever grateful to Thistledown's Al Forrie and Jackie Forrie, brother and sister, for going out on a limb for me.

I'm also profoundly indebted to book editor Michael Kenyon, a novelist and poet himself, for his skill and diligence, reining me in at times or empowering me with encouragement.

My thanks also to The Writers' Union of Canada for guidance provided by its manuscript evaluation service and to Valerie Laws, the union's administrator. She's a treasure of support for aspiring novelists. And thank you for a wealth of resources to the Greater Victoria Public Library, Nellie McClung branch. Also to computer guru Dan Russell (ABC Business Services) who keeps my word processing machinery in good working order. And to the city of Victoria itself for providing a setting for the story.

The reference to the dual levels of pity is drawn from Stephan Zweig's novel, *Beware of Pity*. Attribution is due to the late Terence David Pratchett, English comic novelist and an Alzheimer's victim himself, for sizing up his condition as two diseases rolled into one — the dementia itself and even more devastating, the affliction of knowing that he had it and what lay ahead for him.

Other sources of inspiration: Alice Munro's short story "The Bear Came Over the Mountain" and the movie that grew out of it, *Away from Her*, directed by Sarah Polley. Also Charles S. Pierce's novel, *Hard to Forget*, a better book than mine, and *Jan's Story*, Barry Peterson's account of his wife's decline into Alzheimer's.